TARK'S TICKS GAUNTLET

A WWII NOVEL

CHRIS GLATTE

SEVERN RIVER PUBLISHING

TARK'S TICKS GAUNTLET

Severn River Publishing
www.SevernRiverBooks.com

This is a work of fiction. Names, characters, businesses, places, events and incidents are either the products of the author's imagination or used in a fictitious manner. Any resemblance to actual persons, living or dead, or actual events is purely coincidental.

ISBN: 978-1-64875-565-1 (Paperback)

ALSO BY CHRIS GLATTE

Tark's Ticks Series

Tark's Ticks

Valor's Ghost

Gauntlet

Valor Bound

Dark Valley

War Point

A Time to Serve Series

A Time to Serve

The Gathering Storm

The Scars of Battle

164th Regiment Series

The Long Patrol

Bloody Bougainville

Bleeding the Sun

Operation Cakewalk (Novella)

Standalone Novel

Across the Channel

To find out more about Chris Glatte and his books, visit

severnriverbooks.com/authors/chris-glatte

For my Family

1

"You sure we're on the right beach?" asked Staff Sergeant Tarkington.

Sergeant Gonzalez answered testily, "Yeah, I'm sure." In the darkness he glanced at Major Nieto, the leader of the Communist Guerrilla unit who'd guided them there. Nieto didn't say a word, just continued to stare into the vast darkness of the South China Sea. They spread his 150-man force of guerrillas throughout the area, making sure there were no Japanese forces nearby.

They'd successfully escorted the Americans from the interior and gotten them to the west coast of Luzon without being detected. The Japanese were undoubtedly scouring the valley where they'd lost nearly an entire company of soldiers. Moving that many people, even during the rainy season downpours, wouldn't go unnoticed by the locals. Eventually, the Japanese would ask the right person, or apply enough pressure, until someone mentioned the group of armed fighters.

Major Hanscom said, "Since the fall of Corregidor, the Japs have probably intensified their naval presence. Any shipping, even submarines, will have to run a gauntlet in and out."

Sergeant Gonzalez nodded his agreement. "It's only the second night. They gave us a five-day window."

Tarkington said, "Japs find us, we'll have our backs to the sea. Have to swim or die."

The stoic Filipino Communist leader nodded, "Not good. If not tonight, we leave. Too dangerous here."

Major Hanscom nodded his understanding, "You've already done enough, Major. I'm thankful for your support."

Tarkington checked his watch, the luminescent dials barely discernible past the condensation coating the inside. "One AM," he muttered. The small group of leaders were sitting on a small, sandy beach. The rest of Tarkington's GIs, Tark's Ticks, spread along the beach, keeping close vigil.

The day before had been the first day in nearly a week they'd actually been able to rest. They were beyond exhausted. They'd left the village, moving only at night, but got little sleep during the day, having to stay hidden from the heavy presence of Japanese patrols.

Fleeing the valley and the village where they'd spent the past few months had been bittersweet. It forced the villagers to leave or risk the horrible retribution of the Japanese. They'd gone their separate ways with barely a word spoken. Tarkington knew they didn't blame him and his men, but it still pained him knowing it forever changed their lives. He wondered if the small, hidden village deep in the valley would ever return to its former self. When, and if the war ended, would there be anyone left to inhabit it? Would anyone remember? The thought left a pit in his stomach.

He was pulled from his thoughts by PFC Henry's southern drawl, "Light out there. Ten o'clock."

Everyone stood at once, seeing the flashing beam far out to sea. Sergeant Gonzalez slapped Major Hanscom's back. "Hot damn! They made it!"

Hanscom couldn't keep the grin off his face, but it disappeared when he thought of Staff Sergeant Miller. He made the agonizing decision to leave his critically injured NCO with the villagers. They'd put his unconscious body into the bottom of a cart and stacked goods around him to keep him hidden. Hanscom doubted he'd make it. He needed urgent medical care, but he didn't see any other choice. Leaving him in the village for the Japanese to find would most likely end with him being used for bayonet practice. At least leaving him with the villagers would give him a fighting chance, assuming they could get him to some kind of medical facility. He wondered if he was still alive.

Gonzalez was nearly dancing as he watched the flashes from the darkness. "Yep, that's it. That's the correct sequence. It's them alright. I'll give them the return signal." He pulled a flashlight from his backpack and clicked it on and off with the appropriate sequence.

Tarkington ordered, "All right, get the boats to the water."

Major Nieto ordered the same thing in Tagalog and soon the GIs and Filipinos had the two hidden fishing skiffs pulled from cover and their bows nudged into the warm waters of the South China Sea.

Gonzalez hefted the backpack holding the radio with extra batteries and trotted toward the boats. Major Hanscom and Staff Sergeant Tarkington turned to Major Nieto. Hanscom was the first to shake his hand. "Guess this is goodbye, Major. Can't thank you enough for all you've done for us. I'll pass it along. You're sure you don't want the radio?"

Nieto shook his head, "I have radios." He held up two fingers, "Two radios."

Tarkington was next. Nieto had a powerful grip and pointed at Tarkington's waist, "Trade sword."

Tarkington gripped the leather handle of the war trophy, shaking his head, "Nope. I'm keeping this, Major. We've been through a lot together. Besides, you doubled your weapons and ammo after scavenging the battlefield."

Nieto hung onto the handshake, gripping harder, but Tarkington matched him until Nieto finally released. He pointed at Tarkington, "We meet again someday, Tarkington."

Tarkington shrugged and grinned, "I hope so, Major."

Nieto barked an order in Tagalog and the resistance fighters hustled off the beach and disappeared into the jungle. As they watched, Major Hanscom asked, "What was that all about?"

Tarkington shrugged, "Dunno. You feel like he was threatening?"

Hanscom nodded, "Yeah. I got that feeling. Well, nothing to do about it now." He slapped Tarkington's shoulder, "Let's get off this island."

Tarkington nodded, following the major to the boats. He unslung his Type-100 submachine gun and placed it inside the wooden boat, then stepped inside and took a seat in the center. The men pushed the boats off the sand, and they glided gracefully into the placid, warm water.

The submarine would flash the light every two minutes and Sergeant Gonzalez would answer with his own flash. Soon the men's strong paddling got them close enough that they could see the black outline of the submarine's mast, then its elongated shape. Soon they were butting up against the black metal and the voice of a sailor greeted them, "You boys fancy a ride?"

They hustled off the deck of the submarine and sailors corralled them toward an open hatch. As Tarkington waited for the men to shimmy down the ladder, he took one last look at Luzon, the island that had been his home for the past two years. He'd had some magnificent times there before the war, but all he could remember at the moment was the pain and suffering, and all the friends he'd lost.

Once inside the cramped space, they moved quickly to an out-of-the-way compartment and soon they felt the sub accelerate, then tilt forward, and dive beneath the surface.

Two sailors stayed with them, one a Pharmacist Mate. He went over them as though inspecting farm animals at the slaughterhouse, noting any wounds needing attention. He scowled and scrunched his nose, as though they stank to high heaven. All of them had multiple cuts, dings and bruises and having him gouge and touch them didn't earn him any friends.

"What's the big idea?" asked PFC Vick, when the sailor saw the dirty bandage covering the remains of his seeping bullet wound, and ran a thumb over it.

"What's under the bandage?" he asked.

"Whaddya think? A wound," answered Vick, testily.

Without preamble, the Pharmacist Mate, whose nameplate said "Wilkins", yanked the bandage off. It was stuck on by the juices from the wound and when he yanked, it pulled the puckered skin, causing it to bleed.

"Yow! Dammit, man!"

The other sailor immediately shushed him, "Keep your damned voice down. Jap destroyer hears you, our goose is cooked."

PFC Stollman, who was watching Vick's discomfort with some amusement, asked, "What d'you mean? How's a Jap gonna hear us? We're underwater."

The sailor looked at him as though he were no smarter than the countless rivets holding the submarine together. "Sound travels a long way in water and the Japs have good sonar. They can pick up lots of noises, even our voices, particularly yelling. So keep your voices low or we'll have more Jap depth charges on us in no time."

Vick winced as Wilkins dabbed the bleeding wound with ointment. "You got depth charged already?" he asked in a whisper.

The sailor, whose nameplate said "Unterman," nodded, "Yeah. Couple days ago." He licked his lips, remembering. "Awful. Don't ever want to go through that again."

Sergeant Winkleman got suddenly agitated, looking around the confined space as though searching for an exit. He asked, "What happens if one explodes close? I mean, what if there's a breach? How do you get out?"

Unterman gave him a sour look, "There's no getting out unless we're on the surface, which we wouldn't be, if we're being depth charged." He looked at the others, who watched him closely. "If there's a breach," he shrugged, "we die. Either drown or crushed by the pressure as we go down."

Winkleman ran his hand through his suddenly sweaty hair, "We'll keep our voices down."

Unterman nodded and grinned, "I'll need to stow your weapons too. Can't risk accidental discharges." The GIs stared at him as though he'd asked them to remove one of their eyeballs. "Can't use 'em down here anyway." He pointed toward the ceiling, "Japs are up there, not in here."

Tarkington nodded, "Unload 'em and hand them over, guys." The GIs unloaded clips and worked bolts, expertly expelling bullets.

The exotic Japanese weapons clearly fascinated Unterman. He stacked them and stepped back admiring them, "Those are beauts. You ever want to trade, just let me know."

"Show us where you're stowing them, sailor," said Major Hanscom.

Unterman gave him a look. None of the scraggly men had any insignia, so he had no idea of rank or even service branch, but he could tell the man was older and must either be an officer or an NCO. Unterman nodded, "Yes, sir," and when he didn't get corrected, noted it in the back of his mind for later.

An hour later, the GIs felt the angle of the submarine change again, this time angling upward at the bow. The two sailors were still there. Wilkins had finished tending Vick's wound and gone through each man, cleaning and bandaging their minor wounds.

Another sailor, whose nameplate read "Hurst," hustled down the hall and motioned the GIs. He wore a white shirt, covered in grease stains. As the GIs approached he held his nose, "Damn, you guys stink." He shook his head and said, "Lieutenant Commander Staub wants to talk with the officers and NCOs." Hanscom, Gonzalez, Tarkington, and Winkleman continued following the grubby sailor.

Tarkington heard Machinist Mate Unterman say, "Come on. I'll show the rest of you where you'll be bunking."

Tarkington ducked and weaved through the tight hatches, which seemed to come every couple of yards. They finally entered the bridge area and Hurst held them up before entering the room. "Here they are, Skipper."

Lieutenant Commander Staub continued looking through the sights of the periscope, moving a few degrees every few seconds, but answered, "Fine, fine. Be with you in a moment."

Tarkington took in the scene. There were sailors dressed haphazardly, manning stations intently. Some, he noted, didn't have shirts on at all. All of them had a thin sheen of sweat streaked through with grease marks. The air was stale and warm. The distinct odor of unwashed bodies permeated the air, and he realized their own stink must be terrible if he smelled it over the sailors'.

The skipper ordered, "Surface."

"Surface, aye," answered an officer hunched over a good-sized table with a chart pinned to the top. "Angle on the bow, two degrees positive."

Another sailor sitting behind a steering wheel answered, "Two degrees positive, aye."

The slight upward angle was barely noticeable. The skipper stepped away from the periscope, slapping the handles upright, sending the tower into the deck. He smiled at them, "Welcome aboard The Eel, gentlemen. I'm Lieutenant Commander Staub."

The NCOs snapped off salutes and Staub returned them quickly. "So, who's who?"

Major Hanscom smiled and introduced himself and the others. He introduced Tarkington last, and Staub looked him up and down when he did. "So, you're the man responsible for this fiasco?"

Tarkington scowled, "Fiasco, sir?"

"Yes, yes. This entire operation came straight from the top. Instead of sinking Jap shipping, I'm ordered here to rendezvous with you and your men, putting everyone aboard at risk." Tarkington stood, at ease, with his hands clasped behind his back, staring past Staub's head. Staub continued, "The Japs have spread quite a net around Manila Bay, extending all the way to Mindanao Island. We attracted their attention and were nearly sunk."

When the silence lingered, Tarkington responded, "I'm sorry to hear that, sir. It was not my decision. I can assure you, we'd rather still be killing Japs on Luzon."

Staub, who was of average height and sported a dark, well-manicured mustache, nodded, "MacArthur and his staff want you back and will put my men's lives in danger to make it happen. I wonder what's so special about you?" Tarkington adjusted his gaze, staring into Staub's bitter eyes. Tarkington didn't reply, not sure if the officer expected him to or not.

Major Hanscom interrupted the staring match, "We're all following orders, Commander."

Staub's gaze shifted to Hanscom. He stroked the edge of his mustache and nodded, "Yes, Major. I suppose we are." The sub jolted slightly and flattened out, pulling Staub's gaze away from the raggedy soldiers. "Give us fifteen knots, Lieutenant Gilson, and get the spotters topside."

"Aye, Skipper," answered the officer near the charts. Now that he wasn't hunched, Tarkington noticed he was tall and bean-pole thin. His cheeks were sallow and his eyes recessed deeply into his thick eyebrows, reminding Tarkington of a character from *Frankenstein*. He relayed the order.

Soon sailors scurried up ladders, spun lugs and thrust open hatches, allowing the night air in and the fetid air out. The sailors disappeared out the hatches. Staub glared but gestured for them to follow as he went to the ladder, "Come on up."

Hanscom gave Tarkington a quizzical look, conveying his confusion over the officer's personal issue with them. Tarkington gave him a muted shrug and followed him up the ladder. The fifteen knots blew in their faces as they stood beside the skipper on the conning tower. It was still the middle of the night. There was a sliver of a moon which darted in and out of cloud cover. The sea was calm, with just a slight swell. The bow of the Gato class submarine sliced gracefully and easily through the black, shimmering water.

The Lieutenant Commander took a deep breath and blew it out slowly, relishing the freshness. It seemed to help his mood. "The nights out here are pleasant, wouldn't you agree?"

Hanscom answered, "Yes, it's cooler than inland. Guess it's the sea effect."

Staub grasped the rounded edge of the conning tower while glancing behind him at the three sentries jammed into skinny platforms with binoculars to their eyes. "We should be okay tonight. Sometimes the screws and the passing hull make the sea light up with phosphorescent algae. It's like a beacon for any aircraft that happen by."

Hanscom asked, "Still a lot of enemy aircraft out here? We didn't see much on the island after Corregidor fell."

Staub shook his head, "Not much, but that's because we're inside their net. The closer we get to Mindanao, the worse I expect it to get." He glanced at his watch. "The timing's not in our favor at the moment. We've got a better chance of slipping through at night. It'll be close, but I don't relish sitting here all day waiting for tomorrow night. This water's clear and relatively shallow—a spotting plane's dream." He looked out over the vast darkness, "That's what happened on our way here. Spotter called in a destroyer and gave us hell. We got lucky. The way I figure it, we'll be through the worst of it right as the sun's coming up, then we can submerge and operate on battery power for a few hours until we're well away."

Hanscom nodded his understanding. "Makes sense."

"I have strict orders to get you men out with as little fanfare as possible, which means no offensive moves. We had to pass up two choice Jap merchant ships on the way here. Whatever they're carrying could've been the difference between victory and defeat."

Staff Sergeant Tarkington shook his head. He didn't remember when he'd slept last and couldn't keep the irritability out of his voice, "Like I said earlier, sir, this wasn't my idea. We're *all* following orders...sir"

Staub gripped the metal rail until his knuckles turned white and seethed, "MacArthur and his inane pet projects..." He shook his head, "Drives me crazy, Staff Sergeant."

Major Hanscom saw Tarkington getting irritated. If he was even half as tired as he was, they were heading for a breakdown. Winkleman hadn't spoken a word; his eyes were half shut. He looked as bad as Hanscom felt. "Sir, we've been awake for...well, I don't even know. Mind if we get some shut-eye?"

Staub nodded then sighed, "Be my guest. Ask Lieutenant Gilson to get you set up, then send him up here."

Major Hanscom nodded and without another word, they descended through the hatch, leaving the surly skipper sulking on the conning tower.

2

The GIs crammed into bunks, two men per, and laid head to toe. They were tired enough that it wasn't a problem. Tarkington, Winkleman and Hanscom had scrunched their way between the slumbering GIs, and despite having to crawl over the top of them, none of the exhausted soldiers had stirred. Tarkington slipped into a dreamless, black sleep.

The sound of a blaring horn, emanating throughout the confines of the submarine, pulled him from the silky abyss. He sat up and thumped his forehead into the bunk above, only two feet up. For a long moment, he had no idea where he was. He must be in the jungle, but no, that wasn't right; he was in some kind of bed. Home? No, not comfortable enough. And what the hell was the blaring alarm? The words coming from the overhead intercom system reminded him where he was, "Battle stations, battle stations, battle stations."

The narrow hallway was filling with sailors leaping out of nooks and crannies and dashing to their assignments. It impressed Tarkington how fast they moved through the space. He thought if he tried running as fast as they were, he'd surely run into a wall and wouldn't make it through the hatches without injury.

The klaxon continued to wail and the red light pulsed until it finally went to a steady red. "What's going on?" asked PFC Raker, sleepily.

"Dammit, get your damned Yankee feet outta my face," complained PFC Henry in his southern drawl.

Major Hanscom, who was on the lowest bunk, waited until the foot traffic stopped, then slithered his way out. He hit the floor, not able to make his legs work in time. He cursed and pulled himself to his knees, the metal floor grinding into him painfully. "Stay here. I'll check it out." He gripped the bunk as though recovering from an all-night bender and stumbled his way down the hallway.

Tarkington jabbed Winkleman who was still softly snoring, "Wink, wake up. Come on Winkleman, wake your ass up." He punched him in the side but still got no response. "Shit," he muttered. He got to his stomach and pulled himself across Winkleman's back, the next bunk up making it a tight fit.

That woke Winkleman. He suddenly thrashed, bucked and punched. Tarkington rolled off the bunk like an egg squirting out the ass-end of a chicken and landed on his bare feet. "Dammit, Wink! It's just me!"

Winkleman peered over the edge of the bunk at Tarkington. "What—what the hell's going on?"

Tarkington barked, "Get the men rousted and ready for..." he hesitated, "Whatever." He struggled to get his sandals on, finally cramming his toes beneath the leather straps. It felt as though they'd shrunk four sizes, but he figured it was more likely that his feet swelled from the long hours of combat, followed by miles upon miles of hiking.

He made it into the next hallway, squeezing his broad shoulders through the hatch sideways, when he saw Major Hanscom trotting back his way. The red light made it appear like he was covered in blood, and Tarkington had a momentary flash of Eduardo's bloody body tangled up with Vindigo's in the bottom of a foxhole.

Hanscom nearly ran into him, but pulled up just in time, "We're under attack."

"Attack? Depth charges? Haven't heard any explosions."

Hanscom shook his head, "We're not underway. Parked in a little natural bay. Jap plane flew over low, and Lieutenant Commander Staub's sure they saw us. He's shooting for deeper water."

"Parked? Thought we were..."

Hanscom interrupted, "Lost an engine soon after we hit the rack. With less speed, Staub thought it best to hide for the day and sneak out tonight. Jap plane put a crimp in his plans."

"What are we supposed to do?"

Hanscom shrugged, "Told us to stay out, and I quote, 'of the damned way.'"

Tarkington shook his head, "Why's he got it in for us so bad?"

"Beats me. The Navy got their asses kicked at Pearl. Probably still bitter."

Tarkington led the way back to the others. The men were pulling themselves from bunks, wiping tired eyes and yawning. They'd gotten five much-needed hours of sleep, but it wasn't nearly enough.

The boat lurched forward, making them grasp for handholds. They could barely feel the increase in speed as whatever engines still worked turned the screws. The sudden heavy clanging of metal on metal made them all duck. They were well familiar with the unmistakable hammering of bullets impacting metal.

Tarkington cursed, "Shit!" He looked around frantically, "Where the hell're our weapons?"

Hanscom pointed, shaking his head, "Won't do us any good down here."

Tarkington said, "Show me."

Hanscom pushed Sergeant Gonzalez toward him, "Show him, Gonzo." Gonzalez nodded, pushing past Tarkington, who followed close behind. "Just bring sidearms, Sergeant. Not enough room in here for rifles."

Tarkington nodded and muttered, "Yes, sir." Now that they were back with their armed forces, he had to remember to defer to officers. He'd been in command so long, it felt odd reverting.

Minutes later, he and Sergeant Gonzalez were back, passing out pistols. "Don't chamber rounds yet. That might keep the sailors happy," said Tarkington.

Once everyone had weapons, Sergeant Winkleman asked, "What now?"

The submarine was still moving, but it was obvious from the flat angle that they were still on the surface. Tarkington answered, "Sit tight. If they need us, guess they'll let us know."

The chattering of a large caliber weapon firing made them all glance at the ceiling. Another followed immediately. The second one sounded like it was toward the bow. It had a staccato pattern, firing every other second. Hanscom had to raise his voice over the din, "Anti-aircraft gun, if I'm not mistaken."

They cringed, and the beads of sweat on their foreheads, reflecting the red light, made it look as though they were bleeding. PFC Stollman shook his head, "Hate being down here like damned sardines. Feel helpless."

Another flurry of loud clangs as more bullets slammed into the hull. The guns continued to fire both fore and aft. "Taking a beating up there," shouted Gonzalez.

They held on as their speed increased. The guns stopped; soon after, they felt the angle shift steeply, as the sub slipped beneath the surface. The dive angle changed, not as steep but still down. The hammering bullet impacts were replaced with the creaking of the hull as the pressure increased on the outer skin. After a few more minutes of descent, the angle finally flattened. The men relaxed, still wondering what the hell was going on topside.

Hanscom stood and stretched his back, "I'm going forward. Need to know what the hell's going on."

Tarkington nodded, "I'm coming with."

The red lighting changed back to normal, the blaring klaxon silenced long before. Hanscom and Tarkington poked their heads into the nerve center of the submarine. Some sailors sat in front of complicated-looking devices, flicking and turning knobs, others wore headphones, concentrating on sounds. Everyone looked stressed.

Lieutenant Commander Staub saw them enter and asked irritably, "What are you doing out of your bunks?"

Tarkington's jaw rippled, and he was about to retort, but Hanscom put his hand on his shoulder and stepped in front of him, "Just wondering what's happening, Skipper. We're not used to submarine operations, and the men are getting anxious. Anything we should know? Anything we should do?"

Staub's face changed, and he waved them to the chart table. Tarkington and Hanscom nodded to the XO, Lieutenant Gilson, who hovered over the chart holding a grease pencil in one hand, two more tucked over each ear. Staub stabbed at the chart with a thick finger. "This is Mindoro Island," he moved his finger north, "We picked you up here. As you can see, we made good time before the damned number two engine quit." He waved his hand as though dismissing it, "The Chief Engineer's working on getting that fixed, but with the slowdown we couldn't risk penetrating the Jap net during the day, so we pulled into this little bay. As far as we knew, it's a deserted area, and the bay kept us out of sight from any passing shipping. Unfortunately, a Jap float plane went over us at 500 feet. Popped out of nowhere and before we could take evasive maneuvers, came around and strafed us." He gazed at them, "You heard that, no doubt."

Hanscom nodded, "Indeed. Are your men okay? We heard AA fire."

Staub shook his head, "Gunner's Mate Malone took a bullet in the leg, shattered it bad." His voice caught in his throat, "Gunner's Mate Yuncy went overboard." He looked at the floor and shook his head, "Couldn't stay on the surface to recover him."

Tarkington pinched the bridge of his nose. "Damn. Was he hit?"

Staub nodded, "Yeah. The Mae West life vest kept him afloat, but Perkins saw him face down." Silence permeated the room. Finally, Staub continued, "No actual damage to the hull, that's the only good news. It's likely we'll have company soon, though. The plane got away scot-free. He'll radio the contact. We're trying to get as far away as possible. We finally found deep water, but our electric motors put out half the knots of our diesels. Hopefully, that'll be enough."

Tarkington focused on the chart and asked, "So, where are we now?"

Staub looked annoyed, so Gilson answered, "Here," he pointed to a spot off the west coast of Mindoro Island. "We're heading southwest, and once we're here," he ran his finger along the intended path, and continued, "we'll turn south, shoot the gap between Cuyo and Palawan. Should be dark by then, and hopefully the number two engine'll be fixed and we'll run on the surface at twenty knots. Once we're in the Sulu Sea, we'll be hard to find."

Hanscom shook his head, whistling low, "These charts are something. How accurate are the depths?"

Staub shrugged, "Estimates, at best. We can't take the normal routes, the Japs know them too well, so we travel less-known areas and the charts," he tilted his hand back and forth, equivocating, then continued, "The real problem though's the water clarity. On a cloudless day without chop, we're visible from an aircraft unless we're at 200 feet. Makes daylight travel hazardous, especially this close to Jap territory."

Hanscom nodded, "Thanks, Commander. We'll get out of your hair. It'll put the men at ease knowing what's going on. Let us know if you need anything." He pointed at Tarkington, "His men are experts in all kinds of weaponry. If you need any replacements for the men you lost...well, we're available."

The corners of Staub's mouth turned down, and he nodded, "Yes, hopefully we won't need them." He stroked the edges of his mustache, "But it's a good idea to get them trained on the deck guns just in case." He looked over his shoulder and addressed the XO, "Put Ensign Romero on it, Gil."

Lieutenant Gilson nodded, "Aye, aye, Skipper."

They stayed submerged for the rest of the day, crawling at three knots to conserve battery power. Occasionally, Lieutenant Commander Staub ordered periscope depth, searching for surface vessels and landmarks. The sea was calm, and the day was bright and clear—not optimum for staying hidden. If the Japanese sea plane had radioed their position, there were no vessels close, or they'd been unable to find them.

Tarkington and his men slept most of the day. In the evening, sailors roused them, wanting to reclaim their bunks after long hours on duty. The GIs got the full tour. The Gato class submarine was over 240 feet long, and they filled every square centimeter to capacity with gadgets and or supplies.

They ate in shifts, using the tiny mess hall in ten-minute blocks. It was the only way to get all three shifts in and out quickly. The food was exceptional. They crooned over spaghetti with marinara sauce, thick slices of bread, and even vegetables. Even before the Japanese invasion of the Philippines, they hadn't eaten like this.

When darkness fell outside, Lieutenant Commander Staub took them to the surface. The GIs could feel the increase in speed and the slight shudder as the bow sliced through light swell.

They were given awkward and bulky Mae West life jackets and invited topside. The night air was warm, the skies clear, and the sliver of a moon and bright stars provided plenty of ambient light. Tarkington and Hanscom watched from the tower as the sailors showed the GIs the ins and outs of the surface guns, which comprised a 3-inch deck cannon, a 20 mm Oerlikon, and a spindle mount on the stern for a .50 caliber. They fired no shots, not wanting to attract unwanted attention, but after some intensive training, the men felt they could at least help if needed.

Lieutenant Commander Staub pointed to a silhouette of land in the dark distance to the west, "That's the tip of The Calamian Islands. They'll be off our starboard bow the rest of the night. We're in the Mindoro Strait, which is plenty deep, and leads straight to the Sulu Sea."

Hanscom asked, "Is it patrolled?"

Staub nodded, "Undoubtedly. We didn't come through this way, though, stayed west in the South China Sea, but the currents are wrong for the return trip." He leaned forward, resting his elbows on the railing, "Hopefully the Japs won't be as thick here, because of the currents, but there's a lot of shipping between the islands which could be a problem for us as we approach the Mindanao and The Sulu Archipelago. They might not all be Japs, but being spotted by anyone in here would be dangerous."

Hanscom shook his head, "I'm understanding just what kind of undertaking this has been for you and your men. It's a wonder you were only a day late for the pickup."

Staub explained, "We got the word while patrolling toward Japan. We were 400 miles from the rendezvous point, but yes, it was still quite a feat. That's why they gave us a week long window. Even that was probably too short."

Tarkington asked, "Did you get the number two engine working?"

Staub smiled, something none of them had seen yet. "Yep." He pointed at the slicing bow, "You're looking at twenty knots. We could do more, but we've got a long way to go yet."

A sailor yelled from a lookout 20 feet up the mast, "Skipper, the algae's glowing."

Staub cursed and turned toward the stern. The others did the same and saw there was a bluish-green track of phosphorescence coming off the twin screws of the Gato class sub.

Staub cursed, "Damn, stuff's like an arrow pointing straight at us."

Gilson, the XO, stiffened noticeably, "Shall I have the men bring up the other guns, sir?"

He thought about it for a second, then asked Major Hanscom, "Your men able to operate the guns?"

Hanscom deferred to Tarkington, who nodded, "Of course, Commander."

Staub nodded to Gilson, "Bring 'em up, Gil."

"Aye, aye, Skipper." He relayed the message over the radio handset and in less than two minutes, the .50-caliber machine gun arrived from the bowels and got mounted onto the spindle.

Tarkington cupped his hands and yelled to his men, who were lounging on the deck enjoying the first night of peace and calm they'd experienced in weeks, "Look alive, Winkleman. Get the men to the guns."

Winkleman nodded, stood, and slapped the GIs' backs, "Stolly and Vick to the 50, Raker to the 20 millimeter." As the men got themselves off the deck, Winkleman called up to Tarkington, "Trouble?"

He cupped his hand and called back, "Boat's churning up phosphorescence. If there's Jap air patrols out, they might see us."

Two hours later, Tarkington and Lieutenant Gilson were the only two men manning the conning tower. Lieutenant Commander Staub and Major Hanscom had gone below to get some shut-eye. Sergeant Winkleman was sitting on the deck between the 50 cal position, which was behind and out of sight from the tower platform. Tarkington could hear their voices drifting up but couldn't make out the words. He hadn't heard so much talking from Winkleman since they'd left Luzon two days earlier. Being out of the tight confines of the sub was having a positive effect on him. That and a couple hours of sleep.

The big deck gun was below and forward a few yards, its three-man crew watching the skies. In front of them, farther toward the bow, sat the 20 mm Oerlikon, which PFC Raker was taking a turn on. Tarkington strained to see Raker, but he was just a dim outline in the darkness. The sea was gentle tonight, but there was still the occasional spray from the bow, and Tarkington wondered if Raker was cold. He wouldn't be one to complain.

He turned to Lt. Gilson, "Men working the 20 millimeter get cold up there?"

Gilson focused forward and shrugged, "Sometimes. 20 knot wind and sea spray can be cold even if it's hot out. Think your man needs more clothes?" He reached beneath the railing and grabbed a rubber navy bag. He unrolled the top, reached in and handed him a rain slicker. "Take this to him. It'll keep the wet off."

Tarkington took it and nodded, "Thanks. I could use a walk anyway. Legs are getting stiff up here." He went to the ladder, swung himself onto it and descended to the main deck. The sailors on the deck gun watched him pass, giving him a wave. The deck was wide and stable, but he wondered what it would be like during a storm or heavy seas. Hazardous, no doubt.

The three sailors manning the deck gun didn't glance at him and Tarkington wondered if they were sleeping, but put his suspicions to rest when he heard a sailor messing with the gun sights.

He made his way forward until he saw Raker lying on his back with his hands clasped behind his head and his legs crossed. He really did look asleep, but as Tarkington approached Raker arched his neck looking back, "That you, Tark?"

"Yeah, it's me." He sat beside him, handing him the raincoat, "Need this? Thought you might get cold."

He took it, balled it up and placed it beneath his head. "Ahh, now that's more like it. Thanks, Tark. Just staring at the stars, beautiful night."

"And looking for Japs, no doubt."

Raker grinned, "Of course." He held out his hands to the expansive sky, "Anything crosses this chunk of sky, I'll see it. The rest of the guys are scanning the area behind."

Tarkington sighed; it really was relaxing. The warm air was infused with the perfectly cooling sea spray. The heavy gun mount blocked most of the 20 knot wind. He arched his neck and looked at the stars. The moon traveled east and was low in the sky. "I see what you mean. It's nice out here."

Raker said, "Sure beats the mud on Luzon."

Tarkington looked around, "Where's the ammo for this thing?"

Raker pointed at a round drum-like structure on the top right. "Just one drum of 60 rounds. The guys worried I'll burn up the barrel, so just left me with the one."

"60 rounds? That's all?" He glanced at Raker, "Won't you burn through that pretty quick?"

Raker nodded and itched his nose, "Yep. Shoots 450 rounds a minute, so I'll be out in a couple seconds."

Tarkington shook his head, "Don't make a whole lot of sense."

He made a move to get up, intending to see about more ammunition, but Raker stopped him with his hand on his arm. "It's better this way, Tark. The last guy got splattered all over the deck. Less time I'm out here, the better."

Tarkington relaxed and grinned, "Guess so. Probably shouldn't be out here at all, that being the case."

"Best seat in the house, as long as the Japs don't show up."

3

Lieutenant Naga changed course, banking his Aichi E13 reconnaissance/bomber float plane toward Mindoro Strait. He, along with his navigator, Sergeant Ming and, his gunner, Sergeant Masaki, normally turned west, patrolling the South China Sea, but today Captain Ung had changed his flight orders. There'd been a sighting the day before, a US submarine taking refuge in a bay off Mindoro Island. Naga didn't put much stock in it as the report was from Lt. Yin, someone he didn't trust to report the weather, but when he saw the damage his aircraft had taken, he understood they'd come across something. He thought it more likely to have been one of the American fast patrol boats, what the imperialists called PT boats. Either way, the sighting was significant and changed his normal search pattern. He had to admit, the change in scenery, even at night, was refreshing.

The Aichi's engine purred, and the controls responded beautifully. The cooler night air gave his flight surfaces more bite and buoyancy. There was good visibility from the stars and crescent moon, and through the rear-view mirror he watched his navigator arranging maps and pens—and when he'd just organized everything, Naga banked the plane into a 35 degree turn, causing Ming to clutch his neatly-arranged instruments or risk losing them into the tropical air.

Ming's voice sounded strained over the internal radio, "Let me know before you do that next time, Lieutenant."

Naga grinned and replied, "Oh, excuse me, Sergeant. Did I upset your things?" The sarcasm in his voice was unmistakable. Naga watched his persnickety navigator in the mirror, noticing the gunner in the rear, grinning.

Ming shook his head, not hearing the sarcasm or teasing tone, "No sir, well some, but I'll be ready next time, sir."

"Yes, I'm sure you will be, Sergeant," Naga replied, smiling. He enjoyed flying more than anything he'd ever done in his young life. The power of the Aichi was a joy to feel beneath his feet; the power of freedom coursing through the stick and rudder pedals was intoxicating.

Having the two sergeants along was also a joy, particularly since he'd lucked out and been assigned two men he respected, and more importantly, had senses of humor. It wasn't always these two, but this week it was, and he'd been having fun with them. Ming was more serious, but that made it more fun for Naga and Masaki to gang up on him.

With the course correction, he flew straight and level, arcing his head to the right. Even in the low-light conditions, the view was amazing.

From 800 meters ASL, he could see the distinctive southerly flow of the Mindoro Strait. The flow, in fact, was the reason he hadn't patrolled this way yet; any vessel coming from the south, which was where the enemy was, would have to fight that current, so his patrols had concentrated on the northerly flowing South China Sea. Those patrols had mostly been endless hours of boredom, the view never changing from the blue and green expanse.

He'd only recently moved to night operations. This new patrol route would take them over beautiful islands and various reefs, all of which were shrouded in darkness. Hopefully, he'd come across whatever Lt. Yin had attacked.

The dark, expansive sea, whisking beneath his green-painted wings, looked endless and vast. He wondered, not for the first time, how he'd ever find anything out here. This was his eleventh patrol, and he'd yet to find anything more interesting than floating debris.

During his sixth patrol he called in what he thought was the periscope of a submarine, but upon closer inspection, turned out to be a discarded metal container. When he realized his mistake, he had the embarrassing chore of correcting himself over the radio.

He'd given into Sergeant Masaki's pleading, allowing him to open fire upon the container. It had been a daylight patrol, and Masaki had fired his 7.6 mm gun as Lt. Naga circled it slowly. Watching the great geysers of water and the sparking metal was exhilarating, but also unsatisfying. Naga desperately wanted to add his own efforts to the war effort.

He glanced at his gauges; he'd burned through half his fuel. He was nearing the point where he'd need to turn back toward home along an alternate route. Fuel was never a tremendous concern for him. The Aichi's two large pontoons allowed him to land on any strip of water, but the embarrassment would be far worse than the danger imposed by having to ditch a non-pontoon airframe.

Sergeant Ming's voice cut through his thoughts, "What's that?"

Lieutenant Naga glanced in the rear-view mirror, seeing Ming staring left and pointing. Naga swiveled and saw what he meant. Greenish-blue algae was glowing down there. That wasn't unusual, this magical place was full of environmental surprises, but its straight-line track *was* unusual.

They were flying south, and the track seemed to get brighter the farther they went. Naga was thrilled, "Something's passed through here recently, and we're getting closer." He tilted the aircraft slightly to get a better look, but the track extended all the way to the horizon.

"Shall I call it in, Lieutenant?" asked Ming.

Lieutenant Naga shook his head, "Not yet. Could just be a whale or a large school of fish. Maybe even a local fishing boat." He didn't want to report something that turned out to be nothing. He'd already been dressed down once for a false report. The shame he felt still burned in his gut. He wouldn't make a report until he had something concrete.

Ming nodded and said, "Our radio check-in is coming up soon, anyway."

Naga checked his gauges again, satisfying himself that they could follow the algae track for at least another half hour. Hopefully, it would lead him straight to a fat target. "There's no scheduled local shipping, is there?" he asked his navigator.

"No, sir. There's nothing in my notes about that."

Sometimes, despite the warnings, locals would venture out in their small barges and outrigger canoes, but whatever they were following was big enough to churn up the algae kilometers after passing. Naga felt his heart pound in his chest; this was it. This would be something more than flotsam and jetsam. This would be an enemy vessel. He could feel it in his bones.

Naga glanced at his knee-board and flipped a few pages, stopping on the pre-attack checklist. He shone a small, red flashlight and keyed the mic, "Sergeant Masaki, check weapon."

Masaki checked his weapon, pulling the bolt, assuring he had a round in the chamber. "Gun checks out and is ready, sir," his voice was all business.

Naga continued, "Check safety belts are fastened and secured." He didn't wait for compliance, knowing his men were checking and following along. "Headgear secured."

"Check."

"Loose items secured."

"Check."

"Radio check..." he hesitated, still wary of calling in a bogus report. He studied the glowing algae. It was getting brighter and brighter the closer they got to whatever was causing it. He nodded to himself and continued, "Make the call, Sergeant Ming. Tell them we're following a promising algae track."

Ming nodded his understanding, "Yes, sir."

Naga went over the weapons he had at his disposal. Besides the 7.7 mm, Type-92 machine gun in the back, he had one 90-kilogram bomb hanging off his one hard point. Normally, the Aichi didn't carry bombs, used instead for long-range reconnaissance, but since Lt. Yin's sighting, they'd been patrolling with the 90-kilogram bomb strapped to the underbelly and Lieutenant Naga was happy about that.

He nearly tilted the plane into a tight bank when he pulled his eyes off the gauges and saw a black shape at the point of the phosphorescence. It looked like a black rocket spewing color out the back, and for a moment his spatial awareness altered. He quickly recovered and nearly choked trying to

get the words out, "There—I see—I see it. Eleven o'clock." He could feel the
two sergeants shift eagerly left. Naga's voice went up an octave, "It's—It's a
submarine. An enemy submarine." He momentarily had no idea what to
do, then his training took over and he ordered, "Call it in, Sergeant." He
turned the plane gently away from the sub, at the same time gaining alti-
tude, hoping to make the radio transmission crystal clear. His primary
mission was to spot and report enemy activity. Attack was secondary. "Keep
your eye on it, Masaki."

"Yes, sir," Sergeant Masaki responded, a slight tremor in his voice.

Tarkington was still lying on his back alongside PFC Raker near the bow-
mounted 20 mm, when he thought he caught a faint noise. He stiffened,
and Raker asked, "What's wrong?"

Tarkington sat up and put his finger to his mouth, cocking his head to
the side. Raker sat up too and Tarkington asked, "Hear that?"

Raker concentrated, then nodded, "Yeah, sounds like..." he looked up,
"an engine?"

Tarkington got to his feet, turning toward the tower. No one else was
reacting. The deck gunners were as still as stone. He could see the outline
of the sailors high up the tower slowly searching side-to-side, but no one
was acting like they were hearing or seeing anything unusual. The sound
was more distinct now, growing in intensity. "They can't hear it. Engine's too
loud back there." He searched the sky—it was difficult to pinpoint—but he
got the impression it was coming from behind.

Tarkington turned back to Raker, "Get on the gun. I'll warn the others."
Tarkington took off at a sprint. When he got close enough to the curious
gunners, he hollered, "Plane! I hear an airplane!"

They watched him with bemusement. The sergeant they'd pulled from
the darkest of jungles had finally flipped his lid. He heard Raker yell,
"There! Six o'clock high!"

Tarkington saw it and pointed. A second later all three sailors on the
tower pointed and yelled, "Jap Jake! Jake, six o'clock!"

Raker was the first to fire. He rotated the 20 mm Oerlikon aft and depressed the trigger, sending a flame three feet from the barrel, hurling a short but intense stream of tracer fire.

Raker's brief bursts marked the general vicinity of the plane and the deck gunners laboriously slewed the cannon.

The plane was visible against the dark backdrop of the stars. It was diving, closing fast, but angling so it would pass off the port side. Raker sent a long stream of tracer, which seemed to walk from back to front, but slightly low. The plane shot upward slicing closer and soon there were winking flashes coming from it.

Tarkington flung himself to the deck yelling, "Cover!" The sea erupted in geysers as the 7.7 mm rounds impacted. The plane's rear gunner walked the rounds across the deck, tearing up planking and zinging bullets into the night air.

The 50-caliber, manned by Stolly, answered with lancing streams of fire, which seemed to chase after the dark plane as it zipped past. Henry and Vick were close by, helping with the ammunition. A loud boom erupted as the three-inch deck gun finally fired.

Raker was suddenly beside Tarkington, "You okay?" he asked. Tarkington nodded, got to his feet, and they ran past the still-adjusting deck gun.

A blaring alarm broke through the sounds of machine gun fire, and Tarkington heard the deck gun loader yelling, "Lock her down! Lock her down! We're submerging!" He had to reach out and punch the nearest crew member's shoulder, breaking his concentration. They rotated the gun back to center, quickly covered the barrel and ran for the hatches. A spent brass casing rolled side-to-side. Normally, they'd police it up, taking it below, but tonight it would be lost to Mindoro Strait forever.

The 50-cal suddenly stopped firing and Tarkington ran past the conning tower, seeing Vick, Stollman and Henry coming his way, carrying the heavy weapon and ammo. The barrel was red hot. "Come on," Tarkington urged.

He hustled them to the open hatch, and they passed the smoking gun into the hold. Sailors with thick gloves handled the weapon and hustled them out of the way. Tarkington glanced toward the bow which was washing with seawater. He saw the dark shape of the airplane angling down, coming straight for them. He wondered why he wasn't firing, but didn't ponder the thought for too long. He went through the hatch, and a sailor lugged it with a hard pull and quick spin.

The deck angled farther into the waves. Tarkington grinned and was about to comment, when there was a violent clang, followed with an ear-shattering explosion. The sub lurched and seemed to roll 90 degrees, sending Tarkington flying into the metal wall. He hit his head, seeing stars. He dropped to the ground, warm blood tracking down his cheek. His vision was blurry and he couldn't seem to keep the darkness at the edges from creeping in. The last thing he remembered seeing was Lieutenant Commander Staub desperately gripping the handle alongside the conning tower, yelling into the mic, "All stop! All stop!"

Lieutenant Naga waited until Sergeant Ming finished relaying the submarine sighting to headquarters. He'd taken the Aichi up another 200 meters, then turned back toward the submarine. With the radio message complete, he keyed the mic, "Sergeant Masaki, I'll bring you alongside. Sweep the deck, then I'll line up and drop the bomb before they can submerge."

Sergeant Masaki responded with a tight, "Hai."

Naga eased the plane closer to the sub and increased the throttles. He wanted to be within easy range of the Type 92 machine gun, but not so close to be an easy target for the deck gunners. In the darkness, he couldn't make out if there were any deck guns, but he had to assume there would be. He wondered if this was the same submarine Lt. Yin had attacked.

The Aichi was in perfect attack position. He got an excellent look at the conning tower and decided it was most likely an American Gato-class submarine. Suddenly the night lit up as a gun near the bow opened fire. He kept the plane steady despite the huge globes of tracer rounds lancing toward him. He glanced in the rear-view mirror, seeing Sgt. Masaki leaning into the gun, "Not yet, Sergeant." The quick burst from the bow was most likely 20 mm fire. The Aichi wasn't as thin-skinned as some other planes in the Japanese arsenal, but it wouldn't be able to sustain a hit from the 20 mm cannon.

He pushed the throttles to full power. The night lit up again with a long burst from the bow gun. The tracers were mesmerizing as they floated toward him and he thought sure, he'd die any moment. The awful sound of bullets punching through metal made him cringe, and he instinctively pulled up. The controls surfaces reacted well, and he decided the huge pontoons had taken the brunt. He edged the plane closer and yelled, "Now, Sergeant!"

Sergeant Masaki had his shoulder pressed firmly into the stock, sighting down the barrel at the looming shape. He fired, watching his rounds impact along the base of the hull. He adjusted, walking the bullets up the length of the sub's deck. He noticed more winking flashes of return fire, but kept the trigger depressed. The power of the gun was intoxicating. He felt like a god doling out justice. He pivoted the gun, keeping it centered on the sub's conning tower, finally stopping when the plane's tail interfered.

Lt. Naga pulled up, keeping the Aichi's engine pegged to full power. There was a slight stuttering in the engine. He glanced at his gauges; there was something wrong, but there was no time. He had to drop the bomb before the sub disappeared beneath the waves. He'd deal with the engine when he had more time. He only hoped the bomb release mechanism worked.

He arced upwards, watching his speed decrease, then turned back toward the submarine. The incoming fire had been intense, and he'd felt many impacts, some close enough to make his seat vibrate. Now the sub was silent. The winking flashes of fire, gone. He knew why: the submarine was making an emergency dive. He'd have just enough time to make his drop.

He pulled the plane back around, noting that the flight controls were a little sluggish. He fought the stick, lining up the dark sub which was approaching fast. He could see the whitewater washing over the deck as the sub angled toward the depths. He pushed the throttle, not feeling the normal surge of power. He worked the rudders at his feet, fighting to keep the plane straight and level.

The sea was glowing with phosphorescence, churned up even more by

Sergeant Masaki's fire. He clutched the red knob with his left hand, keeping his right firmly gripped on the stick. He leveled off, struggling to keep the sub lined up, but the plane wanted to slip to port. He fought to keep it on course. Sweat beaded on his forehead dripping to his goggles, which thankfully, hadn't fogged up. The sub's bow was beneath the surface. He yanked the bomb release handle and felt the plane jolt upward as it was suddenly 90 kilograms lighter. He pulled up, putting distance between himself and the imminent explosion.

Fear streaked through him like a flash of lightning as he thought the bomb failed to explode, but relief flooded his system when he heard and felt the concussive blast of detonation. The night lit up and he couldn't keep the joy from his voice, "Banzai!" he yelled.

He looked into the rear-view mirror, seeing the back of Sergeant Masaki's head as he tried to see the results of their attack. Lt. Naga leveled off, turning left, hoping to see a burning, dying American submarine, but instead glimpsed the conning tower disappearing beneath the waves. "Fire, Masaki! Fire!" There was no response. He continued slicing toward the sea, trying to get closer, giving him a better shot, but still nothing.

Sergeant Ming yelled, "Masaki! Masaki!"

Naga twisted in his seat, trying to get a better view, but the mirror was better, so he refocused his attention on it. "What's wrong? What's happened?"

He saw Ming unstrap his safety harness and get to his knees, facing Masaki's position. "He's hit. Oh no...Masaki!" he yelled.

"Help him! Help him!" he watched in horror, the mirror like a movie screen.

Ming leaned out the cockpit trying to help, but finally gave up and sat back into his seat, his face in his hands. "He's gone, sir. He's gone."

Naga pulled his eyes from the mirror, slamming his fist against the console. He shut his eyes, but the sound of the engine coughing brought him back from his grief. He pushed the pain away, concentrating on flying the stricken aircraft. Something was definitely wrong. "Call headquarters. Tell them we attacked with guns and bombs and damaged the submarine, but we took damage and may have to land out here."

Naga heard Ming working the radio. He put it out of his mind, trying to keep the plane in the sky long enough to figure out what was wrong. The oil gauge was dropping fast. He glanced at the port side wing, noticing fluttering fabric where a bullet had torn through the aileron. The smell of acrid smoke made him lean out inspecting the engine cowling. The smoke was coming out the seams, getting thicker every second. He checked his airspeed; he needed to put the plane down before the cylinders seized and burned.

Ming's frantic voice cut through his concentration, "I can't raise anyone. The radio's not working!"

"Keep trying but be ready for a forced landing. I'll get us as close to land as possible." Naga nursed the plane, cutting power enough to keep them from stalling. He angled the plane downward, but he was only 300 meters above the sea, not much room to balance speed with power. The engine sounded awful. The oil pressure gauge was at zero and the engine temperature gauge in the red. He cut the engine, and the propeller continued spinning with the wind. A second later, it ground to a sickening halt. Naga pushed the nose down, trying to maintain speed, but the Aichi wasn't known for gliding, especially with the heavy pontoons.

He watched the angle simultaneously with the airspeed, feeling for the stall point. He was right on the edge; he could feel it in the seat of his pants. The sea was coming up fast. "Brace," he barked.

He hauled back on the stick and the nose lifted slightly, just enough to stall the plane's flight surfaces. He was too high. The feel of the nose dropping forward uncontrollably, combined with near freefall, was sickening. The plane crashed into the sea; the pontoons dipping deep, stopping forward momentum suddenly and violently. The plane flipped forward, dipping the hot engine into the water with a hiss. The doomed Aichi's tail continued up, slicing through the night, until finally resting upside down with a tremendous splash. The cockpit submerged along with the struggling occupants. The bullet-riddled pontoons filled with sea water, providing little buoyancy, and the plane disappeared beneath the waves in under two minutes.

4

Tarkington awoke with no idea where he was. There was a red glow, and he was in a tight space, and for an instant he thought he might be in a coffin. A flash of panic gripped him, and he could not move. The sound of yelling—some close, some distant—brought it all back. He was on The Eel. They'd been making their way south and had been attacked. He was waking from a nightmare straight into another.

He lifted his head, and the throbbing pain made him touch his forehead. He felt a sizeable lump topped with a gash. It hurt like hell and he wondered how long he'd been out. He lay back, testing the rest of his body. Nothing else seemed out of whack. He glanced across the aisle seeing another man, a sailor, bandages covering his entire head. There was an IV stuck into his arm. At least I'm not as injured as that poor bastard, he thought.

He grimaced, making himself swing his legs from the bunk. He sat on the side of the bed. The move made his head pound, and he felt nauseated but fought the urge to lie back down. He needed to find out what the hell was going on. He surmised the damned Jap plane had bombed them, but how bad was it? Obviously not as bad as it could've been. He was still alive.

"Whoa there, Staff Sergeant." Tarkington opened his eyes a slit, seeing Pharmacy Mate Wilkins coming toward him, holding a tiny syringe full of liquid. Tarkington shied away and grumbled something unintelligible. Wilkins went to the man across the aisle and poked the needle into his arm, pushing the contents of the syringe into him. Then he turned to Tarkington and kneeled in front of him. "Take it easy, soldier. You got knocked out."

He touched Tarkington's forehead, running his finger over the gash, causing Tarkington to pull back and slap his hand away. "Knock it off. What the hell's the matter with you?" he slurred.

"You've got a nasty gash that's gonna need stitches, but the swelling's gotta go down first." He reached behind him, pulling out a wet cloth rag. "I stole some ice. Hold this on the wound."

Tarkington gingerly placed the rag on the wound, not able to keep from wincing, "What happened?"

Wilkins kept working on the injured sailor, poking and prodding the bandages covering his face, like he was playing with clay. "We got strafed and bombed by a Jap Jake."

"Jake?" Tarkington asked.

"It's what we call that type of plane. No one can pronounce the Jap name."

Tarkington nodded, "I mean what happened after that? How long was I out?"

Wilkins looked at his watch, "About an hour and a half. You had me worried."

When Wilkins didn't keep talking, Tarkington raised his voice, "And...?"

Wilkins glanced at his tone, but finally answered, "Skipper says we took some damage. It's pretty bad. Had to surface and shut off some forward compartments. Bomb hit the starboard bow plane. Tore it off and holed the hull forward of the torpedo room. We weren't going fast, and the skipper stopped the engines right away. If he hadn't, we'd be on the bottom by now. It's a miracle, really. If the bomb hit another few feet toward the hull, it would've hit the torpedo room and we'd all be dead. As it is, we're unable to dive."

"That's bad, right?"

Wilkins nodded grimly, "Yeah. It's bad." He indicated the injured sailor, "King was up there in the torpedo room. It knocked the shit out of those guys." He shook his head, "Some didn't make it. Thrown around like rag dolls."

Tarkington murmured, "My God." He shook his head, imagining what that must've been like. "Sorry to hear that."

Wilkins nodded, continuing to work. "Yeah." He picked at the palm of his hand, "So far this fucked up mission's cost us four men." He tilted his chin toward King, lowering his voice, "Assuming he makes it, which is anybody's guess."

Tarkington pressed the ice into his forehead. His wound seemed petty now. He wanted to tell Wilkins that they hadn't asked to be rescued. If he'd had any say in the matter, he'd still be on Luzon. But none of that mattered. Wilkins needed to blame someone, no matter how wrong it was. Tarkington could take it if it helped him work through the pain.

He kept the icepack on his forehead and stood. He gripped the rail, steadying himself. Wilkins protested, but Tarkington shook his head and walked past him murmuring, "Take care of King."

Tarkington emerged from sick bay trying to ignore his pounding head. While he was unconscious, someone had removed his old shirt and now he wore a light blue sailor's shirt. He made his way forward past tight, confined spaces, until he emerged into the bunk area.

Sergeant Winkleman was the first one to notice him. "Tark, you're awake. How d'you feel?"

"Like they ran me over with a deuce and a half." He looked at the other GIs, nodding at each and noticing a few were missing, "Where's Vick and Henry?"

"Up with Gonzalez and Hanscom. They needed some help with the forward compartment," Winkleman answered. "Raker's on the 20 millimeter again."

"What's the situation? We still underway?"

Winkleman nodded, "Far as I know, but limping along. That bomb tore off the bow plane and ripped open a forward compartment. There was flooding, but Staub shut down the engines quick. They say if we'd been

going faster, we'd be on the bottom. There's still minor flooding, so it's dragging. Skipper's worried that Jap plane's telling all his buddies about us. He
expects trouble, and we can't dive."

Tarkington nodded, "Get the rest of our weapons. I'll be damned if I'm
going down with just a sidearm."

Winkleman reached behind his back and pulled out Tarkington's
captured submachine gun, "Way ahead of you, Tark." Tarkington grinned
and nodded his thanks. Winkleman added, "Got your sword. You want that
too?"

Tarkington shook his head, "Nah, get in the way down here, but keep it
close."

Stollman asked, "You going topside?"

Tarkington shrugged, "Gonna talk with the skipper. Come along."

Winkelmann and Stolly got to their feet, and Tarkington noticed a
bandage across Stollman's arm. It was stained red with blood. "You okay?"
he asked.

Stolly nodded, "Yep. Bullet grazed me. Hurts, but nothing serious."

They moved down the corridors nodding at sailors who mostly scowled
back, as though this whole shitty war was their fault. When they got to the
bridge, Tarkington held them up while he poked his head inside. He saw
the XO, Lieutenant Gilson, standing over the chart table. He motioned for
the others to follow and approached, "Lieutenant Gilson."

Gilson looked up from the map and grinned, "Good to see you back on
your feet, Staff Sergeant." His eyes went to the wound which Wilkins had
covered with a gauze strip. "How's the head?"

Tarkington replied, "I'll live."

Gilson pointed at the submachine gun strapped across his back.
Winkleman and Stolly had left their longer rifles in the bunk area, "You
expecting trouble?"

Tarkington shrugged, "Just feel naked without it, I guess. Would've been
nice to shoot back at that Jap plane. What d'you call 'em? Jakes?"

He nodded, "Yes, the Aichi sea plane. Easier to call 'em Jakes."

"You expecting more of them?"

Gilson nodded, "They don't work alone normally. His base is around
here somewhere, and there'll be more. Hard for us to hide, not being able

to dive and all. We've altered course, but they'll find us when it gets light," he glanced at his watch, "in another two hours. We're working on patching the hole. We'll need a drydock for the bow plane." He motioned toward the ceiling, "Meanwhile we've got all the guns manned. Your man, Raker's on the 20-mil. He did well. Think he might've even hit the bastard, or at least thrown his aim off."

"Does he have more ammo? He only had one drum last night."

"Yeah, plenty. We assigned GM Hedgewick to help him with that."

Tarkington focused on the map, "So, where are we?"

Gilson pointed, "The attack happened here. We've turned northeast, heading back toward Cuyo Archipelago. They'd expect us to keep steaming south, or even west toward Palawan, but Lieutenant Commander Staub's trying to trick the bastards."

Tarkington nodded, "Think it'll work?"

"It'll be close. The Japs'll search south and when they don't find us, they'll spread in every direction. If we're not detected by nightfall, we've got a chance. I think their planes will probably find us; the trick'll be avoiding their ships. We've got enough guns to fight off their planes, but if we get into a shooting match with anything bigger than a patrol boat, we'll lose."

Tarkington looked the map over and nodded, "Know anything about Cuyo? Is it occupied? With Japs, I mean?"

"It's a series of islands, all tiny. There's nothing strategic about them, so we don't expect Japs. We'll be able to hide there until nightfall, then push for Mindanao tonight." He pointed at the large land mass southeast of their position.

"Why Mindanao?" asked Winkleman.

Gilson shrugged, "There used to be facilities there. Probably don't have spare starboard bow planes," he joked, "but might be able to shore us up some." He looked around and lowered his voice, "Also, there's a growing resistance there. Led by some ex-mining engineer. An American officer. Fertig's his name, or something like that. He was in the Army reserves and called up right before the Japs invaded. Now he's leading and organizing resistance, and—from what I've heard—been pretty damned successful."

Winkleman grinned and slugged Tarkington's arm, "Now that sounds familiar, doesn't it?"

Tarkington ignored him and asked, "Facilities to repair the hole?"

Gilson shrugged again, "Hopefully patch us well enough to dive, yes. It'll be awkward with only one dive plane. Don't even know if it's possible." He shook his head, "If we can't dive, it'll be suicide to continue. A month ago? Maybe. But the area's crawling with Jap surface vessels now, and we have to run it on the surface in daylight at least some of the time. Perhaps they'll send another sub for you."

"Can't imagine we're all that important, Lieutenant."

"Someone thinks you're important enough to send us."

Tarkington had been wanting to ask about that since Major Hanscom told him the news a little more than a week before. He leaned in conspiratorially, "Any ideas on that, sir? I mean, why us? Why not this Fertig character? He's an officer, at least."

Lieutenant Gilson frowned, "That's above both our pay grades, Staff Sergeant."

Gilson's tone made Tarkington stiffen, "Yes, sir," he replied. "Mind if we go topside? I'd like to check on my men."

Gilson nodded, "Of course. Be my guest."

The early morning air was brisk topside, but the sea air was refreshing after being inside the stifling submarine. The weather had changed. Instead of endless bands of stars, there was a thick layer of clouds, which made the night feel very dark. Despite the cloud cover, the sea was still relatively calm, and he could see the white froth as the bow cut through.

There were no lights shining on the sub for obvious reasons, and the three of them made their way forward using the metal railing. Tarkington could just see the outline of the deck gun. The 20 mm, where Raker was, was virtually invisible.

They continued following the railing until it suddenly ended near the very front. Tarkington stopped, leaned forward squinting and could see a jagged hole. There was movement, and he strained to see who it was. He heard Henry's unmistakable drawl, although he couldn't understand what was being said. It was coming from the open forward escape hatch behind him. Tarkington went to it and cupped his hand beside his mouth, "That you, Henry?"

The talking stopped. Henry emerged from the hatch, wiping his hands on his soaked pants. Vick followed him topside, and they stood in front of them. "Yeah, it's me," Henry answered.

Vick asked, "How you feeling, Tark?"

Tarkington involuntarily touched his forehead, "I'm fine. Just a bump on the head."

Henry chimed in, "You were bleeding like a stuck pig, but head wounds are like that, I guess."

Tarkington waved it away, like a pesky fly, "How's it look down there?"

Vick shook his head, "Shitty. Some leaking. Vick and I don't have a clue what we're doing."

Three more figures emerged from the hole and stood beside them. Through the darkness, Tarkington recognized Hanscom and Gonzalez. The third man was a sailor.

Hanscom shook his head, "A lot of water coming in."

The chief engineer looked down, shaking his head, "It's not too bad. Once we stop, the sea water won't be getting forced in."

Winkleman pointed at the twisted metal where the bow plane had been, "Really did a number on it, didn't it?"

The sailor nodded, "Luckily the hole's above the waterline, but there's still water coming in, especially since we're pushing 15 knots. Can't slow down though. Japs're looking for us."

Tarkington asked, "You guys done down there, then?"

The sailor, a broad-shouldered older man, nodded, "We did everything we could think of. Gotta get back to my duty station." He slapped Henry's back and said to all of them, "Thanks for helping. Means a lot," his voice cracked. "Good men died down there." He walked back toward the conning tower, his head down and shoulders sloped. They'd all lost friends in the war and knew exactly how he felt.

Hanscom sighed and said, "I'm heading in, see if I can rustle up some chow." Gonzalez nodded and walked with him, but the others stayed put.

Tarkington said, "I wanna check on Raker."

Henry pointed forward, beyond the hole. "He's up there."

The outline of the 20 mm Oerlikon was just ahead, and just like a few hours before, Raker was on his back with his hands beneath his head, staring at the ominous clouds. Beside him sat a sailor. He wasn't quite as relaxed.

Raker heard their footsteps and peered their way. When they were close enough, he addressed the sailor. "See, this is what I'm talking about, Hedgewick. No matter where you go, you can't get away from things you don't like."

Henry shook his head and drawled, "Shiiit, Raker. You're one to talk."

They sat down beside Raker and the hapless Gunner's Mate Hedgewick, who looked at them nervously. Raker sat up and slapped the sailor's shoulder, "Don't worry bout them none. They're harmless...so long as you ain't a Jap."

Hedgewick didn't say a word, obviously intimidated by their presence. He'd heard the scuttlebutt. These guys had been through the wringer from the beginning. They were killers. The few times he'd seen them in the confined halls of the submarine, the most notable thing about them was their eyes. They were the eyes of much older men, yet he knew they couldn't be much older than his 19 years. After being depth charged, strafed, and now bombed, he thought himself a combat veteran, but these men were on a different level.

Winkleman grinned, "Hey, this is us. Tark's Ticks, all together and in one place."

Silence, as each man thought about the one missing member. Eduardo's body buried on his home island, alongside the man he'd died fighting beside: the village elder, Vindigo.

Hedgewick felt like an intruder. He stood up shakily, dusted off his blue dungarees, and mumbled something about having to use the head. He walked off into the night, leaving Tark's Ticks to ponder their situation.

Henry pointed to the submachine gun on Tarkington's back, "Now that's an excellent idea."

Tarkington nodded, "Wink pulled 'em outta the locker." He sighed, "I don't know what will happen over the next few days, but I don't want us caught with our pants down. Gilson told me the plan, and it's a good one. Staub's trying to throw the Japs off our trail by doing what they don't expect. Gilson thinks the Jap planes will find us again, but he's hoping their navy won't. I know it's probably against their rules, but I want you guys armed and ready to either fight, or get the hell off this floating coffin when the time comes."

The GIs nodded, and Winkleman asked, "You gonna run it past Lieutenant Commander Staub?"

Tarkington shook his head slowly, "Nope. Better just to do it and ask for forgiveness later. Besides, he's got enough to worry about."

5

The men of Tark's Ticks watched the sun rise off the port side bow. Despite the danger daylight brought, the scene was awe-inspiring. Shafts of golden light lit the clouds yellow, pink, and red.

Tarkington looked back at the conning tower, seeing Lieutenant Commander Staub staring back at him, his binoculars dangling from his neck. He was sure the impromptu meeting on his bow was grating on Staub. "We better break this up. Looks like the skipper's gonna shit himself."

Hedgewick returned with another sailor walking alongside. He nodded at them as he passed and addressed Raker, who still stood with the Oerlikon gun. "Taylor's here to relieve you, Private."

Raker nodded and hustled after Tarkington and the others, "Looks like I'll be joining you below decks."

When they got to the hatch, Tarkington motioned that they should descend, "Go on ahead, I'm gonna speak with Staub."

The GIs disappeared belowdecks and Tarkington went to the tower, looked up and called out, "Okay to come up, Skipper?" Lieutenant Commander Staub looked over the edge and motioned him up, then continued scanning the sea with the powerful binoculars.

Tarkington pulled himself onto the bridge platform. Lieutenant Gilson and two ensigns were with the skipper, all scanning different sectors of sky. Tarkington snapped off a salute and Staub returned it quickly, then continued scanning. "Lieutenant Gilson told me he filled you in on the plan."

Tarkington nodded, maintaining his at-ease stance, "Yes, sir. I hope it works out for us."

Without taking his eyes from the binocs, Staub stated, "You've armed yourself, Staff Sergeant."

"Yes, sir. I figured since we're on the surface anyway..." he let the thought fade, then added, "Us ground pounders feel naked without them nearby, sir."

Staub ignored the answer. He pulled the binocular strap over his head, handed them to Tarkington, and pointed, "See that outline of land there?"

Tarkington put the glasses to his eyes and worked the focus until the blur crystallized. He could see the stark outline of an island. It was small, with another one nearby, "Yes, I see it."

"That's the first island in the Cuyo Archipelago. Once there, we'll hope-fully find some out-of-the-way bay to lie low in."

Tarkington looked at the sky. It was still cloudy, but it was breaking up and looked like it would clear soon. "Too bad the weather's clearing."

Staub's scowl deepened, and he nodded, "Yes, cloud cover would've been better."

Tarkington handed the binoculars back, careful not to let them drop to the deck 15 feet below. An excited voice from the lookouts above almost made him do just that, "Plane, ten o'clock high!"

Tarkington turned the way the lookout was pointing, not seeing anything but clouds and bits of blue sky beyond. All eyes turned. He glanced down to the deck gun crew. They were cranking the wheel system as fast as their arms allowed. The loader held binoculars, searching franti-cally so he could better direct their aim.

One of the young ensigns sang out, "I see it! I see it! Moving west to east, maybe three thousand feet. Looks like another Jake. It just went into a cloud."

Lieutenant Gilson asked, "Did he see us?"

Lieutenant Commander Staub ordered, "Cut engines to half speed."

Gilson picked up the handset, repeating the order, and Tarkington felt the sub slow noticeably. Staub said, "No need to show them a large wake."

Tarkington looked behind and saw the diminished wake, but thought the pilot would have to be blind not to see them. For a few long seconds there was nothing. The only sound was the thrumming of the engine and seawater lapping against the hull. Then, so faint he thought he might be imagining it, there was a distant hum.

The same ensign called out, "There! He just popped out the other side."

Lieutenant Commander Staub nodded and—keeping the binoculars glued to his face—ordered, "Nobody fires until we're sure he's seen us." Lieutenant Gilson yelled the order to the deck crews, who were slowly tracking the distant target which was little more than a dot to the naked eye.

Tarkington squinted, holding his hand out to block the sun shining through the clouds. He saw a tiny sparkle and imagined the sun must have reflected off the canopy glass.

The ensign cursed, "Damn. It's turning our way."

"Has he seen us?" demanded Lieutenant Commander Staub.

Another few seconds of silence then Lieutenant Gilson nodded, "I think so, Skipper."

Staub ordered, "All ahead full. Maintain course."

The ensign confirmed Lieutenant Gilson's assessment, "He's definitely coming our way, Skipper."

Staub nodded, "I agree." He leaned over the bridge and yelled, "Let him get closer."

Tarkington leaned over, watching the gun crews. They looked anxious but excited to get some payback. The sound of the plane's engine was unmistakable now, and he looked up, shading his eyes. He could see the large pontoons, which seemed bigger than the plane itself. They reminded him of clown feet, too big for the body.

The ensign yelled, "I see a bomb. He's armed."

The plane was slicing toward them, getting larger by the second. Tarkington unslung the submachine gun, holding it at port arms. He knew he had as much chance of hitting the thing with a rock as he did with the submachine gun, but holding it made him feel better.

The plane leveled off at 2000 feet, then turned away. Staub yelled, "Fire at will!"

The ripping buzz-saw of the 20 mm, combined with the roar of the three-incher, made for a deadly symphony of destruction. The 50-caliber, mounted aft, didn't have a shot. Tarkington could see the fiery deck gun round slicing toward the plane. It disappeared into a cloud, missing badly.

Smoke enveloped the tower, filling the air with the familiar smell of combat. The plane jinked side-to-side, then dove, throwing the gunner's aim off. In another couple of seconds, it was streaking low and fast straight away. The 20mm gun crew continued hammering away, sending up arcing balls of tracer rounds. The plane was soon out of range and out of sight. Silence. The only sign of the brief exchange: their ringing ears and rolling, empty shell casings.

Lieutenant Commander Staub ordered, "Keep an eye out, but he probably won't be back. He'll be scrambling ships and more planes." He scanned the looming archipelago and added, "Change course to 130 degrees. We'll shoot for Mindanao while they're looking for us in the Cuyos."

"Aye, Skipper."

Lieutenant Commander Staub kept the men vigilant, scanning the sky for more enemy planes as they cut southeast into the Sulu Sea. They passed various points of land, mostly tiny atolls surrounded by shallow reefs. The adrenaline had worn off and Tarkington lost concentration. They had seen nothing for three hours.

Raker was on the 20 mm again, and Stollman, Vick and Henry were taking their turns on the stern fifty cal. Tarkington was thinking of heading below to get some chow. The navy food was an enormous step up from anything they'd eaten on Luzon, except for the tropical fruits. He'd gorged on steaks, vegetables and eggs, and didn't see any reason not to take advantage of the navy cook's largess.

He noticed Raker in the bow waving and pointing at his ears, as though hearing something. Tarkington leaned forward, straining, but heard nothing except the sound of the lapping waves against the hull. Lieutenant Commander Staub asked, "What is it, Staff Sergeant?"

Tarkington pointed at Raker, who was now swinging the 20 mm's barrel down and traversing to port. His assistant, Gunner's Mate Hedgewick, cupped his hand, yelling, "Boat," and pointing.

Everyone swiveled, looking toward the nearest island of the Cuyo Archipelago. The sentries above the bridge called out, "Surface vessel, eight o'clock, closing fast!"

Staub focused his binoculars and cursed, "Damn. It's one of their motor torpedo boats. A small one. A T-14." He was immediately on the horn, "Attention, T-14 torpedo boat closing fast from the rear port quarter. Turn to 090, maintain speed."

Tarkington felt the submarine heel over, turning back toward the oncoming boat. If the Japanese boat kept its course, all the sub's guns could fire on it without risk to one another. He glanced behind, seeing Stolly aiming the fifty cal toward the oncoming target. It'd be within the big weapon's range in a matter of seconds. It was already within the bigger deck guns' range.

Staub leaned forward onto the rail, "Fire at will!" The booming deck gun fired sending a shell passing off the small boat's starboard side, exploding harmlessly 200 yards beyond and sending up a huge geyser of sea water. Raker leaned into the 20 mm cannon's shaped shoulder mounts and thumbed the trigger, sending a quick burst. He adjusted, firing again.

The sea erupted around the boat and it turned hard to port, trying to stay directly in front of the submarine's bow, in an attempt to lessen its exposure. This immediately blocked the three-incher from engaging. Staub was on the horn, "Maintain this turn."

There was a winking muzzle flash coming from the top of the MTB's small bridge area and 25 mm rounds from the mounted auto-cannon tore into the submarine's thick skin with loud hammer blows. Tarkington ducked behind the mast's metal rail, hoping it was thick enough to stop the heavy caliber ordnance. Staub was still giving orders, "Load port side bow torpedo tubes and all aft tubes." Tarkington looked at him questioningly. It would be tough to hit something as alert and quick as the MTB with a torpedo. Staub ducked and shrugged, "Might get lucky."

For the moment, Raker was the only one able to return fire. He adjusted aim, walking the rounds forward, finally catching up to the streaking boat. The geysers of water and skipping 20 mm rounds surrounded the target, and it was momentarily shrouded. Tarkington, whose eyes were just above the lip of the rail, could see flashes as the 20 mm shells found their mark.

The Japanese skipper changed course again, this time turning straight into them. The bow sliced through the spray of water like an emerging warrior through smoke. The winking flashes continued and tracers whizzed past the tower, barely missing.

The sub's continued turn brought the rest of the guns into play just as Raker's 60-round drum emptied. The momentary pause didn't last long. The decisive crashing of the three-inch deck gun ended it.

The MTB's wildly swerving maneuvers saved its life, as the shell demolished the sea it had just vacated. The fifty added to the cacophony. Tarkington felt relief, knowing his men were still in the fight. There was no armor protecting them.

Staub, crouched alongside, heard something in his headphones, nodded and ordered, "Fire one and two!" Raker pointed over the railing and Tarkington saw two streaks of bubbles whooshing from the bow on slightly different tracks. "Mark tens are out." He keyed the mic and ordered, "Fire three!" Another whoosh of bubbles and a third torpedo streaked away.

The MTB turned back to its starboard, desperately trying to stay directly in front of the sub's bow. Staub keyed the mic, "Maintain this course, stop the turn." The deck gun didn't have time to fire again. By now, Raker had reloaded. He swung the hot barrel, trying to keep up with the fast boat which was now broadside. He depressed the trigger, sending massive shells streaking just over the top of the MTB's mast. He adjusted, walking more rounds into the hull which sparked like shattering crystal.

Black smoke billowed from the rear and the boat's bow mushed into the sea, sending up a wall of water from all sides. It wallowed and turned slowly. Raker overshot, but quickly adjusted and for a moment he and the Japanese gunner were in a shootout, both making hits.

Staub was on the radio, "Hard to port." The submarine immediately turned hard left, rolling the hull to starboard so severely that Tarkington thought he might tumble from the conning tower like ice stuck to the bottom of an emptying pitcher of lemonade.

Raker's fire stopped as he struggled to stay in the strap connecting him to the gun. Tarkington hoped his men manning the machine gun weren't in the drink, but there was no way to check until they completed the turn.

Staub ordered a stop to the turn and the sub righted itself, the jagged hole in the bow causing the entire sub to wallow. The enemy boat was smoking from the rear and dead in the water. The 25 mm had ceased firing, the gunner either hit or reloading.

Staub stood, and Tarkington joined him. "Look at the torpedo tracks," he exclaimed with barely-contained glee. Sure enough, the first and second torpedos were on collision courses: the first with the bow, the second with the stern.

The gun crews recovered from the hard turn and firing resumed. The doomed MTB was an easy target and there was no return fire. The sea all around the boat erupted, masking it from view. There was an explosion which shot through the fountains of water sending up a huge billowing black cloud. The rumbling explosive concussion swept across the bow, creating an unnatural breeze. Staub yelled, "Cease fire! Cease fire!"

It seemed to take forever before they could see the results through the curtain of water. It was descending from the sky like some crazed rainstorm, full of bits and pieces of boat and bodies. When the view cleared, the boat was simply gone. The only thing remaining was a burning patch of sea and an oily streak. Staub was beside himself with pleasure. He slapped Tarkington's shoulder, "That's what a mark ten torpedo does to a small boat!" The sounds of cheering from the deck gunners added to the festive feel.

Tarkington could see that Raker was okay, so he leaned over the rail, looking for Vick, Stollman and Henry. All of them were pulling themselves off the deck. Tarkington yelled, "You guys okay?" Stollman shook his head slowly, finally giving him a thumbs up. Tarkington breathed a sigh of relief and turned back toward the skipper who was pumping his fist, grinning ear to ear.

The reverberations from the massive explosion were still rattling through their heads when a whistling sound pulled them from the celebration. There was a panicked yell from a sentry, "Jake!" followed seconds later with a crushing explosion which pushed Tarkington to the metal floor then into the mast, reopening the gash on his forehead and making him woozy and lightheaded. His ears rang, blocking out all other sound, and the world seemed to move in slow motion.

Lieutenant Commander Staub sprawled on the floor and looked to either be dead or unconscious. The ensign beside him lay perfectly still as though he were a mannequin and Tarkington noticed he didn't have a head. He wondered if it were rolling around like an abandoned basketball after a game.

The simple act of gripping the top rail and pulling himself to his feet was agonizingly slow. By the time he did, the air was choked with acrid smoke and he coughed incessantly, sending shots of pain through his chest. He tried to call out, but his throat felt dry as pumice, and he gave up.

He peered over the rail, seeing a fresh gaping hole. This one where the conning tower met the deck. Through the smoke, he caught glimpses of fire and even the occasional view of the innards of The Eel, as though he were a medical student watching a particularly messy surgery from a balcony. There was no sign of the deck gun. There was a smoldering body nearby, all that remained of them.

He swayed, gripping the handrail, trying to see through the smoke where Raker had been. The smoke burned his eyes, and he closed them. He dropped to his knees, coughing. Lieutenant Commander Staub moaned. He was alive. Tarkington put his hand on his chest and shook him, trying to wet his tongue enough to speak, but it was no use. He wondered if he'd somehow burned his throat. Perhaps he'd sucked fire into his lungs past his voice box.

He heard yelling, cutting through his ringing ears as though someone was calling across a great distance. He stood again. Wind blew the smoke to port, giving him a moment of relief and allowing him to see. The bow was down slightly, and he noticed sea water slapping over it occasionally. He could see the 20 mm gun was still in place, but he couldn't see Raker or his loader.

Men were emerging from a forward hatch, like gassed ants. They stumbled and tripped, some going to their knees, vomiting. A thin wisps of smoke rose from the open hatches. More and more dazed men emerged.

He heard a familiar voice, "Abandon ship! Get to the boats!" He looked toward Lieutenant Commander Staub, who was staring in disbelief at his headless junior officer. He hadn't given the order; it was Gilson. Lieutenant Gilson was somewhere down there, and Tarkington was thankful someone could still take charge.

He put his hand on Lieutenant Commander Staub's shoulder and tried to yell over the roar of his ringing ears and dry throat. "It's time to go," he managed to croak.

Getting from the conning tower to the deck 15 feet below wasn't easy. The ladder was still intact, but it was twisted and the metal was hot in spots from licking flames. Tarkington and Staub helped each other over the side and when other survivors saw them, they shook off their own injuries, rushing to help.

More and more men emerged, some dragging dead or dying men along with them. Those that could, helped organize. The sub was listing to starboard, toward the already damaged bow dive plane. The hole was mostly underwater as the stricken sub lost buoyancy and was quickly submerging.

Tarkington led Lieutenant Commander Staub to his XO, who'd been below decks when the bomb exploded. "Skipper! Thank God!" Gilson exclaimed. "I thought you were dead."

Staub shook his head, "Re—report."

"She's going down! Engines aren't responding and we're taking on water —well—everywhere. We can't keep her afloat, sir. She's hit too badly."

Staub leveled his gaze, "Casualties?"

"Unknown, but at least six below decks." He glanced to the charred remains of the gun emplacements. "I don't think the gun crews made it, at least not the three-inch crew."

Staub swallowed and croaked, "Hulsey didn't make it," he thumbed toward the conning tower. "His head," he stammered, "Well—he's dead."

Tarkington croaked, "Seen my men?"

Gilson nodded, "Winkleman, Hanscom and Gonzalez were with me at the dining hall." He pointed, and Tarkington saw them helping with the wounded. They were so blackened by soot, he hadn't recognized them at first.

Tarkington stumbled toward them, hearing Staub concurring with the order to abandon ship. Winkleman saw him coming and stood to greet him, "Tark, you're alive! Thought for sure everyone in the tower would have bought the farm."

Tarkington's throat still burned, but he managed to ask, "The others? On the guns. Seen anyone?"

Winkleman nodded, "Raker's over there, he's wounded—broken arm. Were the others in back?" Tarkington nodded, not wanting to speak again. Winkleman said, "Stay here. They're bringing rubber boats up. We'll find 'em." The wide-eyed Sergeant Gonzalez trotted after Winkleman. They gave the gaping, still burning hole a wide berth, shielding themselves as they passed.

Tarkington couldn't keep himself from collapsing to the deck. Major Hanscom noticed, reaching out to him, "Are you wounded?"

Tarkington shook his head, and mouthed, "water."

Hanscom instinctually reached where his canteen would normally be. Not finding it, he looked around, but there was no water. Tarkington shook his head, waving it away as a minor inconvenience.

There was yelling and Tarkington saw sailors rolling out two black rubber boats. There was no way they'd hold the entire crew of 60 men, less now, and he wondered if there were more coming.

He gazed through the smoke, seeing a not-too-distant island poking from the clear green waters. He wondered if it were the same island where the Japanese boat had come from. Were there others? He figured he could've easily made the swim, even two weeks before. But now, in his exhausted and probably shell-shocked state, it seemed impossible.

CO_2 charges filled the rafts quickly. Paddles, stowed inside, plopped into the center, seven per boat. Tarkington had no idea how many men survived the attack, but he was damned sure it was over 14. Two soot-covered sailors strode past, handing out Mae West life jackets. Tarkington put the odd-shaped thing on, pulling it over his arms, which were aching and burning.

He was so dirty that he couldn't tell if he'd been burned or simply singed. Either way, it hurt. Hanscom saw his quavering hands and helped him cinch the life preserver. Tarkington glanced back, remembering how Stollman and Henry had complained mightily about wearing the life vests, and how Vick had been like a worried mother explaining their virtues. He wracked his brain trying to remember if they'd been wearing them during the attack, but came up empty. He hoped to God they had been. If they'd been thrown from the sub, it might be the only thing keeping them alive.

At that moment, Sergeant Winkleman trotted around the corner, followed by Gonzalez. They both looked white as sheets and Tarkington braced himself for more grim news. Winkleman kneeled beside him and shook his head, "There's no sign of 'em Tark. The gun's there. It took some shrapnel, but there's no sign of them."

Tarkington saw the pain in Winkleman's eyes and nearly let emotion get the better of him. He gritted his teeth, took a deep breath and croaked, "No bodies though. Probably got thrown off when the bomb hit. We'll find 'em."

Sailors were pushing the rubber boats over the side, the sea getting closer and closer to washing over the deck. Wounded men were being loaded. Tarkington took another look aft, then refocused and said, "Let's help with the wounded."

He shuffled his way toward the sailors, Hanscom giving him support. Lieutenant Gilson and Lieutenant Commander Staub were in charge, directing the loading. Staub saw them coming and waved them closer, "We've only got two boats. We'll put as many men in as possible, but we don't want to wallow. Are you well enough to swim alongside?"

Winkleman answered for him, "He can barely walk. He's burned and needs to ride."

Tarkington wanted to protest but his throat was still dry and the less he said the better. Staub nodded, "Get in the second boat, Staff Sergeant." He pointed, and Tarkington stepped in that direction, helping another wounded sailor along the way.

Hanscom asked, "Any more men below?"

Gilson answered, "We've recovered everyone that can be recovered." He looked around at the sailors. Some were unconscious, some gasping and crying out, clutching wounds. Most, simply dazed. "Any sign of the guys manning the rear guns?"

Hanscom looked pained, shaking his head, "Tarkington thinks they got thrown into the sea. No bodies."

Staub looked at Tarkington, who was now helping Raker to step into the raft. Raker held his left arm close to his body. His life preserver was scorched, and some of the floatation was seeping out the back. Staub pursed his lips, "We'll need paddlers. With the wounded, probably four paddlers per boat and a rudder-man. The rest'll have to float alongside or swim. We'll put ropes off the back if we have to." He pointed to the closest shimmering island. It looked deceivingly close. "That's our destination."

The Eel suddenly angled down much steeper, and the rubber boats were unexpectedly floating away. Men standing on deck were suddenly up to their waists in seawater. "We gotta go right now," barked Staub. He lunged for the nearest boat. "Grab the sides, or you'll be sucked down with her."

Winkleman, Gonzalez, and Hanscom waded to the nearest raft—the one carrying Tarkington—and latched onto the sides, their feet still on the submarine deck. Tarkington was searching for his lost men, straining to see past the sun's bright reflection off the water.

The GIs alongside were suddenly floating, the sub sinking away, hissing as water entered the burning hole. Winkleman found a sturdy metal D-ring to hold on to along the edge of the raft, directing Hanscom and Gonzalez to do the same. More men were scrambling toward the rafts, swimming frantically.

Lieutenant Gilson's booming voice from alongside the other raft barked, "Paddle! Get away from her!"

A sailor behind Winkleman suddenly yelled in panic, "I'm caught! I'm stuck! Help!"

Winkleman looked back, seeing a dark-haired sailor waving frantically, only his shoulders out of the water. He was near the conning tower, which was still eight feet out of the water. It was obvious what had happened: he'd stepped too close to the hole and gotten snagged on the jagged edges.

Winkleman didn't hesitate. He pushed off, taking powerful strokes, and was soon beside him. The sailor latched onto Winkleman, pushing him under. He fought for the surface, but the sailor was out of his mind with panic, clutching at anything to keep himself from going under.

Winkleman gave him a savage punch to the stomach, which loosened his grip, allowing him to break free and swim to the surface. He stayed out of reach of the sailor's grasping hands. The sailor was up to his chin now, his eyes sheer terror. Winkleman breathed in and out quickly, hyperventilating. It was an old trick his uncle taught him when they'd dive for abalone off the California coast. He doffed the life jacket and took a deep breath, submerging and swimming through the clear water to the panicking sailor's feet.

The problem was obvious; a thick cord wrapped tightly around the sailor's leg. Winkleman reached for the knife he normally carried, but remembered taking it off. It was probably still on the bunk 20 feet below.

The sailor was kicking and thrashing, but Winkleman went to work trying to free him. The cord was wrapped tight, and he couldn't get enough slack to loosen it. His vision dimmed when he took a knee to the face, momentarily stunning him. He raged inside. *If this stupid son-of-a-bitch would stop thrashing I could help him.*

Winkleman felt their downward descent. He looked up, seeing the sailor's head was underwater now, which made him thrash more. Winkleman's lungs burned. He had one chance. He tackled the sailor's leg, holding tight, then pulled him downward, trying to give himself some slack. He felt himself being pulled down farther. He worked frantically, but the sailor continued to thrash and he wasn't making progress. His ears ached as he went deeper.

He had to leave now, or he'd be too deep to make it to the surface. Panic welled in his gut but he calmed himself, remembering his uncle telling him that rushing and panicking burned more oxygen. He glanced up, seeing the sailor looking down at him, his eyes huge, tiny air-bubbles streaming from his nose. His eyes had changed from panic to pleading. It tore at Winkleman, but he had to save himself or they'd both die.

He tore his eyes away, found the metal hull and lunged upward with every ounce of remaining energy. He rocketed past the sailor who clutched at him, his eyes beseeching him to save his life. Winkleman's strong strokes pulled him closer to the surface, but not as quickly as he hoped. The downward pull of the water being dragged with the descending submarine was having an impact. Thankfully, the descent of the sub was slow, but he was still having to fight against the current and suddenly the surface seemed a long way up.

His lungs burned like fire, and he couldn't keep the panic from welling up inside. He hastened his stroke. He was burning through oxygen quicker, but he couldn't keep himself from doing it. His vision blurred; the surface still seemed so far. Too far. He took one last feeble stroke, reaching for the golden light. The light suddenly blocked, and he saw a silhouetted hand reaching out for him. *God?* he wondered. How nice.

He came to seconds later on the surface, held by Sergeant Gonzalez, who was trying to put his life-jacket back on him. Gonzalez felt him trying to help and exclaimed with relief, "You're alive! Thought I recovered a body."

Winkleman finished donning the preserver and lay upon his back, allowing Gonzalez to swim him toward the rafts. He stared at the blue sky, knowing that the sailor's terrified, beseeching eyes would never leave him. He muttered, "I—I couldn't save him. I couldn't save him." Gonzalez didn't respond, just kept pulling him through the warm water.

6

An hour later, they were still struggling to paddle the rubber rafts to the island. The Eel had slipped beneath the surface as though some ghostly crew was still manning the controls. Despite their efforts, the island didn't seem much closer than it had when they first started. It didn't help that the men hanging alongside the rafts acted like heavy anchors.

When it was obvious they weren't making good headway, they brought men into the rafts one at a time. The eight-man rafts weren't meant for taking a whole crew off a sub. They were for the occasional mission onto islands to collect coconuts, fruit, or fresh water.

With significant effort, they got most of the men into the rafts. Only six remained in the water, and they were strong enough swimmers to keep up with the rafts by side stroking.

To keep the paddlers from getting fatigued, they switched positions every ten minutes. Their headway increased dramatically, but the island still seemed far away. Winkleman—despite nearly drowning—insisted on swimming. It helped him keep the accusing eyes of the sailor from driving him crazy.

The longer they exerted themselves in the sweltering sun, the thirstier they became. No one had water. Unlike soldiers, sailors on subs didn't carry canteens.

Tarkington scrunched as small as he could make himself, trying to ignore his nagging thirst. Besides that, he felt better than he had. His hearing returned, although his head still throbbed. He wasn't sure which incident had been worse, the first or second, but he was damned sure not going to complain.

It was his turn to take up the paddle. He did so eagerly; the work taking his mind from his discomfort. He found it helped not to watch the elusive island, but to keep his head down, counting each stroke. When he got to 1,000 he'd allow a glance. During one such glance, he saw a flash of something from the corner of his eye. He turned and was about to discount it as his imagination when he saw it again.

He stopped paddling and pointed, "Plane! Plane at ten o'clock high."

Everyone stopped paddling, and the second rubber boat, 20 yards back, caught up quickly. They saw the lead boat's occupants pointing, and soon everyone stopped paddling. As people saw it, they'd point it out to those who hadn't until everyone was staring and pointing.

Tarkington glanced at the island; they were much closer—he figured 500 yards. He called back to Lieutenant Commander Staub, "Gotta be Japs looking for survivors. We gotta keep paddling."

Staub nodded his agreement and motioned them, "Let's go, let's go! Keep paddling! We're almost there."

The swimmers put their heads down and stroked steadily. Winkleman considered himself an excellent swimmer, but he felt fatigued. He did the best he could.

The paddlers had figured out early to keep their strokes steady and in sync. Anything else was counterproductive. Tarkington called out a steady cadence and the paddlers were soon stroking steadily, pulling the raft ever closer.

Tarkington glanced at the plane which was getting closer, but not in such a way that meant someone had spotted them. The pilot was probably still over the area where the submarine went down. He wondered if perhaps the pilot could see the wreckage through the clear water. He doubted it, they'd been in deep water as far as he knew.

The water here was shallow though—only 20 feet. They'd been paddling over the top of a beautifully vibrant and colorful reef for the past

15 minutes. He hoped that—from above—their black boats would blend into the reef bottom. He didn't want to bet his life on it though.

The plane circled a few times then moved southeast, ever closer. Tarkington figured they had another ten minutes, at their current pace, before they'd have to deal with the white breakers, which he figured were 50 yards from the beach. If the plane didn't spot them soon, they might make it.

His shoulders were screaming and Hanscom must've felt the same because he ordered, "Switch!"

Tarkington gladly handed his paddle to the next man in line, and shifted his position, monitoring the plane. He pulled his submachine gun off his shoulder and checked the breach. Hanscom pointed, "Might just come in handy. Besides that, there're just sidearms."

Tarkington shrugged, "I hope it doesn't come to that. We'd be fish in a barrel." The plane went into a slow turn and Tarkington could hear the engine's noise change slightly, "What's he doing?"

Hanscom repositioned himself, "Doesn't look like he's spotted us yet."

Tarkington scowled, "He's spotted something. He's going lower and slowing down." He saw winking flashes and seconds later the sound finally reached them, "He's firing at something." He exchanged a worried glance with Hanscom. The firing continued for a long burst, then stopped. The plane went even lower, nearly out of sight, then arced up steeply, finally leveling off and slowly circling. "It's gotta be them."

Hanscom pursed his lips, shaking his head, then said, "You don't know that, Tark. Besides, seeing three men from a plane's nearly impossible, especially men who don't want to be seen. Could've been anything. Hell, maybe they're shooting up sharks. I'm surprised we haven't seen any ourselves."

Tarkington called back to the other raft, "You got a compass on you?"

Gilson nodded and croaked past a swollen tongue, "Yeah."

"Take a heading on that. I'll bet it's my guys."

Gilson nodded, pulling out the compass and yelling back, "I'll do it, but it's gonna be next to useless. There're currents and we're still drifting too."

Tarkington nodded his understanding but yelled back, "I'm going after them once we've dropped off the wounded."

Lieutenant Commander Staub clenched his jaw and was about to remind Tarkington how the chain of command worked, but Lieutenant Gilson touched his shoulder and said something Tarkington couldn't hear. Staub barked something back at his XO, but didn't address Tarkington.

The plane finally left the area, but Tarkington kept the paddlers at the same cadence, wanting to get to the beach quickly. The second boat slacked off a little, but stayed within 30 yards.

The reef shallowed, and as they neared the beach, it was obvious they'd be dealing with some significant breaking waves. The swell, which seemed nonexistent in deeper water, was enough to make the next 100 yards difficult.

Tarkington held the paddlers up just outside the breakers. The second boat nudged up against them and Staub stood, using Gilson's shoulder for support. He scowled, "Looks dangerous. If we capsize, we'll be cut to ribbons on the reef."

Winkleman, who was still swimming alongside, hefted himself into Tarkington's boat. He had the most experience in the ocean. He was panting from the exertion of swimming and his head felt waterlogged. "Gotta wait for the right sequence. The waves come in sets. There's usually time between each. Just gotta figure it out, then go like hell during the lull."

While they waited, sitting just outside the breakers, they also watched the island. The beach sand was pearl-white and the jungle beyond was lush, but didn't look as impenetrable as some. There was no sign of anyone, enemy or otherwise.

They rafted the boats up side-by-side. They were overcrowded and the swimmers—not wanting to risk being scraped along the reef—had squeezed into the rafts. Winkleman was on his knees, watching the undulating sea coming from behind. After a few minutes he yelled, "Okay, now! Stay straight. Rudder from the back."

Winkleman was in back, a paddle dragging behind, keeping the boat straight as the men paddled in quick, powerful strokes. The raft lurched forward, Winkleman calling out the cadence now, "Stroke, stroke, stroke."

He looked back, seeing the other raft falling behind, but still coming on strong. Gilson was in back, acting as the rudder man.

The clear water turned to churned-up white foam. This was the impact point. Another 15 yards would put them beyond where the breakers formed and into the more sedate, already-broken waves. Winkleman glanced back, seeing the swell building. He yelled, "Go hard! Pull!" The men were exhausted, but they put everything they had left into it. Despite that, it still felt as though they were paddling through syrup. The overloaded raft was low in the water, making it sluggish.

The swell hit the shallows and grew until it finally crested. Winkleman yelled, "Hold on!" The men stopped paddling, leaning into the raft, clutching the slippery tubes. Winkleman kept the rudder in place as the waved crashed just behind them. The whitewater overtook them, pushing the raft forward as though they'd sprouted an invisible engine. Winkleman couldn't keep himself from whooping, "Yaaahoo!"

The wave continued to carry them toward the beach, the raft skimming over the sharp reef. He turned, and the joy melted away. The second raft would not make it. The next wave in the set was building behind them and Winkleman knew it would break on them, instead of behind them.

He yelled, "Keep it straight!" The men were paddling like mad, but the wave crashed over the stern, enveloping Gilson. He couldn't keep the paddle ruddering, and the raft immediately turned sideways, sending sailors away from the wave and digging the front tube low into the water. The crashing whitewater lifted the other side and threw it over the top, capsizing them.

Everyone on the lead raft saw the second raft go over. Winkleman cranked on the paddle, turning his raft sideways on the now-benign wave. He yelled, "Paddle forward!" The men were dazed, watching for bobbing heads, but snapped into action, digging their paddles in and pulling themselves from the wave that was giving them a free ride into the beach.

The second raft was still upside down and was surfing in on the now-broken wave. Heads popped up behind the raft. Men who'd been thrown and were still in the impact zone of oncoming waves were thrashing their arms, struggling to stay on the surface.

The next wave crashed over them, driving them deeper into the sharp reef. The capsized raft tumbled toward the first and Tarkington yelled, "Grab it!" Two men jumped onto the bottom and tried to turn it right-side up while it was surfing in.

Winkleman steered, and the exhausted men paddled back toward the breakers. More heads were popping up, some bleeding from fresh wounds. They stood in the shallows and struggled forward, but the incessant breakers knocked them down and they'd come up spluttering, sporting more wounds. Some weren't able to stand, their life-jackets floating them, and they tumbled with the broken waves, like so much driftwood. The men on the raft hauled them in and soon were too full, forcing the uninjured back into the water to help whomever they could find toward the beach.

Finally, both boats, and everyone who'd been on them, sprawled on the beach. One sailor, who'd been unconscious from the initial air attack, was dead. They found him washed up on the beach, facedown and unresponsive. Everyone from the capsized raft was banged up to some degree. The cuts on their arms, legs, torsos and faces looked as though they'd been attacked by razor blades. The capsized raft had one sizable hole which had deflated one of the four compartmentalized chambers, leaving that segment flat and floppy. They found all the wooden paddles, but two were broken.

The sun beat down upon them like an angry god. None of them wanted to move. Tarkington sat up after catching his breath. His tongue was thick with thirst and he was sure he wouldn't be able to speak. He stood on shaking legs, kicking Winkleman as he passed. "Come on," he tried to say, but it came out as an uninterpretable bit of nonsense.

Winkleman felt the kick and knew what Tarkington meant. He pulled himself to a sitting position, looking around at the sprawled, exposed men. He forced himself to his feet, feeling as though he was asking his body to climb Mt. Everest rather than simply stand up. He followed Tarkington, kicking each man, helping them move toward the shade only 20 yards away.

Finally, they were all under the cover of the overhanging scrub trees and bushes. Tarkington never remembered being this thirsty. Every fiber, every cell, seemed to call out for water. His tongue felt foreign, as though he had a stale, dry fish in his mouth, threatening to block his airway. All he wanted to do was lay down and forget everything, but he knew if he did so, he probably wouldn't wake up. *Fuck it,* he thought, giving into the urge.

He was nearly in the oblivion when the image of Henry, Vick, and Stollman flashed through his mind. He forced his eyes open. He had to save them. They were still out there. The Japanese plane firing on them was proof of that. They needed his help and there was still one operational raft.

With great force of will, he pushed himself to his feet. His vision was blurry. None of the others were awake, some looked gray and dead, but he knew it was from extreme dehydration. He felt weak as a newborn kitten. How would he make it past the breakers? *Hell, I can't even make it to the raft.*

Along the edge of his consciousness, he saw a small brown person squatting in the jungle scrub. He held a long spear, staring at him with bright shimmering-brown eyes. Tarkington shook his head, thinking he was imagining things. But when it didn't fade away, he tried bringing his submachine gun from his back, but he couldn't lift his arms. The thought of bringing it to his shoulder, aiming and squeezing the trigger was like an impossible fantasy. Something only a superhero could do.

Without remembering it happening, Tarkington was suddenly on his knees. His vision was dimming but the little man was still there, standing now, holding the spear and walking toward him. This was how he'd die, a spear in the gut, as though he were a character from the Genghis Khan book he'd read in school. He hoped he wouldn't feel it; he always thought it would be a painful way to go.

The little man strode straight up to him until he was only feet away. Tarkington felt like a vassal about to lose his head to the hangman. He briefly wondered about his odd fixation on ancient history. But instead of spearing him, or lopping his head off, the man set his spear down carefully and lifted a bloated leather pouch, tilting the tip toward Tarkington's mouth. Sweet water hit his cracked, swollen lips, and he instinctively opened up, gulping down mouthfuls of the finest tasting water he ever remembered drinking.

He immediately felt better, his body responding to the water like a dry sponge dropped into a river. More spear-carrying men emerged from the jungle, moving among the sleeping sailors and soldiers, coaxing them awake with drops of water upon their lips. Most lunged involuntarily, seeking to suck every drop from the water bladders. Their saviors only allowed a few mouthfuls though, knowing too much too fast would make them sick.

Tarkington watched the other men come back to life as though they were being resurrected from the grave. The natives continued doling out water, and soon Tarkington's debilitating thirst was an unpleasant memory. His body still felt sore and weak, but his vision cleared and he felt human again. The natives spoke little, but what he heard he recognized distantly as Pidgin, a combination of Tagalog and English.

Tarkington stood, testing his balance, which was still off a little. The other sailors and soldiers scattered around the beach stayed down, nursing countless cuts and bruises. Tarkington plodded along the beach, his boots sinking into the sand, which was as white and as fine as sugar.

He teetered in front of Hanscom, who squinted up at him. Tarkington's throat still felt raw as he spoke, "Need to go out for Henry and the others. I need paddlers."

Hanscom stared up at him as though the staff sergeant had lost his mind. He shook his head and uttered back, "I—we can't go back out there, Tarkington."

Winkleman, who was on his back nearby, sat up and wobbled to his feet. "I'll go," he stated.

Hanscom scowled, shaking his head, "You need to rest first. You're wounded."

"They'll die out there."

"You don't even know if they're alive. If you go out there, you'll die too." He pointed to the crashing waves, "You won't make it past the break." Hanscom struggled to his feet, clutching his aching knees. "Just wait a minute. Let's talk to the natives first. Maybe they know something."

Tarkington watched the natives still moving from man to man, delivering water from the bladders. "They're speaking Pidgin, I think."

Hanscom nodded, pointing to Sergeant Gonzalez, "Gonzo's our linguist."

Gonzalez pulled himself upright, squinting up at them. He extended his hand and Winkleman stepped forward, helping him to his feet. Winkleman kept holding on after Gonzalez no longer needed his help and looking him in the eye, said, "Never thanked you for saving my life at the sub... Thank you."

Gonzalez nodded back, "You woulda done the same thing."

The moment passed, and Gonzalez shuffled up the beach to one of the natives. He smiled and addressed him in stilted Tagalog. The native responded, but soon the language changed to Pidgin and the conversation went back and forth much smoother.

Gonzalez was nodding and smiling, piquing everyone's interest. When the conversation finally ended, Gonzalez's smile couldn't be broader. "Henry, Vick, and Stollman are okay. They're on the other side of the island. These guys saw the smoke from the sub, then the Japanese strafing. They have outrigger canoes and went out to investigate. They found them out there."

Tarkington couldn't keep the emotion from overtaking him. His eyes stung, and he pinched the bridge of his nose. "That's—that's incredible!" Winkleman reached out, steadying him. Tarkington felt like he might drop to his knees and was thankful for Winkleman's support. He shook his head, his eyes glistening, "I can't believe it. Ask them to take me to them."

Gonzalez relayed the request and the native's smiles broadened and they nodded, motioning them to follow. None of them were in any shape to hurry though, and despite Tarkington's glee, he could only manage a shuffle.

It was obvious not everyone could make the trek, so those who could were helped along by the natives. The others stayed put; the natives promising to return with help and even makeshift stretchers. Lieutenant Commander Staub, Lieutenant Gilson, and Pharmacist Mate Wilkins stayed with the injured men. Despite the good news, the sailors were lamenting the loss of over half the crew and The Eel herself.

The natives led them along a well-used trail, which wound along a band of cliffs, eventually ending in a relatively large, protected bay. The sea was calm and flat here, with none of the waves along the west coast.

The short walk, about a mile, was hard on the fatigued men, but they put their heads down and ground it out. The natives explained to Gonzalez that they'd come from the much larger Panay Island approximately 50 miles southwest. They traveled in huge outrigger canoes and spent a week on this island spear fishing. Something they did a couple times each year.

At the edge of the jungle, there were ten small thatch and wood huts sitting upon stilts. The huts faced the bay and Tarkington thought it would be a wonderful place to pass the time while sipping a beer. Three men reclined in chairs on the front porch of the nearest hut.

Tarkington recognized them immediately and called out in his raspy voice, "You worthless scalawags! Knew you were loafing."

The three stood slowly, obviously as sore and fatigued as everyone else. Henry's sideways grin and Cajun drawl was music to Tarkington's ears, "Well, looky here. Thought we got rid of you sons-of-bitches."

They eased themselves down the rickety steps, stepping onto the soft warm sand in bare feet. Hugs, handshakes, and backslaps ensued.

Stollman pointed at Raker's arm. He'd fashioned his shirt into a sling. Stollman asked, "You okay?"

Raker shook his head, "Broke my damned arm. But never mind that. What the hell happened to you all? We looked high and low for ya."

Stollman shrugged, "When that bomb hit, we got thrown like rag dolls. I mean, it *launched us*. I must've been 20 feet high. We all were." He shook his head, continuing, "Those damned life-jackets saved our asses. Vick got knocked out and would've sunk like a rock if not for the floatation. By the time we found one another, the damned sub was too far away to swim to. We yelled and waved, but it was no use. Sub was on fire, and everyone was obviously preoccupied. Pretty soon, we couldn't even see it anymore, just the smoke and even that stopped."

Stollman looked at them. They were completely wrapped up in the story, so he continued. "Then we kinda rafted together and started swimming. We could barely see this here island. We were at it for hours but weren't getting any closer. And, to make matters worse, we attracted a bunch of sharks. Huge, nasty fucking things. We knew we were gonna die out there. We were just too damned tired." He paused, looking at Vick and Henry, who were nodding somberly.

Stollman's eyes hardened and his voice lowered, "When we heard that Jap plane," he pursed his lips and looked them in the eyes, "Well, we had a discussion." He blew out a lengthy breath then continued, "We could hunker down and die of," he held out fingers, counting them off: "drowning, exposure, thirst, or shark-bait." He paused, finally shrugging, "Or try getting their attention, and spend the rest of the war as prisoners." He looked at Vick and Henry, "We decided we had better chances with the Nips, so we waved and lo-and-behold, they saw us." He shook his head, "We shoulda known. Those yellow-bellied bastards did a couple fly-bys, waved, then the rear gunner opened up on us. He was walking the rounds around us—playing with us.

"I think the gun must've jammed cause the gunner started smacking it and jerking around in back, obviously pissed." He grinned, "The pilot came in for a landing, either gonna take us prisoner or shoot us with his sidearm. Luckily, old Henry still had his. He'd used it a few times on the damned sharks. When the plane got close, the gunner jumped onto the pontoon and sure enough, he had a pistol out, so Henry plugged him with his last two bullets.

"That pilot didn't wait around, gunned it and took off out of there like a shot. He left his wounded gunner behind." His smile faded as he remembered the scene, "All that blood put the sharks into a frenzy. They tore that guy up. He deserved it, but damn," he shook his head. "We figured we were next, but..." he opened his arms as though presenting a trophy, "these fine fellas showed up, and here we are."

Once everyone was escorted along the path to the bay, the Filipinos lit fires and soon the savory smells of grilled fish filled the air. The men were exhausted but the promise of food kept them awake and soon they were gorging themselves, barely tasting the subtle spices. Grease and chunks of fish dripped from their chins as they devoured the tasty morsels. There was little talking, only grunts of satisfaction. The natives watched, bemusedly exchanging glances with one another. When every morsel had been devoured, they all agreed it was one of the best meals they'd ever eaten.

Stuffed, the men's eyes drooped, but the Filipinos insisted they rouse themselves enough to make use of the huts. There wasn't room for all of them, so the wounded and a few of the surviving officers and NCOs filled them. Everyone else curled into the soft sand and fell asleep. They forgot the harrowing events of the day, at least until morning.

Tarkington lay beside his old friend Henry, staring up at the shimmering stars. The clouds from the morning were nowhere in sight, and the air was comfortable and thankfully dry. The soft purrs of sleeping men were all around them and Tarkington knew he wouldn't be far behind them. He murmured, "Thought we lost you guys out there, Henry."

Henry sighed, chewing on a blade of grass as usual. He talked around it, "Winkleman said you guys were about to take a raft out to search for us."

"Stupid, huh?"

"Probably. But I for one appreciate the thought. Being out there—bobbing around like shark bait—loneliest feeling I've ever had. Just waiting to die. It was surreal. Like nothing I've ever experienced."

"Yeah. I can only imagine." It was more words than Henry normally strung together at once, and that concerned Tarkington.

"What now?" Henry asked.

Tarkington's voice slowed as his body slowly shut down, falling toward the abyss of a deep, black sleep. He mumbled, "Dunno. Just glad we're all together again."

The next thing Tarkington knew, it was just getting light. The sensation of tiny prickles along his back and the sides of his legs made him jolt. Something skittered across the palm of his hand. He flicked whatever it was and glanced to the side, seeing the entire beach moving like a bizarre tapestry of bronze and blue. He thought he must still be dreaming, but the feel of more creatures moving across his body made him sit upright. The once shining-white beach was now full of countless small crabs, all making their way back to the sea. He knew they were harmless, but wondered how long they'd been snuggling up to him. By the feel of it, most of the night.

He brought his knees up, resting his arms across the top of them, and watched the glow in the east getting brighter and brighter, changing the wispy clouds from orange to pink. By the time the first glint of sun rose from the sea, all the crabs were gone—the only evidence they'd ever been there, tiny delicate tracks.

He took a deep breath in and blew it out slow. He figured the temperature was a degree or two cooler from when he'd fallen asleep, but he knew the day would be hot. He rolled his shoulders, feeling the stiffness. He rubbed his arm, noting the burn still hurt, but convinced himself it wasn't more than a first-degree burn. He noticed the Filipinos had left water bladders beside groups of slumbering men. He lifted one awkwardly and squeezed, forcing a thin stream of tepid water into his mouth. He gulped it down lustily. It tasted wonderful.

The sun was up, hanging just a few feet from the shimmering water. He stood gingerly and stretched his body. He felt surprisingly good—stiff beyond measure, but alive.

The men still slumbered all around him and he couldn't help noting how similar they looked to the Japanese soldiers he'd mowed down on the western coast of Luzon. Would he ever be able to see things like a normal person again? He suddenly wished the water bladder was full of liquor; he could go for a stiff drink right about now.

Henry sat up, stretching his neck side-to-side. "Morning," Tarkington growled.

Henry squinted up at him and got to his feet. "I feel like I've been run over by a tank," he mumbled. Tarkington handed him the bladder of water and he took a long squirt, then wiped his mouth with the back of his hand. "Damn, that's good. Where'd the Filipinos go?" He pointed to where the ten outrigger canoes had been pulled up on the beach but were now gone.

Tarkington hadn't noticed their absence but didn't let on. He shrugged, "Don't know, they were gone when I got up 15 minutes ago."

Henry squinted out to sea and pointed, "There they are. Must be fishing already. Early morning's usually best for that sort of thing."

Sure enough, Tarkington saw them maybe a half mile out, still over the reef, bobbing with the slight swell. "Spear fishing, right?"

"That's what they said."

"Ever do that on the bayou?"

Henry gave a sideways grin and nodded slowly. "Yep. Lot of fun, but you had to watch for gators." His face changed, and he pushed sand around with his feet, "Don't know if I'll ever feel safe doing that again. Not after those damned sharks."

"Worse'n gators?"

Henry shrugged, "Well, not really, I guess. I mean gators kinda sneak up on you; you've got some time to move away—but sharks?" He shook his head, "They're just outright killers. I don't even think they were hungry— just wanted to kill for the sheer joy of it." His gaze went far away, recalling, "Their eyes are dead. I can't even describe it."

Tarkington had never seen his lead scout and oldest friend spooked by anything, especially an animal. Growing up, Henry dealt with a variety of dangerous beasts daily while subsistence hunting in the vast and bayou. "You shot a couple of 'em?" Tarkington asked.

Henry shrugged and nodded, "Yeah. turned 'em, but didn't seem to have much affect otherwise. Kept coming back. There was a bunch of them though, so not sure if it was the same one or not."

"That's rough."

Henry grinned and slapped Tarkington's back, "That it was." He strode down the beach, stripped off his clothes, and dove into the greenish-blue water. He stayed under, taking powerful strokes, propelling himself toward the sun.

By midday, the fishermen returned and again they were treated to a delicious seafood feast. Gonzalez was told they planned to cross the 50 miles of sea back to Panay that night and they would be glad to take them along.

Gonzalez relayed the message to Lieutenant Commander Staub and the other officers and NCOs. Staub asked, "Are there Japanese on Panay?"

Gonzalez asked and translated the response, "Cruzado says yes, but not as many as other islands and they're concentrated more in the southeastern area, near the Port Of Iloilo. He says that Hamtic, where they're from, is virtually empty of Japanese."

Staub nodded his understanding, "Makes sense. Iloilo's one of the safest ports in the Philippines. Ask 'em why at night?"

After translating, he replied, "Says the Japanese forbid fishing more than a mile offshore. There are occasional Japanese ships and boats coming out of Iloilo Port and if they're spotted, they'll fire on them. Safer at night."

Lieutenant Gilson asked, "Do they have enough room for all of us?"

The translation took longer and finally Gonzalez said, "It'll be tight, but yes. He says we ate most of their fish, so there's more room than normal. He says we can eat the rest before we leave."

Tarkington shook his head, "Crap, we ate through their supplies?"

Gonzalez answered, "He explained that there's plenty of fish closer inland. This trip is more for pleasure. Something they've been doing for generations. The fish aren't needed in Hamtic."

The men were glad to have the afternoon to laze around the beach eating fish. Tarkington made a point of doing a thorough count of all the weapons and ammo. All the officers had sidearms, but few had extra magazines or spare rounds. The final count was Tarkington's one submachine gun with a 30 round magazine—which he'd painstakingly unloaded, dried out, and reloaded—and ten pistols ranging from service Colt .45s to a .38 Special. None of the Arisaka rifles, or Stollman's cherished Type-96 light machine gun, had survived the submarine sinking. Tarkington realized his prized Japanese Samurai sword was also a casualty. He wondered if someday a treasure hunter would come across it, assuming this war ever ended.

11 weapons, with limited ammo for 26 soldiers and sailors, wouldn't allow them to fight off much if they encountered a Japanese boat, but it was better than nothing. At Major Hanscom's direction, the interchangeable ammo got redistributed evenly, which meant the Colts each had 14 rounds. The .38 and Tarkington's magazine held their own non-interchangeable ammunition.

By the time darkness fell, the men felt reasonably rested. Many had slept most of the day, and those that didn't still felt a thousand times better than they had when they had washed up onto the beach.

The Filipinos waited another two hours, something having to do with the sea currents, before telling them it was time. The outriggers were long, carved deeply, and felt incredibly stable. They scrunched into them, knees tucked tight to their chests with the man in front using shins to rest their backs upon. The Filipinos sat upon the carved seats, wielding beautiful paddles.

Once everyone was aboard, they pushed off and the prows cut into the calm sea. Tarkington gazed back at the idyllic little beach with the comfortable huts, thinking perhaps he should go over the side. Live out the rest of his life there, away from this cursed war. He turned back forward, shaking his head, thinking, *maybe someday.*

The Filipinos paddled efficiently, not straining nor slacking. Their bare torso muscles flexed and stretched and it was obvious they'd been paddling all their lives. The boats sliced through the sea in near total silence. The only sound was the paddles pulling through the water and the occasional cough or sneeze. Soon the back-and-forth motion of pulling, pausing, and pulling again, lulled Tarkington into a place on the edge of sleep.

Being cramped and sitting on the hard-wood bottom wasn't comfortable. That was the only thing keeping Tarkington awake. Hours passed— the only change, the paddlers occasionally switching sides to spread out the fatigue.

Tarkington spent the time on the edge of oblivion, thinking. His men had been through a lot. From the first Japanese thrust into Luzon, just hours after Pearl Harbor, to the final clash on the Bataan Peninsula, to the hard-fought rain-soaked chaos of guerrilla warfare, and now the sinking of their ride out of it all. It had been a hell of a year. And now, sitting in an ancient dugout canoe somewhere in the openness of the Sulu Sea, watching starlight reflect off water, blurring with each powerful paddle stroke.

He tried to think of home. What were his parents doing at that moment? Did they know he was alive? How must it be for them not knowing his fate? And what of his little brother? Was he still in school? Was it even something that still went on, or were they shut down because all the young men were at war? He had no idea.

Images of men he'd known: friends, soldiers—all dead—flashed through his mind. Their fates playing out before him like a deranged theater of the macabre. The moment of death, or its aftermath, tattooed onto his mind forever. Some he couldn't help: men blown up by mortars or artillery, or gunned down because they didn't take cover fast enough, or simply in the wrong place at the wrong time. Others *were* his fault. Men following his orders, like Fernandez. The kid was barely a teenager. He should've been playing marbles on the school grounds, but instead was feeding the worms in a dead village, full of other people who'd died because of his actions.

He pictured his kid brother again. Pictured him with his right hand raised, wearing the uniform of some branch of the US armed forces, vowing to uphold the righteous values of America. *No*, he seethed to himself, wanting to reach across time and space and shake him, scream at him, *it's not what you think, Robert. Stay out of it at all costs!* He clenched his jaw, trying to dispel the image, but it wouldn't go away. His younger brother volunteering to fight. Just like his older brother. His own example would get him killed too.

Tarkington's vision focused, like a telescope being adjusted from fuzzy to perfect. He lifted his head, looking at the stars. They'd been blurred with the motion of the water, but the sky was crystal clear and with the clarity, so too cleared his mind. With the light, warm wind whipping past his ears, he vowed to himself that he'd end this war in any way that he could. If it killed him, so be it, but he'd kill whoever needed killing. He was already blooded, already ruined. He'd never be able to live a normal life. No matter the scene, even the very stars he looked at now reminded him of nights laying in ambush, the terror of waiting followed by horrific violence. Nothing would be the same for him, so why not *use* him? Use the rest of him up, so men like his brother Robert wouldn't have to fight.

8

One Month Earlier

Colonel Fertig awoke from a light sleep, his eyes flickering open. The shabby room with the leaking roof was still dark this early in the morning. He would've liked to slip back into sleep, but once he woke there was no going back, as though his body knew what it needed and signaled his brain: time to wake up.

Sometimes he wished it wasn't that way, but for most of his life, he'd averaged just five hours of sleep. When he was working for the mining company, it was good for his career. He'd arrive early and leave late. His coworkers often teased that he never left. Despite that, it was why he'd risen so quickly through the managerial hierarchy.

Now, however, his early waking was more of a burden. There'd always been things that needed doing before, but now that the war was in full swing, he found he rarely knew what to do with his time. Besides keeping out of sight from the Japanese, his days were boring.

He'd fled to the Misamis Province of the southernmost Philippine Island of Mindanao when the rest of his US Army unit surrendered or found a way off the island.

He was a reserve US Army officer, carrying the rank of Lieutenant

Colonel. He got called back to active duty when it became obvious the Japanese might be "up to something," as General Winningham had phrased it. Fertig wondered what had become of that old war-bird. Last he'd seen him, he was taking a ship north to Luzon, only days before the Japanese invaded.

He swung his legs over the rickety bed frame stacked with frond leaves and covered with a sheet which had seen better days. The leaves were probably due for an upgrade, but comfort wasn't all that important to him. He'd sleep as well on the dirt floor as on the bedding. It was another one of his peculiar sleep habits; he'd get his five solid hours of sleep regardless of the comfort level.

Although his days weren't as filled with the seemingly endless minutiae of working for a mining company in a far-off exotic locale, he hadn't been idle.

He stood, stretching his tall frame side-to-side, feeling the familiar pop and crunch of joints and bones. He performed ten minutes of four calisthenics exercises; always the same four, sometimes varying their order, but never the count.

Once done, he opened the solid wood door; the hinges squeaked badly, reminding him once again to have someone grease the damned things. The town was dark and still, and not just because of the early hour. The Japanese, although not on this section of Mindanao in force, imposed strict light restriction rules. It wasn't a monumental problem. Many of the homes only had lanterns anyway and kerosene had become increasingly scarce.

From the darkness a small woman appeared. His six-foot-two inch frame towered over her, making her seem childlike, melting her 60 years of life momentarily. She arched her head back, muttering something he didn't quite catch. She was always awake before him, and he wondered if she ever slept.

"Morning, Lana," he uttered. She held out a bundle of firewood, which he took from her graciously. "Salamat," he said, thanking her. He'd been in the Philippines long enough to be fluent in their language. She lingered, and he asked, "Is it time already?" She nodded in the darkness. He sighed and re-entered the room, the hinges protesting loudly. He placed the wood in front of the little stove, and crouched in front, shoving short lengths of wood inside, then lighting the duff beneath with his Zippo lighter. Light emanated, illuminating Lana's smiling features.

"One month payment," she said.

He grinned, shaking his head, "You know you're worse than landlords in the states? At least there, they wait for a decent hour."

She held out her gnarled right hand. She only had three fingers: the thumb, index and pinkie. He'd always wondered how she'd lost them, but doubted she'd tell him if he asked. She was a woman of few words and less emotion.

She repeated herself, "One month. Pay now."

The dry wood she'd brought crackled as the fire took and a puff of acrid smoke wafted out. He shut the iron door, careful to keep the bottom air holes open. He stood to his full height, reaching into his pant's pocket and pulling out a few coins, which he dabbled through in the low light. She reached up, like a child reaching for candy, pulling his hand down to her level. She took what he owed, impatient with him. He only paid her in US coins, and he wondered if she knew the exchange rate. He wouldn't put it past the sly old gal. She never took more than he owed—a month's rent for the rundown, leaking room put him back 20 US cents—and she supplied firewood, washed his clothes, and sometimes cooked his meals.

He shook his head, stuffing the rest of the coins back into his pockets, "You're putting me in the poorhouse, Lana."

She shook her head, pointing her misshapen index finger up at him, "You're a rich man, Colonel." With money in hand, she left him to heat water for his morning tea.

He watched her go, the door squeaking, "Can we get the door fixed?" he asked.

Without looking back, she said, "Door works fine. It open and close."

He chuckled. She was right; it did its job. He scowled, *if I could get the same work out of Anthony, I'd be thrilled.*

The sun was up and Fertig had been awake for hours going over plans for the day. Colonel Anthony Rodrigo was in town waiting for him at the central building. Fertig stood, placed his wide-brimmed straw hat upon his unruly red hair, and pushed the door open, stepping into the bright sunlight.

The normal hustle and bustle was somewhat diminished today. He wondered if it had anything to do with the upcoming meeting. It would be a momentous day, one way or another.

He strode through the streets, greeting townspeople he knew with hearty handshakes, nodding and smiling at those he knew less well. He had little to fear from the Japanese; they didn't have a large presence here. The few that were kept to their small, under-manned compound. Their presence tolerated only because Fertig convinced his burgeoning resistance to leave them alone. If attacked, he explained, the Japanese would send a larger force, possibly forcing them out of their towns and villages. As long as they stayed confined to their compound, Fertig and the others could live almost as though they had before the invasion.

By the time he got to the central building, Fertig had an entourage of men and women surrounding him. Each of them was a part of his network of resistance members.

Inside, with his own entourage of young men carrying rifles and machetes, Colonel Rodrigo awaited. Before the Japanese invasion, *Colonel* Rodrigo had been *Lieutenant* Rodrigo in the Filipino Army. He'd given himself the new rank in an attempt to put himself on equal footing with Fertig, who he considered to be a rival, rather than an ally. His youth was immediately obvious, however, making his rank seem silly and far-fetched.

Before entering, Fertig exchanged a brief word with his second-in-command, Juan Gonbono. He'd been a schoolteacher before the war and he and Fertig were kindred spirits in both their incessant drive and high intelligence. "You're okay with this?" Fertig asked.

Juan nodded somberly, shrugging, "It's only a title. If it means he'll join us, so be it."

Fertig nodded; they'd been over it many times before. He leaned in so only Juan could hear, "He'll be away in his sector anyway. Our relationship will remain the same."

Juan nodded, slapping his old friend's shoulder, "I know." His face grew serious. It was the same face he'd seen when forced to kill. "Are you sure you want to go in alone?"

Fertig shrugged, "I'll be fine. If he kills me..." he leaned in close again, "make sure he doesn't leave here alive." Juan nodded, deadly serious.

Fertig touched his shoulder and went up the steps. He stopped briefly on the porch, turning and waving to his compatriots, who returned his wave with worried looks.

Fertig entered the central building, leaving the townsfolk to wander, waiting for the results of the momentous meeting between the two leading resistance groups. None of them felt good about letting him go in alone, but it surprised none of them. It was the tall American's way.

Less than an hour later, Fertig and Rodrigo stepped from the central building side-by-side. Behind them, Rodrigo's guards hovered, their rifles slung over their shoulders, scanning the crowd of onlookers suspiciously.

A silence hovered over the crowd. Fertig grinned, scanning the sea of eager faces. The sun was at its zenith, blazing down upon them. Normally, they'd be tucked under shade trees or near the water, but the momentous meeting had everyone's attention.

Fertig glanced at Colonel Rodrigo's young, stoic face, then addressed the crowd in Tagalog: "Today is the day Colonel Rodrigo and his brave fighters join us in our struggle against the Japanese invaders. With our combined forces, we can coordinate our efforts, assuring our success." There was a murmuring of relief from the crowd.

Fertig continued, "As before, Colonel Rodrigo's fighters will remain across the peninsula, concentrating their efforts from Malabang. We will remain in the shadow of Mount Malindang, here in Ozamiz. Colonel Rodrigo will operate under my command, which will allow us to coordinate our attacks." He paused, and a cheer went up. His grin widened, letting them rejoice. When things died down, he continued, "We will continue to grow our forces, stockpiling weapons and food. Nothing will change for the moment, but when the time comes, our combined forces will strike the enemy." Another cheer and Fertig held up his hands so he could continue. "The Japanese are strong, but their time is short. The might of the United States and all her allies will prevail. When the time is right," he held up a finger, pausing, "and not before, we will be an integral part of taking back the Philippines." A raucous cheer and this time Fertig let them continue. Rodrigo's smile faded, however.

Fertig turned to his new partner, smiling. Rodrigo quickly smiled back, but it didn't reach his eyes. Fertig had no illusions that the man wasn't still dangerous despite their new agreement. Rodrigo was a man of loose morals, a hot-head. He'd do what needed doing to survive, but Fertig knew he'd betray him as soon as he could get away with it.

For now, Rodrigo needed the alliance for his own survival. His band of cutthroats had drawn too much attention to themselves. The Japanese swept through their town, rounding up every military-aged man and carted them off in chains.

Some had returned with tales of torture and death, but most didn't return at all. Rodrigo's once-robust force was reduced by over half. To make matters worse, the remaining townsfolk turned against them, forcing them out. Their bare-bones, disease-infested camp, whittled them down further. Many men disappeared in the night, taking their skills west, joining Fertig's fighters.

Fertig didn't need to take in Colonel Rodrigo, but after discussing the young man's overtures to join forces, he and Juan Gonbono decided it would be good to have eyes and ears across the peninsula as an early warning system. It would also be helpful to keep Rodrigo's ill-fated attacks under control. So far, the Japanese had left Fertig's section of Mindanao mostly alone, but there was only so much the Japanese would put up with before they struck, and Rodrigo was only making it worse.

Before the Japanese sweep of his forces, Rodrigo had complained loudly about Fertig's complacency. At first, this drew younger, more hot-headed fighters to his cause. Fertig counseled patience, but Rodrigo would have none of it and he blatantly attacked a Japanese convoy.

His poorly-trained men disabled one truck, inconveniencing the convoy for an hour. They'd expended most of their ammunition and—despite Rodrigo's claims to the contrary—sources said the Japanese didn't suffer a single casualty. Disabling the truck had cost five men killed, six wounded, and one captured. Not a good trade. The attack had been disastrous. Two days later, after torturing their captives to death, they swept through the village.

Soon, Rodrigo and his henchmen, accompanied by two of Fertig's trusted soldiers, left Ozamiz. They crossed Panguil Bay at its narrowest point using dugout canoes.

Fertig sent his two men with the intent to not only bolster Rodrigo's forces but also to monitor him. Fertig made sure they understood the dangers they were taking upon themselves. If Rodrigo betrayed him, the first thing he'd do was kill them. They'd volunteered despite the danger.

After the meeting, Juan Gonbono joined him inside the central building to discuss the details. "So, that went well?" he asked.

Fertig nodded, "Yes, as well as could be expected. He'll do what I say... for now."

Gonbono shook his head, "I trust him even less than I did before. He's a boy in a man's role."

Fertig shrugged, "I wish there were another choice, but he's what we've got. I wouldn't have hired him to take out the trash."

"You could order his replacement."

Fertig looked sideways at his long-time friend, "He'd go straight to the Japs, rat us out immediately." Gonbono lowered his head, looking over the top of his glasses the way he used to look at students who were being particularly dense.

Fertig sighed, knowing what Gonbono was suggesting. Since being forced to watch the Japanese rape and kill his wife, his old friend developed a dark side which hadn't been there before. He didn't blame him; he had every right to his dark side. Gonbono's only goal was to make the Japanese pay. If it meant killing a fellow Filipino who made that goal more difficult, he wouldn't hesitate.

Fertig pursed his lips, nodding, then said, "We'll see how things go first."

9

The crew of The Eel and the GIs reached land in the wee hours of the morning. Tarkington jolted awake when the bow of the canoe abruptly met the shore. He didn't think he could fall asleep, but he obviously had. They'd all stumbled from the boats, glad to be out of their cramped positions.

The Filipinos led them through the quiet streets filled with single-level, blocky houses. Moving quietly was instinctual for the GIs, but the sailors stumbled along, not worried about noise or staying out of sight.

The Filipinos finally urged them to stay quiet and out of sight. They told them that the vast majority of Filipinos abhorred the Japanese occupiers, but there were always bad seeds who would use every situation for their own advantage. Staying out of sight decreased the chances of betrayal. They went quieter, although still too loud as far as the GIs were concerned.

Finally, the Filipinos led them to an abandoned factory-like building on the edge of town. The rusted-out equipment and grasses growing through cracks in the concrete floor told them the factory had been defunct long before the invasion. The Filipinos got the word out to trusted friends and family, and soon the soldiers and sailors were set up with sleeping mats and even thin blankets.

Before anyone could lie down and go to sleep, Major Hanscom had Tarkington and Winkleman assign men to two-hour watch cycles. Tarkington put men outside along each corner of the sprawling building, armed with pistols. He kept his submachine gun close, found an unoccupied piece of concrete, and fell asleep quickly.

It seemed like an instant later, but three hours had passed when Tarkington woke, noticing streaking daylight coming through gaps in the walls. The roof was relatively intact, which was probably why the floor wasn't damp. He wouldn't want to live there long term, but the factory kept them out of sight, allowing them to get some rest.

He should've been on guard duty by now; he was scheduled to relieve Henry. Annoyed, he walked to the southern corner and peered out into the bright daylight. Raker turned and waved with his good right arm, his left still tightly bound in the makeshift sling. "Morning, Tark."

Tarkington growled, "I'm supposed to be on guard duty. Henry didn't wake me."

Raker shrugged, "We figured you needed some rest, what with your burn and all."

Tarkington's eyes went to slits, "Bullshit. I don't need coddling." He tilted his chin to Raker's arm, "You're worse off than I am."

Raker nodded, "I know. Wasn't our idea, actually. Hanscom ordered it."

Tarkington looked confused, "Why?" he wondered.

Raker looked around, then leaned close, "You were yelling out in your sleep. Having a nightmare or something." He shrugged, "Think he's worried about you."

"Yelling? Really?" Raker nodded, looking embarrassed. "He thinks I'm cracking up? Is that it?"

Raker leveled his icy gaze and said, "We don't care what anyone says or thinks, Tark. You may not have the rank, but we'll follow you anywhere."

Tarkington stared back, giving him a quick nod, then asked, "Any idea where the good major is?"

Raker pointed his thumb, "Last I saw him was near the north corner."

Tarkington went back into the factory building weaving his way past sailors, some still sleeping, most up and wandering about, checking out their new surroundings.

Tarkington found Major Hanscom speaking with Lieutenant Commander Staub and Lieutenant Gilson. He walked up to them and stiffened. Hanscom stopped what he was saying, "Staff Sergeant Tarkington, good morning."

Tarkington gave him a fleeting grin, more menacing than friendly. "Can I have a word, Major?" Sergeant Gonzalez, who was nearby cleaning his sidearm, noticed the agitation in his voice. He stopped what he was doing and watched.

Hanscom noticed it too. He lifted his chin and turning toward him said, "Certainly, Staff Sergeant."

When it was obvious Hanscom wasn't going to follow him for a more private conversation, Tarkington forged on, "You took me off the guard duty rotation. Why?"

Hanscom gave a furtive glance at Gilson and Staub, then answered, "Oh, yes. Well, I thought you needed more rest."

"If I needed more rest, I wouldn't have put myself on guard duty." He intentionally left off the "sir," making Lieutenant Commander Staub's jaw ripple.

Hanscom gave him a thin-lipped smile and continued, "Well, I thought you'd be happy for a few more hours of shut-eye."

"Not your call," Tarkington replied icily.

Hanscom's face changed from amicable to harsh. "Look," he gazed back at the navy officers and lowered his voice, "You yelled out in your sleep. Nightmares. It's not your fault, something that happens to men who've been under as much stress as..."

Tarkington cut him off, seething, "I'm not a head case, Major. A fucking nightmare? Okay, yeah sometimes, but it's none of your damned business, and until it affects the safety of *my* men, stay the hell outta my way!"

Lieutenant Commander Staub couldn't contain himself a second longer. He stepped alongside Hanscom's shoulder, raising a finger, "Stop this insubordination at once, Staff Sergeant. There's a chain of command and you need to relearn your place in it or by God, I'll..."

Tarkington stepped forward, just inches from Staub's face and hissed, "Or you'll what, Commander? You gonna court-martial me out here? You even know the situation?" Staub was stunned and couldn't speak, having no experience with an enlisted man confronting him in such a way. "Let me fill you in," Tarkington continued, "We're in occupied territory. Something my men and I are intimately familiar with. We've been living and fighting this way for months now. You want to pretend things are normal, as though you're back on your sub or perhaps back in Pearl, dressing men down for not polishing their boots?" He lifted his finger, slowly shaking his head, "That ain't reality, sir. Not out here. You wanna survive? You'll listen to me and my men." He shrugged, "Or you don't, and we go our separate ways. We'll be better off on our own anyway. I won't allow your by-the-book bullshit to put my men in jeopardy."

Staub looked as though his head might explode. He looked at Major Hanscom, hoping the ranking Army officer would put his man in his place, but instead Hanscom lifted his chin and said, "Tarkington's right, Commander. He and his men didn't only survive on Luzon months after the Allied surrender, they also did significant damage to the enemy. It's the reason they sent you here. I deferred to his judgement, and he orchestrated a defense which led to the destruction of nearly an entire company of enemy soldiers." He looked beyond Tarkington's shoulder, seeing the rest of Tark's Ticks on their feet, menacingly facing the sailors who were also on their feet, wondering what the hell was happening.

Silence ensued. The GIs separated from each other as nonchalantly as though it were nothing to be facing overwhelming odds. The sailors looked downright nervous. It was bad enough having their boat shot out from under them and being marooned behind enemy lines, but now they had to fight these guys?

Lieutenant Commander Staub faced Major Hanscom and said with disgust, "You obviously can't control your man, Major. I was giving you the benefit of the doubt. However, it's clear that you're not fit to lead. I'm relieving you." He leveled his icy blue eyes at Tarkington and again raised his finger at him, "You are under arrest, Staff Sergeant." Staub lifted his chin, "Arrest him, Gil."

Lieutenant Gilson stepped forward and pleaded, "Skipper, this is crazy. We're behind enemy lines. What am I to do, shackle him? Put him behind bars?"

"Yes!" Staub screamed in frustration. "That's exactly what *arrest* means."

Lieutenant Gilson took a deep breath and moved toward Tarkington. He pointed at Petty Officer Yankowski, a broad-chested sailor, who looked to be the only sailor eager to take on the GIs. "You heard him, Petty Officer."

Yankowski took one step before the GIs had their sidearms drawn and aimed at his head. Yankowski stopped and gulped, losing some of his swagger. Sailors responded by drawing their own sidearms, but kept the barrels down. Gilson held up his hands, "Easy now. Easy. Put 'em away." The sailors happily complied, but the GIs didn't waver.

Tarkington stepped away, shaking his head, "You're not arresting me. You've made your choice, Commander. You're on your own." He retreated toward his men, gathered his things off the floor while the others kept their sidearms ready. "Wink, get Raker in here. Gather everything up. We leave in five." Winkleman nodded and trotted to the southern corner, bringing Raker up to speed on the situation.

Five minutes later, they moved to the door. Major Hanscom and Sergeant Gonzalez met them there. Hanscom held out up his hand, "This is crazy, Staff Sergeant. You're not *that* far from military justice. You need to be careful."

Tarkington stopped and glanced back at Lieutenant Commander Staub, who was pretending not to notice their conference. Tarkington sneered, "You know as well as I do, those guys have no chance out here. We need to blend in, get away from prying eyes. You remember what happened on Luzon. The Japs aren't the only threat out here."

"I know, but this is all new for Staub."

Tarkington sighed, "You and Gonzalez can come along if you want."

"I can't just abandon these men."

"It didn't have to go this way. Staub made his choice."

Hanscom placed his hand on Tarkington's shoulder. "You can't expect him to throw away an entire career of military training just because the situation changed. If everyone did that the entire thing would fall apart, and the Japs would be walking the streets of L.A. by now." Tarkington glanced at Staub who was discussing something with his XO. Hanscom pleaded, "Let me talk to him."

Tarkington considered, then shook his head pushing Hanscom's hand off, "He won't listen to you; he's stripped you of your rank, Major."

Hanscom shook his head, "He can't do that, we're the same rank...at least I don't think he can. Navy and Army," he shrugged, "Well, I'm not sure."

Tarkington stepped past him, "Good luck, Major." At the door he paused, glancing outside, making sure the way was clear, then moved out quickly to the edges of town and into the low scrub of the countryside.

Hanscom watched them go, feeling suddenly vulnerable. "Dammit," he cursed under his breath.

Once Tarkington was out of the village and concealed in the surrounding scrub, he felt better. He had no reason to suspect the Filipinos. They hated the Japanese as much or more than they did, but he didn't feel safe in confines of the factory.

Tarkington waved them close, "These surrounding hills are good observation points. Let's find somewhere and hunker down for the day, see how things pan out." He looked at each man. They looked tired but determined. "Look, I didn't like how that went down, but..."

Stollman interrupted, "We didn't either, Tark. Staub can run a sub, but he's a fish outta water out here. Him not understanding that," he paused, shrugging, "well, he'd get us all killed."

Tarkington nodded, "I agree, but I don't like leaving them on their own like that. Hanscom and Gonzalez know the score, but Staub tried to relieve him, so who knows if he'll listen."

Henry asked, "So what's the plan? Keep an eye on 'em?"

Tarkington sighed and nodded, "For now, yeah. We'll see what happens and help 'em out if we can."

It didn't take long to find a spot with suitable cover and a view of the town. The dilapidated factory was the closest building. Not much had happened since they left. The sailors still stood guard, at least on the corners the GIs could see. They watched Filipinos enter and leave throughout the morning. It was difficult from this distance to know if they were the same men who'd ferried them there. The fishermen seemed to understand the need for secrecy. The possibility of an opportunistic individual looking for an in with the Japanese was a distinct possibility.

From their vantage point, the townspeople seemed to go about the daily business of life. There were no curious gatherings of people trying to get a look at the Americans holed up in the abandoned building. They either weren't interested, or the fisherman had kept it to themselves. It was also a relief not to see any sign of Japanese soldiers. Once in a while they heard the distant thrumming of a boat's engine, which they assumed to be Japanese patrol boats, but they never saw them on the sparkling sea.

Tarkington assumed the submarine battle with the patrol boat hadn't gone unnoticed. He wondered if the Japanese bomber had relayed the submarine's sinking, or if they were still trying to locate it. Had the Japanese pilot reported seeing survivors? Perhaps that is what the boat was out there searching for. He thought about the rubber boats they'd carelessly left on the beach at the first island. Would they be spotted and investigated? Would the Japanese piece together what had happened and send men here? The thought caused a chill, despite the sweltering temperature. The sooner they left this town, the better.

By midday, the men were hungry. The fish feasts over the past few days had been wonderful, but now they had nothing. The Filipinos had left water flasks for them the night before and they'd taken as many as they could carry, knowing they would replenish the remaining sailors. Water wasn't the issue. Being hungry wasn't new to them, though. This was a different island than Luzon, but the vegetation would be similar and they could subsist, at least for a little while. Inevitably, they'd eventually have to reach out to the locals for help.

Not much was happening around the factory building. It was past noon now and there had been some guard duty switches and some light foot traffic in and out, but other than that it was quiet. The GIs hunkered in shaded areas, but the heat was stifling. They were farther south than Luzon, and the difference in temperature was staggeringly obvious. There was no sign of rain, and Tarkington wondered if the rainy season was over or if it was simply different here. The light scrub and low trees suggested less rainfall, but he doubted there could be that much difference. He chalked it up to another of the myriad of mysteries these islands held.

Tarkington's eyelids were getting heavy. He was about to put the men on sentry duty shifts, not knowing what the night might hold, when the distinctive sound of a boat engine brought him fully awake. Everyone looked to the water. Beyond the shining white stucco buildings of the town, the sea sparkled blue and green. They could see lines of outrigger canoes, some of which they'd used the night before. There was a veritable fleet of them. Many had been out in the early morning and returned with whatever fish they'd caught. Beyond them was the distinct cutting wake of a fast boat. It could only be a warship. From this distance it was hard to be sure, but it looked similar to the boat that attacked the sub. It was coming fast.

There were no docks along this town's coast line. The shallow reef extended for at least a quarter mile in every direction, making it impossible for any deep draft vessel to come all the way up to the beach.

Tarkington wished he had the Commander's binoculars, but they rested on the bottom of the Sulu Sea, alongside his Samurai sword. There was little doubt the boat's destination was the town. Tarkington shook his head, "This isn't good."

Raker, whose broken arm was still in the tight sling, asked, "Why they coming here? It's not like they can follow a scent or tracks out there."

Tarkington said, "Bet they found the rafts we left on the beach. Once they figured that out, the nearest villages along this coast are suspect."

Physical pain seemed to move across Henry's face and he slowly shook his head, "Damn. That was stupid."

Tarkington nodded. Winkleman shook his head and spoke before Tarkington could, "We were out of our heads with thirst. Hell, I felt like I was on another planet. Last thing any of us was thinking about was hiding the damned rafts." He guffawed, "Even if we *had* thought of it, none of us had the energy."

Tarkington was about to remind him that after they'd slaked their thirst and eaten, they'd spent the entire day sleeping instead of covering their tracks, but Henry said, "Nothing we can do about it now."

Tarkington bit his lower lip, knowing he was correct but still marking it up as another stupid mistake which might end up killing his men.

Henry pointed at the factory. There were Filipinos sprinting toward it; they'd obviously seen the Japanese patrol boat too. Soon, blue-clad sailors streamed from the rear doorway, led by the Filipinos.

They gathered outside the factory, discussing something with the Filipinos. Tarkington thought he could see Hanscom and Gonzalez among them, but they all wore the same light blue, so it was tough to be sure. No one was being detained or forced as far as he could tell, which made him hopeful that perhaps Staub and Hanscom had come to an agreement. Staub and Gilson were obvious even from here, their khaki-colored officer's uniforms set them apart. *Perfect targets,* Tarkington thought.

"Japs are offloading a dingy. They're coming in," stated Vick.

Stollman shook his head, "What I wouldn't give for my Jap machine gun. Set up on the beach, all them Japs bunched up like that...?" he gave a low whistle, "Problem solved."

They watched the sailors being led into the scrub, the four Filipinos taking them along a well-used track leading due east and disappearing into a low range of jungle-encrusted hills.

They were soon out of sight, and Tarkington had a decision to make. The dingy was halfway to shore. Even from here, their bristling weapons were obvious. Tarkington watched them come, then glanced back at the sailors just going out of sight along the trail. He pursed his lips and said, "Sure'd be nice to have some of that hardware."

10

They watched the ten Japanese sailors spread out and move quickly through town. This wasn't a normal patrol, showing the locals they were in charge. This looked more like an assault and it turned Tarkington's stomach. Once again, his actions were causing pain.

It didn't take long before they herded all the Filipinos in town, with bayoneted rifles at their backs, to the central square. They made them sit in the sweltering afternoon heat, the armed sailors surrounding them.

From their vantage point, they could see a single Japanese officer strutting around the congregation of 100 or so Filipinos. They could barely hear his voice carrying on the wind. He was yelling and sounded angry.

Tarkington was tense. Every time the Japanese officer stopped near a cowering Filipino, he thought he'd pull his pistol or sword and summarily execute them. He'd seen it before. There seemed to be no end to the Japanese propensity for sudden and vicious violence. But it didn't happen this time.

"If these sons-of-bitches start killing, we're going in, numbers be damned," he seethed. No one flinched or balked, even though taking on half a platoon of well-armed sailors with only pistols and not much ammo would be suicide.

Over the next hour, the officer singled out individuals who were shuffled away under guard to a nearby building. It looked as though it was probably the town hall, or jailhouse. Finally, after taking 20 or so, the rest were released. They made their way back to their homes, glancing back toward the building where the others had gone.

With only a few hours before dark, Tarkington mused, "Wonder if they're planning on spending the night?"

Winkleman pointed, "Looks like they're sweeping the rest of the town. Hope they don't find anything in the factory." Sure enough, the sailors were moving in pairs to outlying buildings which were obviously uninhabited, including the large factory.

Tarkington's mind was in overdrive, "If they spend the night, that gives us a few options."

Winkleman asked, "Such as?"

"Smart thing to do would be to fade away once it's dark..." Tarkington paused.

Winkleman added, "But..."

Tarkington nodded, "But—what are they gonna do with the Filipinos they're holding?"

Winkleman shrugged, "Collateral? Further questioning?"

They watched the Japanese troops search the remaining buildings, paying close attention to the two soldiers inside the abandoned factory. After what seemed like a long time, the soldiers finally emerged out the same door the GIs had exited. The soldiers' rifles were off their backs, aiming them into the scrub beyond.

Henry cursed, "Shit, looks like they noticed something."

One soldier leaned down, kneeling close to the ground as though studying something. He pointed, and they exchanged words, both getting more agitated by the second. The kneeling soldier stood, then they both trotted off toward the center of town.

Tarkington shook his head, "Damn. Must've noticed the sailors' boot prints. Different from native sandals."

Winkleman asked, "What're we gonna do?"

Tarkington answered, "Guess we see how they react. It's late, almost dark. Will they try to follow the track tonight or wait until morning?"

No one answered for a long minute. Finally, Henry drawled, "I'll bet they wait. Tracking at night's hard and they'll be wary of an ambush."

Raker added, "We should warn 'em. Let 'em know they're being followed."

Tarkington shook his head, "I think they'll assume that anyway. The Filipinos must have known they'd be followed, or at least have a plan in case they are."

The question was answered minutes later. In the evening light, seven Japanese soldiers arrived near the back door of the factory. The officer stood with his hands on his hips as two soldiers kneeled down, inspecting the ground.

The GIs were well-hidden and far up the hill, but they still held perfectly still and had their weapons ready. They watched the officer gesturing, obviously giving orders. One soldier broke away and ran back toward town. The others stood holding their weapons, listening. They formed a line, directed by a different soldier, which Tarkington assumed must be an NCO. The officer stepped back, watching the five soldiers follow the dirt trail leading into the scrub and jungle beyond.

Soon the officer was alone. He looked around at the surrounding hills, his eyes passing over their hiding place. There was no way he could possibly see them, but it was unnerving just the same. The officer took one last look up the trail, then turned and walked back toward town.

Henry whispered, "What I wouldn't give for my ol' Springfield. Easy shot."

Tarkington squinted at the departing officer's back. "Okay, listen up." The men scooted closer, "Ten Jap sailors came ashore, right?" There were nods all around. "Five of 'em just went into the jungle, probably a sergeant leading them. Including the officer that leaves five guarding the prisoners." Everyone nodded, and he asked, "Figure there's maybe another four or five on the boat? Fifteen crew sound about right?" Nods all around. "I figure the soldier the officer sent back to town has orders for the rest of the boat crew. Probably telling them their intentions. Probably use a flashlight or something to signal, or maybe they've got a portable radio, either way they're in contact with the boat. I'm guessing the officer down there's the head honcho. He decided to pursue without asking someone else first. So, he's the boat captain, which means there's probably a junior officer still out there."

Tarkington rubbed his chin, thinking. Raker finally said, "That all sounds right. So what?"

Tarkington licked his lips and grinned, "So, I think there's a way to free the hostages and kill some Japs."

A few hours later, in the dark of night, Winkleman and Stollman were on their bellies between two outrigger canoes. They'd made their way along the edge of the town, which was eerily quiet and dark. They'd seen no one and were sure they hadn't been seen. They'd crawled across the white sandy beach, keeping to darker sections whenever possible and now they were well-concealed between the boats and ready to move into the sea.

They were both in their underwear, a belt holding a sheathed knife hanging from their waists. Their sun-darkened bodies provided superior natural camouflage. Stollman's lighter complexion blended with the lighter-colored reef bottom. The night was black. There was no moon, the only light coming from the myriad stars overhead, which seemed close enough to touch.

Without a word, they slithered into the sea. The water was only slightly cooler than the air temperature. Their target, the Japanese patrol boat, was anchored somewhere far to their left and a quarter mile out. They couldn't see it, but knew it was there. They hadn't heard the engine start since they first arrived.

They pulled themselves along, careful not to splash. It took a few minutes for Winkleman to get his breathing under control. The fear, coupled with the effort of swimming, could be a lethal combination, but soon they were both gliding along smoothly.

Winkleman looked back toward the beach, surprised at their progress. The white sand was easy to see, the long H-shaped outriggers lined up like toothpicks. Beyond them was the town. There was one dim light, which was near the center of town where the hostages were being held. There'd been no activity, no gunshots or screams, which he took as a good sign. The others hadn't been discovered. He wondered about the US sailors out there in the jungle. Would the Japanese sailors find them and attack? Would they hear gunshots this far out? Probably not.

He was pulled back to the present when he bumped into Stollman, who was treading water. Winkleman stopped stroking, noticing they were beyond the reef and in deep water. The protected little bay had virtually no wave action, even out here where deep water met shallow. He briefly thought of sharks. Did they hunt at night? He thought they probably did.

When they'd gone over the plan originally, Tarkington had Henry accompanying him out here, but Winkleman noticed Henry's discomfort and suggested Stollman might be the better choice. He'd been with Henry during the shark incident, but didn't seem as affected. Indeed, Stollman relished the chance to get up close and personal for some knife work.

Winkleman waved Stollman to follow, and they moved back toward the reef. It would be easier to keep their bearings and not accidentally swim out to sea. They'd follow the reef south. It also allowed them to stop and rest occasionally, since some spots were less than five feet deep.

Finding the reef again, Winkleman leaned toward Stollman's ear and whispered, "Let's move toward the boat. Figure it's 300 yards." Without a word, Stollman moved off, taking long powerful strokes. Winkleman followed, keeping his eyes peeled for the boat's outline.

After long minutes of silent swimming, Winkleman saw it. He gave one powerful stroke, catching up with Stollman, and tapped his bare foot. Stollman stopped swimming and Winkleman drifted alongside him. The saltwater's buoyancy didn't require much effort for them to tread water, but Winkleman worked harder than he needed and forced himself to slow his motions, calming himself. He pointed, Stollman following his gaze. Stollman nodded, seeing the black outline of what could only be the Japanese patrol boat.

Winkleman felt a moment of hesitation. This was the turning point. He could turn around and head back to shore without incident, making up some excuse. He scolded himself, *then what?* He thought. He'd never be a trusted member of Tark's Ticks then. He closed his eyes, forcing himself to glide past Stollman.

They swam slow and steady toward the looming shape, which seemed to be a black cutout against the shimmering, star-filled horizon. There were no lights, and the gentle sound of tiny lapping waves hitting the hull made the scene almost peaceful. The bow faced them, which meant they'd have to swim the entire boat's length to get to the lower stern.

As they neared, Winkleman saw the jagged outline of a mounted deck gun. It wasn't manned, but reminded him of the danger they faced. They were still swimming over the reef; the boat anchored 20 yards into the deeper water. They swam silently, never taking their eyes off the boat. The sudden flare of a flame made Winkleman stop. He let his foot gently touch the jagged reef, hoping he didn't step on something sharp, which was always a danger out here. The flame diminished quickly, and he saw an enemy sailor lighting a cigarette. He was close. Winkleman hadn't noticed him. The cigarette tip glowed into a bright orange.

Winkleman's nose was just above the waterline. He forced himself to calm down, taking normal breaths in and out. After a minute, he pulled his foot from the reef, allowing himself to float. He pulled himself along in an agonizingly slow breast stroke until he was slightly beyond the stern.

They tread water side-by-side, watching the boat. The cherry from the cigarette was still visible, marking the location of at least one guard. Movement near the stern made them both stop breathing. A dark shape moved to the edge and stopped. For a moment Winkleman thought he had spotted them, but his rational mind took over. There was no way. The sound of tinkling water told him what was happening. The sailor was taking a leak.

The sound diminished and soon stopped. Another flare of light as this sentry lit a cigarette. There was no talking, making Winkleman think there were only the two sentries, both nicely marked by the burning tips of their cigarettes. The stern guard moved back into the shadows toward the boat's structure, leaving the stern deck empty.

Winkleman gulped; it was now or never. He nodded at Stollman who nodded back and they moved out over deep water toward the stern.

Tarkington, Vick, Raker, and Henry were positioned near the edge of the beach, hunched in a culvert draining foul smelling water into the sea. They'd made their way along the edge of town, searching for an adequate hiding place, finally coming across the culvert. It provided cover from all directions and would be ideal for their purposes, but the stench was hard to get used to.

Tarkington looked past the white sands to the darkness beyond. The lapping of tiny waves licking the beach was an undulating hiss. The outrigger canoes, where Winkleman and Stollman would start their swim, were well off to the right.

He knew approximately where the enemy boat was anchored but the darkness kept it shrouded. He strained to see past the outriggers for any sign of the swimmers. He knew he wouldn't see anything. If he did, something had gone horribly wrong. *Not* seeing anything was the best scenario he could hope for, and he wasn't disappointed. There was nothing but darkness.

He glanced at his wrist, forgetting he'd lost his watch during the battle on Luzon. He briefly wondered if it was still out there, lying in the fetid remains of a rain-soaked foxhole, keeping perfect time, which no one would ever see. He judged it had been at least three hours since they parted ways. Winkleman and Stollman should be well on their way.

He crawled forward until he was lying beside Henry, who was watching the town. Henry scooted over an inch, making room, and Tarkington whispered, "Anything?" Henry shook his head. The town was as quiet and dark as a morgue. Tarkington nodded and squinted, trying to make out which building the Japanese were holding the hostages. He knew the culvert wasn't directly in front of the center of town, so the building he was searching for would be off to his left. It didn't matter though. When things got started, they'd move wherever they needed to.

Henry tensed and Tarkington froze, knowing his lead scout's senses were nearly supernatural. Tarkington tightened his grip on the submachine gun. The others had their pistols, but the thirty rounds from the submachine gun might prove to be the difference between life and death tonight. He held his breath, trying to see whatever caused Henry to tense.

Tarkington nearly yelled out when Henry suddenly sprang right, as though propelled by electricity. Surprised grunts and scuffling. Tarkington aimed the muzzle in the general direction, not wanting to shoot Henry. The others did the same.

Tarkington finally breathed again when he heard Henry whisper, "Don't shoot. Friendlies." Soon Henry emerged pushing a terrified Filipino, Henry's pistol aimed at his back.

Tarkington whispered, "What the hell's this?"

The Filipino looked at each man, then smiled, gesturing from the direction he'd come from and holding up ten fingers. Raker, who held his pistol in his uninjured right hand, whispered, "Think he's telling us there's ten more of 'em back that way."

Tarkington shook his head, "Dammit. Get outta here," he whispered, giving the smiling Filipino his most severe pissed-off look. "We don't need you," he hissed. But instead of scampering off, the Filipino stood and waved and soon the culvert was filled with more Filipinos, some holding rifles, others cleavers, hatchets, and knives.

Vick tried Tagalog and got a reaction. The short, choppy exchange was easy to decipher and before Vick translated, Tarkington knew he'd be fighting alongside another batch of Filipinos, just like on Luzon. "They wanna help us, Tark," confirmed Vick.

Tarkington lowered his gaze, shaking his head. The last thing he wanted to do was to get more Filipinos killed. He'd failed on Luzon and he didn't want to repeat the performance, but he also knew the Filipino fighting spirit wasn't easily kept down. If he insisted they leave, they might do something on their own and inadvertently mess up the entire operation. Besides that, they didn't have a lot of time. Any second now, Winkleman and Stollman would make their presence known. He whispered to Vick, "Keep 'em quiet. Put 'em in the rear and tell them not to do *anything* until we do." Vick nodded, relaying the message the best he could in his limited Tagalog.

Winkleman and Stollman swam as close to the boat as they dared, then took deep breaths and submerged. They stroked, careful not to break the surface with a splash, propelling themselves into the black water toward the stern.

It was impossible to see the boat in the darkness, the blurriness from being underwater adding to the difficulty, but Winkleman knew it was only a 15 yard swim. Soon there was a looming presence in front of him. He stopped stroking and hovered, reaching out and touching Stollman's arm. They were close enough that they could just see each other's face. Winkleman pointed up, and Stollman nodded. They gently kicked themselves upward, breaking the surface with barely a sound. Winkleman touched the steel of the warship's hull, guiding himself as close to the overhanging lip as he could get. Stollman was beside him.

The gentle swell tilted the boat back and forth slightly, making tiny lapping sounds. Winkleman pointed to the stern. Stollman pushed himself out from under the lip and peered at the deck, five feet up. Not seeing an access point, he moved along the back toward the starboard side. The Japanese had launched the dinghy from this spot. Perhaps there was still some sort of access point.

Winkleman stayed hidden and watched Stollman disappear around the corner. A long minute passed before he came back into view, shaking his head. Stollman swam close and whispered, "No ladder."

They'd discussed what they'd do if there weren't an easy access point. It was risky, but it was their only option. Winkleman licked his lips and nodded. He followed Stollman around the stern, stopping at the lowest point.

Winkleman looked up at the edge. It looked impossibly far away. He looked at Stollman, who was treading water beside him, and shook his head. The plan was to lunge upward, grab the edge, and have the lighter Stollman use him as a ladder. From the bank, it looked possible, but now that they were beside it, the plan seemed ludicrous.

Winkleman motioned that he was going to the other side. Perhaps there was an access point there. They both moved back to the stern, then worked their way to the port side section. There was a segment of rope he could barely make out, hanging a couple inches off the deck. He pointed it out, and Stollman tilted his head with skepticism. It still seemed too far away, but he had to try it. Winkleman whispered, "I'm gonna try."

Stollman nodded, positioning himself close but out of the way. Winkleman went low in the water, his eyes just above the surface, fixated on the bit of rope. He kicked his legs hard, propelling himself upward and reaching. There was no way to do this quietly and the sudden splash sounded like an artillery barrage after the lengthy silence. Winkleman's finger touched the rope, but it didn't budge and he dropped back into the sea with more splashing.

They pulled themselves tight into the boat's overhanging hull, waiting to see if the commotion drew any attention. The clomping of boots across the deck above gave them their answer. It wasn't hurried—either the sentry was being cautious or was simply curious. The steps stopped directly above them and Winkleman imagined the sentry leaning out, searching for whatever had caused the splash. Perhaps he'd think it a large fish, plenty of those around here.

A red-lensed light snapped on, sweeping the water. The sudden sound of a distant Japanese voice made Winkleman hold his breath. He figured someone was asking what was going on. The sentry directly above answered and Winkleman got the impression he wasn't all that concerned. There was curiosity in his voice, not fear. The light lingered for a few more seconds, then snapped off and the boots shuffled away slowly. The sentries exchanged more words.

Winkleman nearly shit himself when Stollman made a large splash, bringing his open-palmed hand down hard on the surface. The light switched on again, this time angling toward the hull. They were still out of sight, the curve of the hull keeping them hidden. Winkleman stared at Stollman with wide, questioning eyes. Stollman stared upward, ignoring him. He was holding the dark five-inch blade, all his attention focused on the sentry.

There was commotion on deck, and soon the light extended down the hull toward them. Winkleman finally understood. The sailor was on his belly, leaning out and down trying to get a better look.

Stollman struck like a lunging viper, grasping the sailor's arm, pulling him from the deck. In an instant, the sentry was in the sea, his yell cut short as he entered the water. Stollman drove the sailor down deep, plunging the knife into soft tissue over and over. Finally, the sailor stopped struggling. Stollman gave one last vicious gouge into the center of his neck and pulled sideways, nearly cutting his head off. He released him to the depths and swam back, surfacing beside Winkleman, and taking a deep breath.

Clomping boots on deck and a questioning voice told them the commotion hadn't gone unnoticed. Winkleman whispered, "Follow me." Without waiting, he took the biggest lungful of air he could manage and pushed himself underwater, following the black hull downward.

Being beneath the hull felt stifling, but Winkleman forced himself to stay calm. This wasn't a big boat; it had a relatively shallow draft. They should be able to get back to the starboard side and toward the reef before having to surface. He took powerful strokes, propelling himself past the hull's low-point, noticing it angling up the other side. He resisted the urge to follow the contour back up, staying deep and stroking hard into the darkness. His chest burned and his brain screamed for oxygen, but he knew they were false signals. He knew how far he could push underwater. He glanced back, not seeing Stollman at first, then seeing movement a couple yards behind. He continued stroking but angled toward the surface. The reef must be close, but he couldn't see it.

His eyes dimmed, dark edges encroaching slightly. These weren't false signals. He slowed his strokes, allowing his body to rise smoothly. The surface came quicker than expected. Careful not to splash, he took in deep, life-giving lungfuls of tropical air. He turned back toward the boat, seeing the inky silhouette. There was movement near the stern. A couple yards back, Stollman suddenly erupted from the water, splashing and pulling in a loud, wheezy breath.

There was yelling from the boat, but Winkleman didn't think it was because of Stollman. A powerful light suddenly bathed the stern of the enemy patrol boat. Winkleman could see the sentry hanging over the port side pointing and yelling. Three more figures dashed through the light, joining him. The panicked yelling increased and Winkleman assumed they'd either found the body or seen the blood. Either way, they'd be searching the surrounding area in seconds. They had to get out of there.

Stollman got his breathing under control and was breast stroking toward him. When he was close, Winkleman hissed, "We gotta get to the reef and move south, fast."

Stollman lurched, his eyes widening, then normalizing as his surprise eased. "Shit, Wink. Didn't see you there."

"You okay?" Winkleman asked. Stollman nodded and Winkleman took another large lungful and went under. He nearly bumped into the wall of the reef, pulling up just before scraping his face. He stayed under, turned and waved for Stollman to stop too. They surfaced, swimming over the reef a few yards before turning south.

A sudden spike of more light thrust out from the patrol boat, adding to the floodlight. The beam aimed at the stern, sweeping the sea. Three sailors bunched together, one holding a long pole which he thrust into the water as though hooking something. Winkleman assumed they'd found the body, and once they saw the multiple knife wounds, they'd know this wasn't simply a man hitting his head and falling overboard. He stroked harder and Stollman kept pace.

11

Tarkington wondered if Winkleman and Stollman had gotten lost. Perhaps they hadn't found a way to get to the sailors, or deemed it too dangerous. It was a shaky plan to begin with. They had no way of knowing whether they could get themselves onto the boat easily. From land, the sides of the gunboat didn't look very high, but perhaps the distance only made it seem that way. They'd entertained taking one of the outrigger canoes, but the chance of being spotted was too great. The option of taking the Japanese dinghy back out was also shelved. That might've worked if someone spoke Japanese. Winkleman was confident he could swim there undetected, but couldn't promise much beyond that.

The hours had slipped by agonizingly slow. Since the Filipinos joined them, there'd been little movement in town. The occasional flare of a sentry lighting a cigarette in front of the town hall, the only excitement so far. The Filipinos kept to themselves, staying quiet and out of the way. Despite initially being angry, Tarkington felt better having a few more men and guns. He just hoped, if this whole thing went off, he didn't get shot in the back by accident. `

A bright light suddenly turned on out to sea, bathing the Japanese gunboat's stern. Tarkington sucked in a breath, hoping he didn't hear gunshots. Distant voices carried over the sea. There was murmuring from the Filipinos—and Vick, the closest GI, gave them a quick shush. They immediately stopped talking.

Tarkington watched for a few more seconds, seeing another more focused light turn on, the powerful beam sweeping the sea toward the stern. Still no gunshots, a good sign for the swimmers.

Henry tapped Tarkington with his boot, bringing his attention forward. Tarkington saw the sentry guarding town hall was no longer sitting, but standing, his dim shape barely visible. The soldier moved toward the sea then stood still, no doubt wondering what had caused his boat mates to break light discipline.

Tarkington growled low, "Stay sharp, won't be long." He slowly pulled the bolt of his submachine gun back, at the same time making sure the safety was on. The rest of his men fidgeted with their pistols, bringing them close to hand.

The sentry continued watching for another few seconds, then turned and opened the door into the building. Soft lantern light spilled onto the porch and the sentry was speaking to someone. He shut the door and returned to his post, watching the light show out to sea. The probe of light was now sweeping the entire area around the boat, as though searching.

Soon the town hall door opened again and two men joined the guard at the railing. They were too far away to hear, but their gestures left little doubt what they were discussing.

Raker got Tarkington's attention and pointed toward the boat. There was a flashing coming from where they guessed the bridge would be. A signal, no doubt. From the porch of the town hall, answering signals. Tarkington wished he knew what they were saying. As far as he could tell, it wasn't Morse code. He wasn't fluent in it, but he thought he would've at least recognized it.

Minutes passed, as did more signals. The sailors reacted to the last signal as though they'd kicked a hornet's nest. Even from here, the GIs could hear yelling and barked orders. Whatever Winkleman and Stollman had done, the Japanese sailors didn't like it.

The door opened and three men hustled out and down the stairs, running toward the beach where their dinghy awaited. As planned, they'd run right past the culvert.

Tarkington got his feet beneath him, ready to sprint forward once they took care of the sailors. He was hoping all—or at least four—of the sailors would've come, but he'd be able to deal with the two left, if he got there fast enough.

Henry was the lead on this. He'd be the first to engage, with Vick and Raker backing him up. It was up to Tarkington and his 30-round magazine to take care of the others before they harmed the civilians.

The thumping boots of the sailors were only yards away. Tarkington kept his eyes glued to Henry's back. The moment he lunged, Tarkington would move. Even though he was expecting it, Henry's quick action still caught him off guard. There was a brief cry of fear, followed immediately with the violent clashing of bodies, then the sharp crack of pistols.

Tarkington ignored the sickening sounds of pain and violence. He was already halfway to the gawking Japanese on the porch. They stood as though frozen, trying to figure out who was firing.

Tarkington churned his legs, running full tilt, his eyes focused on the two enemy sailors. He flicked off the safety, ready to mow them down, but wanting to get as close as possible first.

The one nearest the door reacted first. He pointed directly at Tarkington, saying something while fumbling to withdraw his pistol. The other sailor shifted the muzzle of his rifle Tarkington's way. There was no more waiting.

Tarkington stopped, aimed, and depressed the trigger, spitting rounds at them. The wooden railing splintered, and the sailor with the rifle dropped, taking multiple hits to his legs and chest. The other abandoned his efforts to withdraw his pistol, turning toward the safety of the door. Tarkington took careful aim and as he darted into the doorway, fired a quick burst, shredding the wood door frame and knocking the officer to the ground.

Tarkington sprinted the rest of the way, jumping the six steps and landing on the porch. He glimpsed the unmoving sailor, the spreading pool of blood left little doubt that he was dead or dying. The door had swung partially shut, but the soldier's boot kept it from shutting all the way. Tarkington kicked it the rest of the way open, keeping his smoking muzzle on the man's back. It was an officer. He was still moving, trying to pull himself along, reaching for something he'd never reach.

Tarkington, ever-wary of wounded Japanese, was careful. He could see both the man's hands, which made him feel better. The officer must have felt his presence. He stopped struggling and rolled himself onto his back, facing the Type-100's barrel. A streak of blood leaked from his left eye, a long splinter of wood sticking from it grotesquely. The officer's other eye was full of fear and pain. He stared at Tarkington, biting his lower lip until it bled. He coughed, his breath raspy and labored. Tarkington aimed at his heart, closed his eyes, and pulled the trigger once.

After killing the two soldiers on the porch, he'd waited for Henry and Vick, then entered the main room, finding wide-eyed Filipino hostages staring at them. Their feet were bound. It only took moments to free them. They spoke fast. Too fast for any of the GIs to keep up. Filipinos from the culvert arrived and assuaged their fears.

Henry told him they'd killed the other Japanese without taking casualties, but they'd shot through most of their ammunition. They'd replenished from the dead and now held Type-38 Arisaka rifles, which seemed to be a staple, even for Imperial Japanese Naval troops. They still had their pistols, but only had a few rounds between them. Tarkington reloaded his magazine with spare rounds from the Type-38s.

Urgent signals from the boat crew continued. Tarkington doubted the gunfight inland had gone unnoticed. How would they react? The boat they'd used to come in was already on the beach. Did they have another?

The lights were still blazing, the spotlight now focused inland, squarely on them. He wondered how much they could discern. They were nearly a quarter mile out and even with the powerful light, it was still pitch dark out. Most likely, they'd see darting shapes, which could be anyone. Again, he wished he could signal them, but it was impossible.

Tarkington kneeled over the officer, looking for more ammunition. He asked, "Any sign of our swimmers?"

Henry shook his head, "Not yet."

Tarkington exclaimed, "We gotta get outta here. The Jap patrol might've heard the shots."

Vick called out. He was standing near the waterline with a captured rifle guarding against the possibility of Japanese sailors coming in. Tarkington could just make out what he said, "Who's there? Identify yourself."

Tarkington and Henry turned to the sea, bringing their weapons up. From the darkness, Stollman's voice was unmistakable, "It's me, you asshat. Don't shoot."

Vick answered, "Stolly! Thought maybe you two joined the Jap Navy."

Winkleman's voice was curt and serious, "What's happening? Report."

Vick answered, "Went off like clockwork on this end, Wink."

Tarkington and Henry trotted down to join them, passing Raker who was still rifling through the other dead Japanese sailors. The swimmers finished slogging from the reef to the sand and stopped in front of them, catching their breath.

Tarkington asked, "You good?"

Winkleman nodded, giving him a thumbs up, and when he got his breath back, said, "We're both okay. So it worked?"

Tarkington nodded, "Like Vick said: clockwork."

Winkleman slapped Stollman's back, "Haven't had time to kick your ass yet, Stolly." Stollman grinned, then gave him an "aw shucks" shrug. Winkleman explained, "Stolly got their attention, but didn't bother tellin' me what he was up to. Scared the hell out of me."

Stollman said, "Sorry, Wink. Didn't seem like there was any other way. No time to pass it by you."

Winkleman nodded, "I know. I know. It worked out fine, but damn—I thought our goose was cooked."

Tarkington asked, "How many out there?"

Winkleman answered, "One less than there was. We saw four others. Just like you figured."

They turned back toward the boat, which was still signaling. Tarkington motioned them to follow him up the beach, "We need to get outta here before the other patrol reacts."

Stollman kept his eyes on the patrol boat, "Sure'd be nice to finish 'em off."

Tarkington shook his head, "They'd tear you up with the deck guns before you got close."

Stollman nodded, "Yeah, probably. Just love to get my hands on that boat. That'd get us out of here in a hurry. Reminds me of those speed boats all the rich fellers have on the lakes."

Tarkington pulled up short, mulling it over. He looked at Henry who shrugged back, "We've got plenty of night left."

Raker joined them. He held out an ammo pouch, "Found more ammo. Might come in handy." Filipinos surrounded them—not just the ones who'd helped with the assault and the freed hostages, but from the looks of it, the entire town. Raker tilted his chin at them, "Plenty of extra help too."

Tarkington stroked his chin, then pointed inland, "We could send them out to watch for the other patrol, I guess."

Henry nodded, "I'll lead 'em. Make sure they don't screw it up."

Tarkington considered, then shook his head, "I'll need every able-bodied man for the boat. Raker'll lead 'em. Long as you're up to it with that arm."

Raker shrugged and nodded, "No problem, Tark. You're right, I wouldn't be much use out there. Wouldn't be able to swim if I ended up in the drink."

Tarkington stared at the sand, concentrating. The others kept quiet, familiar with Tarkington's idiosyncrasies. He was deep in thought, not to be disturbed.

A few minutes later, he looked up, as though waking from a dream, and said, "Okay. Here's what we're gonna do."

Raker, 15 minutes later, was leading 15 Filipinos armed with rifles, pistols and machetes toward the trail Staub and the others had used. After conferring with the locals, they decided it was unlikely that the Japanese following the trail would've heard the brief battle unless they were already near the town, and if they were, they would've shown themselves by now.

The Japanese patrol boat still panned the beach with the spotlight and continued the incessant signaling. A half hour had passed since the one-sided battle, and the Japanese boat crew would need to decide soon.

Tarkington figured they must be in contact with their base by now, asking for direction. Iloilo Port, which the Filipinos said was about a 40 minute boat ride from here, would probably send a boat soon.

Tarkington sat in the bow of one of the long outrigger canoes. They'd paddled far around the Japanese gunboat and were now coming from the seaward side. Henry sat in front of him, his newly-gained rifle propped on the bow, aiming at the Japanese patrol boat. There was a second outrigger canoe to their left, paralleling them. Tarkington could just see the silhouette but knew Stollman was in front aiming a rifle with Vick close behind, ready to back him up.

The Filipinos paddled smoothly and quietly. They were still far outside the patrol boat's lights, creeping ever closer, waiting for the signal. It finally came, a signal light flashing from the bank, repeating the same pattern the boat crew had been sending for the past half hour. They had no idea what they were saying, but figured it would keep the Japanese on the boat confused and—more importantly—occupied.

Tarkington looked around the dark sea, listening and searching for any sign another boat was on the way. He knew there wouldn't be lights, but the engine noise would carry for miles. There was nothing but the lapping of sea on the canoe sides. He tapped Henry's back, then signaled the Filipinos to increase their speed. The outrigger surged forward, gliding toward the enemy boat silently.

Tarkington flicked the safety off his submachine gun, watching the stern. Henry and Stollman would take out the gunner. There was only one on the roof of the bridge, manning what was probably a heavy machine gun, similar to the 20 mm Oerlikon. If spotted, the gunner could traverse the weapon quickly, which was why their best shooter was on the task.

They were close enough to hear the four Japanese sailors speaking in harried tones, obviously discussing the signal they were receiving from the beach. When they were 15 yards out, Henry signaled, and the Filipinos stopped paddling, giving him a stable firing platform.

The bark of the rifle split the night. It was followed immediately with a shot from the other canoe. Henry smoothly worked the bolt, chambering another round and firing again. Tarkington had the submachine gun up, aiming at a sailor near the stern who was turning their way. Tarkington squeezed the trigger, sending a burst into him. He aimed low, allowing the barrel to rise, walking the bullets up the doomed sailor's body. The stricken man dropped to the deck, unmoving.

Henry fired again. Tarkington scanned the deck. There were no more targets. The canoe's bow gently hit the side of the patrol boat. Henry stood, grabbing the edge, which was just within reach, keeping the outrigger close.

Tarkington quickly slung his weapon over his back and leaped off the bow, narrowly avoiding Henry. The adrenaline surging through his body allowed him to pull himself up and over the edge, and he tried to slither beneath the railing. He was halfway through when the barrel of his weapon caught and stopped him. For a moment he was half stuck. One of the Japanese sailors sprawled on his back, clutching at a gaping belly wound. He saw Tarkington at the same time Tarkington saw him, and their eyes locked.

The badly-wounded sailor pulled a pistol from a holster with shaking, bloody hands. He aimed unsteadily, but was only a few feet away and couldn't miss. Tarkington squirmed, trying to break free. He pushed himself backwards a fraction of a second before the pistol fired. He felt a sizzling flash of pain, then the coolness of water—then nothing.

12

Major Hanscom wasn't happy to be split from Tarkington and his men. The survivors from the submarine were competent sailors, but they weren't used to land operations and it showed. Hanscom had taken for granted how silently Tarkington and the others moved through the jungle. Now, he and Gonzalez cringed as the Filipinos led them deeper into the wilds, the sailors sounding like stampeding buffalos. If there were Japanese patrols out here or they were being followed, they wouldn't be hard to find.

They moved along the well-used path for hours, darkness finally enveloping them. Their progress slowed, despite the Filipinos urging them forward. The night was black, and even though the trail was relatively straight and the closed-in foliage made it nearly impossible to stray, the constant undulations and crisscrossing vines and roots made every step treacherous.

Finally, the Filipinos stopped them and whisked them off the trail, taking them north. In the darkness the move was sloppy, and there was cussing as men bumbled into one another. The possibility of being separated terrified the sailors, making them bunch up even more.

Hanscom and Gonzalez stayed close to one another but a few yards from the closest sailor. As the Filipinos were managing the move off the trail, Gonzalez whispered, "These guys're gonna get us killed." Hanscom grunted his agreement, keeping watch behind. There were already two Filipinos back there somewhere, watching their backs, but Hanscom thought a little extra vigilance couldn't hurt. Gonzalez continued, "That Staub's a real ball-buster."

Hanscom whispered back, "How d'you mean?"

Gonzalez lowered his voice, "He took your rank. Relieved you."

Hanscom didn't respond for a few seconds, making Gonzalez wonder if he should've kept his mouth shut. Finally, Hanscom sighed, saying, "I'm no lawyer, but my actions didn't warrant his response. And besides, we're in different branches but the same rank."

Gonzalez waited for more, but when it didn't come, he prodded, "So? What does that mean, then?"

Hanscom concentrated on Gonzalez's silhouette, which was all he could see of him, despite being less than a foot away. He whispered, "Staub's like my wife. If she's upset, or she has a strong opinion about something, she'll make a dramatic statement. Just her first thought. She'll be adamant, unwavering. It's just her way." Hanscom grinned in the darkness, picturing her dark hair whipping around her face as she waved her beautifully-sculpted hands and fingers, making her point. "Now, I used to react. You know—try to convince her otherwise. It *never* works. In ten years of marriage, I've learned if I just nod and ignore it, or even agree, she'll eventually come to her own conclusions and change her mind. Without fighting or me having to put my foot down, which doesn't work anyway."

Gonzalez shook his head in the darkness. "I wouldn't tell Staub you're comparing him to your wife," he whispered back. "But what if he doesn't come to his senses?"

Hanscom shrugged, "I'm acting as though nothing's different. We'll see."

Gonzalez nodded, "Well, you should know you're still my commanding officer far as I'm concerned."

Hanscom grinned, "Thanks, Gonzo."

Just then the two Filipinos from the rear appeared like apparitions. Hanscom didn't see them until they were nearly on top of him, and he jolted in surprise, reaching for his pistol. The Filipinos didn't speak English much beyond Pidgin, but they knew the word for danger. The nearest man hissed, "Japs."

Hanscom brought his pistol the rest of the way out, feeling suddenly sick. The nearest Filipino pushed him forward. He stumbled into Gonzalez, who also had his weapon out. Gonzalez asked the Filipino for more information. He relayed it to Hanscom, barely above a whisper. "Says there's a patrol couple kilometers back. Following us."

Hanscom nodded, "Good thing we're getting off the trail."

The news they were being followed made everyone move more carefully. The Filipinos continued leading, taking them up a gentle slope. In the inky blackness, there were no references, but the walking was easy despite being off the trail. The Filipinos urged them forward, wanting them to get to a specific spot before the enemy patrol passed.

The sailors were quieter, but still loud, and Hanscom thought if the Japanese were walking along the trail, still only 30 or 40 yards downslope, they'd hear them easily. He was about to order a halt himself when the Filipinos stopped and passed the word through hand gestures to be silent.

For Hansom and Gonzalez, who were closest to the trail, being quiet meant being *absolutely* quiet. They could still hear the sailors panting for breath, some still adjusting their positions. Hanscom wanted to throttle them himself.

The two rear-guard Filipinos crouched nearby, just the outline of their black silhouettes visible. They had rifles and Hanscom hoped they were loaded and in working condition. He didn't know how many soldiers were coming, but his paltry seven rounds in his .45 wouldn't be enough.

Less than a minute later he heard them. Despite the darkness, they were moving much faster. They didn't talk, but their footfalls and nondescript rustling of clothes and equipment was hard to miss. They weren't loud; indeed, he probably wouldn't have noticed if he weren't straining with every fiber of his being.

He willed the men to keep quiet. One cough or sneeze, one dropped pistol would give them away. The enemy patrol was at the closest point, still moving steadily along the trail. There'd be no reason for them to notice their departure from the trail. They weren't tracking them—it was too dark —but simply following their suspected path.

Hanscom wondered for an instant if perhaps it weren't Japanese at all, but Tarkington and his Ticks. Would the Filipinos have seen the difference in the darkness? Had they even gotten that close, or had they simply assumed? He shook his head; he wasn't about to test that theory.

The patrol passed along the trail, not slowing as far as Hanscom could tell. He realized he was holding his breath and let it out slowly as the unseen patrol passed out of hearing range.

One of the Filipinos moved up the slope; the other leaned in and whispered in Gonzalez's ear. He relayed the message to Hanscom, "He says they're taking us to the top. Some kind of mining operation up there."

Sure enough there was movement, still too loud, as the group got to their feet and continued trudging up the hill. The Filipinos stayed behind with them, keeping their distance from the main group.

The slope steepened and they eventually hooked up with another trail, which wound upward in a series of sharp switchbacks. This one wasn't nearly as well-traveled and came from the east. Hanscom wondered if the Japanese patrol would find its origin and follow it to them. He shrugged in the darkness. *Doubt I'll sleep tonight.*

He was breathing hard by the time the trail finally flattened out. Hanscom saw the dim outlines of buildings against the sky, then noticed the shining stars in the background for the first time that evening. He caught his breath, leaning back, taking them in. They were truly beautiful tonight.

He heard a sailor exclaim through labored breaths, "Thank God that's over. Thought I was gonna puke."

Lieutenant Commander Staub's harsh voice cut through the night, "Can it, Unterman. Sound carries out here."

"Sorry, sir," he whispered back.

Hanscom glanced back at Gonzalez. He could see him better now that they were out of the jungle canopy. He whispered, "Follow me. I'm gonna have a word with Staub."

They wound their way through sailors, some bent over trying to catch their breath, others whispering, discussing the near miss with the enemy patrol. Hanscom saw Staub standing near the Filipinos who were motioning toward the low buildings.

Hanscom noticed Lieutenant Gilson standing nearby. Hanscom stopped beside them and asked, "This where we're spending the night?"

Staub turned and scowled at him, "Hell if I know. Where's that interpreter sergeant of yours?"

Gonzalez stepped forward, "Here, sir." Without being asked, he used his limited Pidgin English, then relayed the words, "Says this is a suitable place. Safe. It's an abandoned mining operation."

Staub nodded, "Good, the men could use some rest. That was a brutal march."

Hanscom added, "We'll need security put out. The Filipinos'll probably do it since they know the area. Can you ask them about it, Sergeant?"

Gonzalez moved beside the Filipino and they moved off, keeping their voices barely above a whisper. In the low light, Hanscom noticed Staub giving him the once over, as though he were something foul a dog might roll in. "The hell you think you're doing, Hanscom?"

Gilson stiffened at the tone and Hanscom leaned in, his hands up, "Keep your voice down."

Hanscom couldn't see it, but he was sure Staub's face was beet red. Staub whispered, realizing the danger, wanting to yell, "I relieved you. You can't give orders."

Hanscom shook his head, stepping closer so he wouldn't have to raise his voice but also because he was feeling a slow burn in his gut. He only came to Staub's chin, but he hissed, "You can do that crap later. Right now we have to work together. Your by-the-book attitude has already cost us our best chance of getting out of here alive. You can try to throw the book at me later, but we need to work together or we're all sunk."

They stared at one another for almost a minute before Staub finally said, "If you're referring to Staff Sergeant Tarkington and his squad as our 'best chance,' then we were never going to make it anyway."

Hanscom shook his head slow, "You *still* don't get it. Now the Japs know we're here, they'll hunt us till they find us. Make no mistake, they're tenacious. Once the word's out, this island's gonna be crawling with patrols. We need Tarkington and his men. They've been living under the Japs for months. Like I said before: they're up to the task."

Staub exchanged a glance with Gilson, who gave him a slight nod. Staub lifted his chin, looking down at the shorter Hanscom, "I'll put our little incident behind us for the time being. You and I don't see eye to eye on how to command, but I can wait on that. As far as your wayward squad— well—they're still my primary mission, despite the circumstances." He shook his head, "But they're gone. If I find them again, I'll have them arrested for disobeying a direct order."

Hanscom shook his head, "Then you won't see them again, and if you do, you'll wish you hadn't."

Staub stiffened again, "Is that a threat, Major?"

Hanscom tilted his head, thinking how to respond. He shifted his stance and rubbed his chin, "Staff Sergeant Tarkington's a hard man. They all are. Being abandoned by their country, left to die or be captured," he shook his head. "It was hard on all of us. Most are still there and I can't even begin to imagine what they're going through. The Japs aren't known for their compassion as you no doubt know.

"I fought beside him and he'd been fighting a long time before I ever met him. He's got a deep hatred for them. He's seen things...atrocities. His leadership has kept his squad alive. They've got a special bond. And out here?" He looked Staub in the eye, "They're dedicated to him— *fiercely* dedicated."

Staub shook his head, not sure how he should take that, so he glanced at Lieutenant Gilson. He straightened up and ordered, "Let's get settled. We don't have time for this right now. The men need to rest and eat, if there's anything worth scrounging."

Hanscom stayed put, watching them duck into the buildings. He gazed at the stars, wondering if Ellie was doing the same back stateside.

The night passed without incident. The Filipinos rotated, taking watch along the obvious routes to the mining camp, but there were no further contacts. Hanscom hadn't slept well, having trouble coming to terms with what he should do next. The more he thought about it, the more he wanted to be with Tarkington, but he couldn't, in good conscience, abandon the sailors. While he stared at the dark ceiling, he wondered how he could make that happen, but came up empty.

An hour before the sun came up, the Filipinos rousted Gonzalez, speaking to him excitedly. The only light was from two ancient lanterns with soot-blackened glass. The conversation didn't go unnoticed and soon Hanscom, Staub, and Gilson huddled nearby, waiting.

Finally, Gonzalez relayed the message, "They're saying the Jap patrol is in the next town, near here. Five of 'em. They're worried that they'll find where we left the trail once it's light." The others nodded, exchanging worried glances. Gonzalez continued, "They wanna ambush 'em instead."

Staub scowled, the low light making his face look craggy and dark, "If we do that, we'll only give our position away."

"There's only five?" Hanscom asked.

Gonzalez nodded, "That's what they said, yeah."

Hanscom added, "We've got more than enough men and weapons to finish all of 'em."

Staub considered, then shook his head, "What if we don't? They'll alert the others, then we'll have a bigger problem."

Hanscom's face stayed calm, "If we lay it out right, there won't be any survivors. We'll also get their weapons and ammo."

Staub shook his head, "Then what? If the patrol disappears, the Japs send a larger force to investigate."

"They already know we're here. That's most likely happening already," countered Hanscom.

Staub crossed his arms over his chest, "No. We sit tight and keep hidden."

Hanscom pursed his lips, not wanting to make things worse. His instincts were telling him to attack—the move would drive fear and caution into the enemy, possibly giving them more time to slip away. The Filipinos were game; they had even more reasons to hate the Japanese than he did, and it was their own backyard. The Japanese sailors wouldn't escape, and if one or two did, they'd be hunted down. He was already walking a tight-rope with the naval officer. Continuing to push him would only make matters worse. So he nodded and waited for orders.

Staub focused on Gonzalez, "Tell them we aren't attacking. We'll stay here until they leave. They won't stay out long, probably didn't bring enough food for a lengthy stay. They'll need to get back to their boat."

Gonzalez exchanged glances with Hanscom, nodded and mumbled, "Yes, sir."

Petty officer Enji of the Imperial Japanese Navy woke from a fitful sleep, rubbing his eyes. He checked his watch; it was 0415 hours. The last time he'd checked, it was 0330, so he must've dozed off for at least a little while. He must've checked the watch a hundred times during the night. He hated every second he was away from his beloved patrol boat. He was a navy man, not a damned ground pounder. He shook his head, wondering how he and the other four navy men ended up here.

He'd done what Captain Yoduki asked of him, leading a patrol to hunt down whoever had made the tracks leaving the abandoned factory. The trail was easy to follow; although once darkness set in, seeing the tracks was impossible without a flashlight, and although the Philippine Islands were occupied, he knew the locals wouldn't hesitate to butcher them if given half a chance, so he kept the lights off and followed the path.

It finally led him to another town, this one smaller than the one on the coast. It was late when they arrived, so instead of waking the residents, he backtracked and set up a hasty bivouac in an out-of-the-way clearing a half a kilometer from town. He'd seen no sign of the men he was tracking. Perhaps he'd have better luck in the light of day.

The other sailors sat up, seeing Enji getting ready to move. They mumbled among themselves, careful to keep their voices low. Enji doubted any of them had slept either. Indeed, the foreign sounds of the jungle at night, even this scrubby little meadow, were enough to keep them on edge. He'd kept one man on guard duty, but it was a formality since none of them had slept anyway.

Enji ordered them to eat their remaining rations; they'd do a quick search of the village, then move back along the trail they'd come in on. Back to the coast and the patrol boat. He was already practicing what he'd tell Captain Yoduki, "no sign of them, sir."

Once they finished eating, they left the meadow and moved along the trail to the village. A few smiling locals met them and ushered them into town. Despite the smiles and overt gestures of goodwill, Enji was sure the Filipinos would've liked nothing more than to slit his throat.

He tried to convey what he was looking for, and there were shaking heads and confused expressions. He gave some buildings cursory searches and was moving out an hour later, bowing and nodding his thanks to the disgusting natives. He didn't enjoy kowtowing to them, but his small five-man force was badly outnumbered and he was sure the Filipinos had weapons close by, despite their illegality.

His men were exhausted, but he kept them moving along the trail, reminding them that in only a few brief hours they'd be back on the coast in the safety of their boat crew.

His legs ached. The long hours of inactivity spent on the boat wreaked havoc on his cardiovascular system. They did calisthenics nearly every day, but it wasn't enough to keep him in shape and now he was suffering. By the looks of it, the other sailors weren't much better off. Despite wanting to push on, he finally called a halt. The men spread out, going to ground immediately, sucking on canteens and wiping sweaty brows.

Petty Officer Enji knew he should put out security, but it would only be a quick stop and he deemed it wasn't necessary. He pulled himself to his feet with a groan, shuffling off the trail to take a much-needed piss. His Type-38 rifle was slung over his shoulder. He closed his eyes, relishing the release. When finished, he opened his eyes, looking up the slope.

The jungle here was sparse, scattered with mostly large trees. Beams of sunlight shone through the leaves, bugs flitting through them like mini-bombers in spotlights over Manila, a scene he'd watched from the deck of the patrol boat. He was about to turn away when something glinted in the light, drawing his attention. It was up the hill a few meters; it looked unnatural. Perhaps it was money. He looked at the trail, his men still sprawled. He'd give them a few more minutes while he checked it out.

He went up the slope, noticing footprints. *Odd,* he thought. He got to the spot, lowering to a crouch. Something was half-buried there. He scooped it up, placed it upon his palm and brushed the dirt away.

All color drained from his face, and his breath caught in his throat. He pulled the rifle off his shoulder, aiming up the hill, expecting to be shot any second. But there was no one there, only trees, sunlight, and bugs. He glanced at what he found again: a small silver button with the letters USN.

13

The morning passed slowly. The inside of the abandoned mining buildings were stiflingly hot. Hanscom and Gonzalez took refuge beneath the shade from the trees near the slope. It was still hot, but at least the occasional breeze cooled the sheen of lingering sweat.

Two of the six Filipinos had gone to the village, seeking news about the Japanese patrol. They'd returned an hour before, saying the Japanese had done a walkthrough, then retreated the way they'd come, presumably along the trail leading toward the coast.

It was a guessing game how long it might take them to get to the spot they'd left the trail, and chances were, they wouldn't notice anything out of the ordinary. But, to be safe, three Filipinos were downslope a couple hundred yards, giving Hanscom and Gonzalez an excuse to be out here, backing them up.

The other Filipinos spread farther along the flanks. One stationed down the trail leading back to the village where the Japanese had bivouacked. All points of entry covered except to the north, which wasn't a likely route.

Hanscom was just finishing cleaning and reloading his eight remaining rounds into his Colt 1911, when one of the Filipinos materialized from downslope. He was moving fast. Hanscom felt his urgency and knew something was wrong.

The Filipino gestured behind him and uttered the one word that cut through language barriers, "Japs."

Hanscom and Gonzalez were immediately off their butts and crouching, clutching their pistols. Hanscom pushed Gonzalez, "Go warn the others then get back here." He nodded and ran in a hunch up the slope. The Filipino darted left to warn the man watching the trail. Hanscom was suddenly alone. *Where are the others?* He wondered. There were still two sentries downslope, but where?

He stayed put, pressing himself against the bulk of the enormous tree, watching for movement. Sunlight streamed through the branches, lighting up the area with a yellowish tint. The insects continued to buzz and click, and he realized he'd become so accustomed to it that he hadn't noticed their constant background noise.

The air felt thicker suddenly, as though pressing against him, restraining his breathing. He realized his breaths were coming in shallow gasps of anticipation. He forced himself to calm down. He closed his eyes, concentrating on controlling his breathing.

He heard someone coming from behind and turned. It was Gonzalez followed by Staub, Gilson, and a few armed sailors. He cringed how their faded blue uniforms stood out against the brown and green background. He was dressed the same way. He waved at them to lower themselves. They slowed, moving more carefully.

When they were beside him, Hanscom smelled their stale sweat. Staub looked downslope, holding his pistol tight. "Where are they?" he whispered, entirely too loud for Hanscom's taste.

Hanscom shrugged, pointing down the hill and whispering much quieter, "Haven't seen them yet."

Staub licked his lips, his dry tongue doing little to help the dryness. His eyes were wide and Hanscom realized the smell of fear was coming off him like he'd bathed in it. He matched Hanscom's tone, "What do we do?"

Hanscom exchanged a quick glance with Sergeant Gonzalez. Hanscom wasn't happy to see Staub scared, but he was glad he was smart enough to know when he was in over his head.

Hanscom whispered, "There's two Filipinos in front of us." He pointed right, "Take two men with you over to those bushes; spread out and stay hidden. Make sure of your targets. If it all falls apart, the rally point's the barracks." He touched Gilson's shoulder, "Take the rest over there," he pointed left. "Use the trees and stay out of sight. Hopefully, the Filipinos will lead them into us."

Staub shared a look with Gilson, who nodded, and they moved off to their respective spots. Gonzalez got onto his belly and moved to the next tree, pulling himself into a sitting position with his back against it. He checked his pistol, then leaned out, peering around the tree trunk.

Hanscom watched the sailors getting into position. They spread wide, assuring one grenade wouldn't take them all out at once. They were crouching behind trees or hunkering under bushes. He could still see them, but he thought from downslope they'd be difficult to spot.

Satisfied, he chanced a look down the hill. Still nothing. He adjusted his aching knees slightly, then froze, catching movement out the corner of his eye. He barely breathed, keeping perfectly still.

There it was again, a slight movement down and to the right, directly in front of Lieutenant Commander Staub and his sailors. He concentrated on the spot. *Was it the Filipinos?* He doubted it; they moved through the forest like ghosts. He nearly choked when the form of a Japanese dressed in khaki and holding a long rifle appeared from around a bush.

The Japanese sailor took a step then froze, peering up the hill, concentrating. After half a minute, he took another two steps and froze again, repeating the slow look around. The Japanese finally glanced over his shoulder, lifting his chin at whoever was behind him. He took four more slow steps, his rifle sweeping side to side.

He saw Gonzalez was motionless. He looked ready to spring. Beyond him, he could just make out Staub and the other two sailors. They were motionless, too, and obviously aware of the threat coming directly at them. He hoped they wouldn't fire too early. Pistols were notoriously inaccurate, and even more so in the hands of nervous young men.

Another form emerged from the jungle, this one more toward his position. He moved as cautiously as the first man, but even from here, Hanscom could hear his labored breathing, reminding him that these were sailors, not soldiers used to fighting in the jungle. He doubted the patrol boat was big enough to have a contingent of naval marines aboard, at least he hoped not.

Another Japanese sailor emerged near where the first man came out. The closest man was still 40 yards from Staub's position. There was a lot of cover between them, and once again, Hanscom wished he'd reminded them not to shoot until they were almost upon them.

His hopes dashed when he saw a quick movement from Staub's position. He watched in horror as a sailor pulled himself to his knees, clumsily aiming his pistol through brambles and bushes.

The Japanese saw the movement and froze for an instant. The next moment the shot and the plume of smoke sent the Japanese onto his belly. The enemy brought his rifle to his shoulder. He fired as the other Japanese threw themselves flat, also bringing their rifles to bear. The submariner yelled out and dropped into the brush.

The two other Japanese fired toward the smoke, working their bolt actions quickly. Staub and the other sailor returned fire, having very little chance of hitting anything with pistols.

Hanscom knew they'd be wiped out unless he did something. Cursing under his breath, he lunged from cover, yelling at the top of his lungs while sprinting down the hill straight at them. His sudden action took the Japanese by surprise and they shifted their barrels his way, trying to line up shots between the trees as he sprinted toward them.

Gonzalez was only a second behind him, running to catch up with Hanscom's crazed charge. He didn't yell and was soon bearing down upon the Japanese who'd first appeared. He was busy lining Hanscom up and didn't have time to react to the new, closer threat. The enemy sailor's eyes bugged out when he saw Gonzalez only a few feet away, aiming his pistol. He slid to a stop a foot away and fired five times point blank. The Japanese sailor's face caved in, spraying Gonzalez with a sheen of blood and brains.

Hanscom was still screaming like a crazy man, running downhill fast, avoiding trees as though time had run out on the clock but he had a chance for the end zone. The nearest Japanese got to his knees, tracking him with his rifle. He fired at the same instant Hanscom passed a tree. He heard and felt the bullet—which would've ended his life—smack into the tree, splintering the bark.

Hanscom adjusted his angle, rushing toward the sailor who was working the bolt action. Hanscom raised his Colt, firing as he ran. Bullets whizzed all around the Japanese, but none found their mark.

Exasperated at his poor marksmanship, Hanscom skidded to a halt and went to one knee, gripping the pistol with two hands and aiming carefully. The Japanese finally chambered a round, bringing the barrel up. Hanscom fired from ten yards and this time his heavy bullet thumped into the enemy sailor's belly, making him grunt and fall forward. His rifle barrel dug into the soft ground. Hanscom pulled the trigger again, but it clicked against an empty chamber.

He noticed the third Japanese rolling from his back to his belly, bringing the rifle to bear. Hanscom's eyes widened. He didn't have time to react, and he was out of ammo. Suddenly, from the jungle behind the Japanese, a flash of movement. The sailor noticed it too and hesitated, giving the attacking Filipino enough time to land on his back and drive a knife into the base of his neck. He withdrew it quickly and drove it home again and again until the Japanese stopped moving. The Filipino looked up from his kill, giving Hanscom a wide, toothy grin.

A second Filipino emerged from the jungle, his long rifle's barrel smoking. Hanscom didn't remember hearing it fire. Distantly, he thought, *how many were there?*

Lieutenant Commander Staub called for a medic, and Hanscom remembered seeing the sailor go down. He gathered himself off the ground, his breathing coming in long gasps. He moved up the hill but his legs felt suddenly weak and he dropped to the dirt, shaking his head.

Gonzalez ran to him, "Are you hit, Major?" He ran his hands over him, searching for a wound, finding nothing.

Hanscom shook his head, "I'm fine. Just need a second."

Gonzalez saw men converging on Staub's position. He shook his head, "Tell me before you pull a stunt like that again, okay?"

Hanscom grinned, shaking his head. "It's all I could think to do. I can't hit the broad side of a barn with a pistol and I've actually practiced. I knew our only chance was to get close."

Gonzalez pointed at the gut-shot Japanese sailor, still leaning over as though praying, a stream of thick blood pooling beneath his knees. "You hit him," he said matter-of-factly.

Hanscom looked at the dead sailor. Shaking his head, he said, "I was aiming for his head."

———

Pharmacist Mate Wilkins couldn't save the young sailor. He'd been hit in each leg. The bullet in his left wasn't bad, but the other had severed his femoral artery, causing him to bleed out quickly. Wilkins tried to pinch off the steady flow of blood but couldn't. After a ten-minute battle for his life, he finally stepped away from the body, bloody, shaken, and defeated.

Hanscom and Gonzalez stayed out of the way, watching from a few yards away. The sailor's death hit his boatmates hard. Lieutenant Commander Staub, who'd been beside him when he got hit, was also covered in the man's blood. He'd kept him alive long enough for Wilkins to arrive, but the incident had shaken him, too.

The six Filipinos hustled down the slope, talking excitedly to Gonzalez. "They say two got away. They ran off, and they want to go after 'em."

Lieutenant Gilson approached, noticing the conference and catching the tail end. His eyes were hard. He set his jaw, looking at the group of downtrodden sailors standing around their dead comrade. He refocused on the GIs and Filipinos, "Let's hunt them down."

Hanscom and Gonzalez nodded. They'd already gone through the dead Japanese sailors' things, taking their rifles and any ammo they could find. There wasn't much, but Gonzalez handed the spare rifle to Gilson who holstered his pistol then expertly worked the bolt action, checking for a chambered round. Gilson addressed the sailor behind him, "Tell Lieutenant Commander Staub we're going after the bastards and we'll meet back here."

The sailor nodded, adding, "I'd like to join you, sir."

Gilson nodded, "Hurry. You can catch up." The sailor, Machinist Mate Rance, ran to relay the message. Gilson nodded to the others, "Let's go."

The Filipinos nodded eagerly, trotting down the hill, past the lined up Japanese bodies. Hanscom kept his eyes up, not wanting to look at the dead men any more than he had to. Gilson spit on them as he passed.

Once down the hill a ways, the Filipinos slowed their pace, talking in murmurs among themselves. Rance caught up, looking relieved. They spread out, continuing down the hill until they reached the main trail. The Filipinos went in different directions looking for signs. Finally, one of them came trotting back, holding up his finger. It was shiny with sticky blood. He was smiling as he waved them to follow.

Gonzalez murmured, "Looks like at least one of 'em's hit."

They trotted along the path in single file. Though Hanscom was near the end of the line, he noticed the splashes of bright blood along the trail. The enemy sailor was losing a lot of blood. Following the blood trail felt primitive and wrong to him, like they were merely hunting animals and not human beings. The more blood the Filipinos found, the more quickly they moved until they were finally jogging.

Hanscom had grown to respect the Filipinos' abilities in the jungles of Luzon, but were they *all* that competent? He wondered if these men were letting the bloodlust get to them. Their pace was worrisome. What if the Japanese were laying in ambush? They'd run headlong into it.

He decided he needed to slow things down. He called out to Gonzalez, "Tell them to slow down, Gonzo. This is dangerous."

Gonzalez nodded, calling out to them, but they either didn't hear or were ignoring him. Gilson and Rance were in front of Gonzalez, running to keep pace with the Filipinos. The trail wasn't wide enough for Gonzalez to pass and physically stop the Filipinos. He called out again without success, and he wondered if perhaps he was getting the words wrong.

Gilson glanced over his shoulder quickly, not wanting to take his eyes off the trail for more than an instant. "I think they know what they're doing," he said between breaths.

Frustrated, and feeling they would be ambushed any second, Hanscom yelled, "Stop, dammit!"

The closest Filipino looked over his shoulder, slowing slightly. Hanscom waved at him, trying to get his attention. The Filipino barked something to the others, and they finally slowed too. Just then, shots rang out. The terrible sound of bullets hitting flesh and the agonized scream of a mortally-wounded man brought his fears to light.

Hanscom and Gonzalez dove off the trail, landing in hard, thorny scrub-brush. Gilson and Rance were slower, but finally crouched, both aiming their weapons forward. The Filipino in front was on his back, writhing in pain, his off-white shirt quickly darkening with blood. The other Filipinos were on their bellies trying desperately to see where the shots came from.

Hanscom noticed a plume of smoke off the trail to the right, across from where he lay. He aimed over Gilson's back. There was a flash of movement. He adjusted and fired, the butt of the rifle slamming into his bicep painfully. He ignored it and worked the sticky bolt action, finally getting another round chambered. He aimed more carefully, seeing another darting shape running straight away. He fired again, and through the white plume, saw the shape drop out of sight, as though tripped.

Rance stood up suddenly, aiming his pistol in the same direction and firing repeatedly until his magazine ran dry. Gonzalez yelled, "Get down!" but Rance was having none of it. Gonzalez leaped to his feet, launched over the cowering Gilson, and rammed into Rance as though sacking a quarter-back. An instant later another shot and another plume of smoke, this time from farther forward. The bullet sliced past Rance's ear.

The shot was met with five more shots from the Filipinos. The onslaught of sound made Hanscom's ears ring. He'd just managed to rack another round when the second Japanese fell forward into the trail, nearly landing on top of Gilson.

Gilson pushed himself away quickly, as though suddenly confronted with a deadly snake. Hanscom raised his barrel, aiming at the Japanese. "It's okay, Commander. I think he's dead."

The nearest surviving Filipino leaped to his feet, sprinting to the body, his smoking rifle barrel ready to fire into the Japanese sailor's inert form, but it was obvious he was already dead. The Filipino glanced at the blank eyes of his countryman lying in the trail; he'd taken both Japanese bullets squarely in the chest. He kicked the dead sailor hard in the ribs, cursing at him venomously.

Half an hour later they were all back at the mining site brooding over their dead. The Filipinos told them they wanted to take the bodies back to their village for proper burial. The Filipinos weren't interested in the American's protestations. No one knew what was happening in the coastal town, but simply walking in with their dead wasn't a viable option.

Hanscom explained that the Japanese had only sent five men to follow them, which meant there were at least that many still occupying the town. For all they knew, they could've been reinforced already and were possibly scouring the area for them. Despite the logic of staying hidden, the Filipinos were unwavering. They were going anyway.

Hanscom asked Gonzalez to allow them some time to decide what they wanted to do, and the Filipinos agreed to wait a half hour.

The officers huddled together discussing options. Staub, who'd recovered from the initial shock of losing the young sailor, seemed more pliable and open to suggestions from Hanscom. *Fear tends to do that,* he thought.

Hanscom started, "I know we'll be walking into the unknown, but I don't fancy us staying out here without the Filipinos. This is a fine spot, but eventually the Nips are gonna come looking for us, especially when their patrol doesn't report back. They'll find this place, which means we'd have to flee overland." He shrugged, "I don't even know which direction we'd go."

Gilson shrugged, "They won't just leave us out here, will they?"

Hanscom shook his head, "In my experience, the locals have been nothing but grateful and helpful, but that was in Manila. Panay? Who knows? So far, I'd say they're like the others, but..." He bit his lower lip then continued, "I think sticking with a known group is the way to go." Gilson exchanged a look with Staub. Hanscom added, "It's not like we'll waltz in there and announce ourselves. We'll be careful, scout it out. Who knows, maybe we'll run into Tarkington and the others."

Staub's face turned from contemplative to dark, "I'm interested in whatever's best for my men. Tarkington's little horror show be damned."

Hanscom cursed inside, wishing he hadn't brought up Tarkington. "I think sticking with the Filipinos is the best thing for all of us."

Staub set his jaw, stewing upon the decision. He finally nodded, "I agree. Get the men ready to go, Gil. We'll need some way to carry Seaman Mankowitz's body."

Gilson exchanged a relieved glance with Hanscom and said, "Aye, Skipper."

14

Tarkington opened his eyes, momentarily confused. Where was he? His addled senses slowly came back. He stared through blurred vision, seeing fuzzy points of light against a black tapestry. He blinked, sharpening the view, realizing he was looking at an endless carpet of stars. It was beautiful, but it did nothing to remind him of where he was. His head throbbed, making him close his eyes. He clutched his hand, feeling soft...*sand*, he realized.

The image of the Japanese sailor bringing the pistol to bear, aiming for his head, then the bright flash followed immediately with searing pain and blackness. *The boat.* He'd been on the boat, but now felt sand. He opened his eyes again, looking to the side. There was movement, and he saw a black outline lean toward him and grin. "You're awake!"

He recognized the voice, "Raker? That you?"

"Yeah, it's me, Tark." He reached over with his uninjured arm and laid his hand on Tarkington's chest. "You gave everyone quite a scare. Thought you were a goner for sure...shot in the head." The image of the pistol flash made Tarkington wince and reach up, wanting to touch the side of his head, but Raker shook his head, "Don't touch it. You're fine, but we just got the bleeding stopped. You don't want to open it up again."

Tarkington gave up trying, "Where am I? What happened after?"

"The guys brought you back. All the Jap sailors are dead. I wasn't there, but the Jap that got you was the last one."

Tarkington stared at the stars, "How long've I been out?"

Raker shrugged, "Long enough to worry. Maybe 40 minutes?" he mused. "The others spread out—some are still on the boat, some near the trail with the Filipinos."

Tarkington swallowed, and it felt like he had broken glass in his throat. "Water?" he croaked.

Raker nodded, reaching to the side, pulling a leather bag close. He helped Tarkington sit up, the movement making him grunt as his head reached a new level of throb.

He drank deep mouthfuls, the cool water wetting his mouth and throat. He thought he could feel it radiating through his blood like some kind of sweet elixir. He forced himself to stop gulping so he could catch his breath.

Raker grinned, taking the bag away and setting it nearby. He lifted a small flashlight and turned it on, shining it onto Tarkington's head wound. He dabbed it with a bloody cloth and Tarkington winced, but didn't pull away. Raker turned the light off. "It looks good. You'll have a nasty scar, but the stitches are holding."

"Stitches?" he slurred.

Raker nodded, "Yeah, one of the Filipinos stitched you up. How you feel?"

Tarkington swayed, trying his best to stay upright. "Like shit. Water helped, though. I keep getting hit in the head, dammit. There a target there or something?" Raker laughed and gave him another pull. He drank deeply. When he finished, he reached out, "Help me stand."

Another familiar voice from his left, "Tark! You're alive," Winkleman exclaimed.

"Help me stand, Wink."

Winkleman and Raker got on either side of him, keeping him steady while he eased himself to a standing position. His body felt as though he wasn't in total control, like it was someone else's and he was trying to figure out how things worked. Winkleman and Raker stayed close but let him test his balance. He swayed, but stayed upright.

"What's the situation, Wink?"

"We took the boat. It's still anchored out there. Vick and Stolly and a few of the Filipinos are still out there. Everyone else is at the trailhead, watching for the rest of the Japs."

Tarkington's head throbbed, making it hard to concentrate. "Anyone— anyone else hurt?"

Winkleman shook his head emphatically, "No. You were the unlucky one." He grinned, "Well, you and those Jap sailors."

A long silence ensued while Tarkington considered their situation. He finally broke the silence, "How much time till daybreak?"

Winkelmann answered, "About four hours."

It hurt to think, but Tarkington tried formulating a plan. They were in a unique situation. They had a boat, which could be a way out of here. Four hours from now they could be well south.

In the morning, afternoon at the latest, every Imperial Japanese Naval vessel stationed at Iloilo Port would come looking for the patrol boat which hadn't checked in. Had they radioed their location upon arrival? Perhaps another damned flying boat would pass over and spot them. Then what?

If they left right now, they could spare the villagers, who could dispose of the bodies and act as though nothing had happened. But if the Japanese *had* radioed their location, the villagers would be tortured and forced to talk.

Tarkington pinched the bridge of his nose. All these thoughts were flashing through his mind like dropped bits of litter. He felt scattered and he couldn't stop the incessant tangents from clouding everything. In the background, like the annoying, incessant buzz of a mosquito, there was something else. *What about the crew of The Eel? What about Hanscom and Gonzalez?*

Tarkington realized Winkleman was talking, his voice breaking through like a breeze pushing through thick smoke. He hadn't heard a word. "What? What did you say?" he interrupted.

Winkleman cleared his throat, "I was just asking what we should do, Tark."

Tarkington lifted his gaze to the stars once again and sighed. "We gotta find Hanscom and the others." It was suddenly so clear to him. "I—we can't just leave 'em out there."

Winkleman nodded, "I know."

Raker signaled the boat, telling them what they intended to do. He'd trained in Morse code, as had Vick. They'd both taken a class offered by the Navy before hostilities with Japan started. The Army offered them a pay increase for the extra training, but neither had ever seen an extra penny. Now it was coming in handy. He received a reply and joined the others. Tarkington ordered him to stay put with the bulk of the Filipinos. He was disappointed but knew—with his arm—it was the right call.

After the violence, none of the Filipinos had gone back to their respective homes, everyone still milling around the beach and city hall as though it were an all-night party. They wanted to build a bonfire in celebration, but the GIs convinced them that would be a bad idea. So instead they filled city hall, bringing in musical instruments, and soon were dancing and carrying on as though the war had ended.

As Tarkington and Winkleman were leaving, Winkleman noticed a few of the local ladies eyeballing Raker, the only remaining American GI, with lustful looks. Winkleman shook his head, "I wouldn't worry about Raker. Looks like the ladies'll keep him company."

Tarkington, whose head still throbbed, glanced back, noticing the same thing. "Son-of-a-bitch'll be useless by the time we get back."

Winkleman's eyes lingered on the scene. The thought of sex was never far from their young minds, even in the throes of survival, but there'd been very few opportunities. Now it seemed Raker was in for it, and Winkleman's interest piqued.

Tarkington shook his head and slapped Winkleman's arm, "Get your damned head on straight, Wink."

Winkleman tore his eyes away, "Sorry. Just—you know—been awhile."

Tarkington knew most of them had been with women, prostitutes mostly. It hurt his head to think of it, so he shifted his concentration to the matter at hand. "We don't got time for that now. Let him have his fun, if he still knows how to use it, but we got work to do." Winkleman sighed, nodding.

Soon they were with Henry and the Filipinos, staged near the beginning of the trail leading east. Henry grinned upon seeing Tarkington up and about. He held out his hand and they shook, the gesture all the old friends needed.

"They know what we're looking for?" Tarkington asked.

Henry nodded, "Yep. I filled 'em in after speaking with Wink," he whispered in his slow drawl.

"Be great if we could get this done before light. I'd love to be back before the boat's moved, but I also don't want to walk into an ambush."

Henry shrugged, "Probably can't have it both ways, but we'll see. They know the score. They've already scouted about a mile in, so the first part'll be quick."

Tarkington nodded, "Good. Get going."

Henry waved and the Filipinos silently moved out, trotting along the trail in single file, keeping a few yards between each man. Tarkington waited until nearly everyone had gone. He took a deep breath, trying to push the incessant throbbing from his mind, and trotted after them. With every step, pain shot through his skull like bolts of lightning. He set his jaw, concentrating on not throwing up.

By morning, Tarkington was questioning his decision to go after the Japanese. They'd made excellent time—the Filipinos keeping a steady, but safe pace. He still felt like shit.

When it was light enough to see, it was obvious the Japanese patrol had come this way. Their distinct boot patterns were easy to pick out in the softer areas of the trail. There were also signs of American boot prints, so they were on the right track, but time was slipping by fast. Tarkington's head still ached. He'd kept from getting sick, but all he wanted to do was lay down somewhere and close his eyes.

He called a halt, and the Filipinos looked back questioningly. Winkleman, who'd stayed behind him in an effort to monitor him, hunched beside him. Soon, Henry trotted up, joining them. Tarkington wiped his brow and took a long drink from his bladder of tepid water. He'd been drinking a lot and wondered if it had something to do with his head injury. Wiping his mouth with the back of his hand, he realized he hadn't peed in a long time, despite all the water.

He shook his head, refocusing on the task at hand. He slurred slightly, "If we don't find them soon, we need to head back. If the Japs aren't already there, they definitely will be by tonight or tomorrow."

Winkleman exchanged a glance with Henry, noticing the slur. "You okay, Tark?" asked Winkleman.

Tarkington looked annoyed. He rubbed the edge of his wound; it still hurt to touch and the constant sting as sweat dripped into it added to his agony. "Another hour. Then we gotta..." he trailed off, the pain and dizziness suddenly too much.

Henry's eyes went to slits, giving his old friend a once over. Finally shaking his head, he said, "You're not well, Tark. You need to go back, now." He exchanged another look with Winkleman, who pursed his lips, nodding.

Tarkington was about to protest, but Henry didn't give him the chance. He gave a low whistle, getting the nearest Filipino's attention and waving them over. Two men trotted over. Henry pointed at Tarkington, whose pale face, and bloodshot eyes alarmed them. He motioned they needed to take him back, mimicking walking with his fingers and pointing back the way they'd come. Their faces darkened, but they understood and nodded.

Henry tapped Winkleman's shoulder. Winkleman nodded, "I'll go with them. You take the patrol. Give it another few hours." He whispered the last part, not wanting Tarkington to hear. "Good luck, Henry."

Tarkington could finally form what he wanted to say, but it came out an angry slur, "I—I'm in charge of this..." He toppled over. Henry and Winkleman caught him and eased him down.

Winkleman cursed, "Shit. We need to fashion some kind of stretcher."

Other Filipinos joined them, seeing Tarkington's condition. Soon, Tarkington was draped onto Carlos's back. He volunteered immediately, being the largest and strongest of them. A rifle, held horizontally beneath Tarkington's butt, and a Filipino on each side—one gripping the barrel, the other the stock—gave Tarkington something to sit on and took some pressure off Carlos's back.

Tarkington's head lolled, and he slurred but didn't struggle and soon passed out again. Winkleman led them back the way they'd come.

Henry watched them round the corner, then waved the others forward. They still had a job to do.

A few hours later, the distant sound of rifle fire made Henry drop onto his belly, his captured Japanese rifle up and ready. The Filipinos were also down, kneeling. The firing was sporadic and sounded like it was coming from up the hill. Henry wondered if perhaps the trail veered uphill from here. So far, it had been fairly flat, with a few ups and downs as it went between valleys, but moved steadily due east. The gunfire was decidedly off their current path.

After a few minutes, the gunfire subsided and finally stopped. The Filipinos looked at him expectantly. It had to be the patrol they were tailing; it was the only thing that made sense. But what was the outcome? It was impossible to discern what weapons were being fired from this distance. They all sounded like distant pops, indistinguishable from one another.

Henry felt the constraint of time pressing in on him. They had to get back to the village then leave before the Japanese sent reinforcements, but he couldn't go back now, knowing his quarry was close. He didn't necessarily want to move forward, not knowing what he'd run into. The prudent thing to do was to hunker down and see what came down the trail.

He signaled, holding his hands up, then put his hand over his eyes and moved his head side to side, hoping he was conveying stop and watch.

Ernesto, the nearest Filipino, a small man with stringy muscles and dark brown eyes framed with thick eyelashes, nodded and spoke low to the others. Henry rose to his feet and, staying in a crouch, moved off the trail and into the scrub grass. He found concealment, making sure he could see down the trail. The others filled in spaces around him, and soon there was nothing but sounds of insects and birds.

Time passed slow. He guessed they'd been in place for half an hour, but it felt much longer. His stomach growled, reminding him he hadn't eaten in a while. He ignored it, knowing it might be hours before he'd get another opportunity. He wondered how long he should stay here. What was his next move?

The decision was made for him, when the unmistakable sound of distant human speech made everyone tense up and lower themselves. There was a slight rise 20 yards down the trail and Henry focused on it, his rifle barrel tucked tight into his shoulder.

Minutes passed and nothing happened. He knew he hadn't imagined the voices—the others had heard it too—but where were they? Was it Japanese, Americans, or Filipinos? He couldn't tell. The voices were too far away to distinguish anything specific. It could've been Clark Gable, for all he knew.

He was so intent on the trail that his eyes blurred, and he forced himself to turn away. It had been five minutes with nothing but normal jungle sounds. He took in a deep breath, deciding he had to go check it out. He waved, getting Ernesto's attention. He hunkered a few feet behind him. He signaled he should stay in place while he moved forward to check it out. Ernesto nodded and passed it along to the men to his right and left.

Henry got his feet beneath him and moved forward slowly to the trail. Normally he'd sneak through the brush, but much of it was dead and brittle and would make a lot of noise. Once on the trail, he felt exposed. He knew there was nothing between himself and the rise. He moved toward it quickly, but soundlessly.

Once close, he got onto his belly and slithered forward, feeling his knees scraping painfully on the hard-pack dirt. He got to the lip of the rise and eased his head over. The trail wound along. There was nothing obviously out of place. He could see maybe ten yards before it turned again. He concentrated on the bushes around the trail.

Suddenly, beyond where he could see, more shots in quick succession. He lowered his head, but when he realized the shots weren't aimed at him, lifted it again, searching. More shots and yelling. He figured the action was at least 60 yards away. He desperately wanted to know what was happening but kept himself planted to the spot. Perhaps whoever was up there would come this way. It would either be the Japanese patrol, in which case they'd ambush them, or it would be the Americans or Filipinos.

Ernesto and two other Filipinos were suddenly beside him, peering over the rise. Henry shrugged his shoulders, answering their questioning gazes. They heard murmured voices, but he still couldn't distinguish specifics and by the other's perplexed gazes, neither could they. Ernesto leaned in close and whispered something which Henry didn't wholly understand but thought to be the equivalent of, "what now."

Henry burned to know what the hell was going on, but running headlong up the trail was out of the question. He decided whoever it was would probably come down the trail. He signaled the others should move up and set up an ambush from this position; it had better fields of fire. Henry could tell the Filipinos wanted to move forward and engage whoever was up there, but they nodded, agreeing to his suggestion.

Henry was pushing the time envelope by staying, but he didn't feel he had any other choice. He decided, if there was no activity over the next hour, he'd need to make another decision: either leave or move forward.

He didn't have to make that decision. He heard sounds of people moving along the trail, coming his way. He noticed Ernesto, off to his right, tense up. It wasn't talking, but nondescript, small sounds: breaking sticks, legs swishing past brush and grass. He eased his rifle stock to his shoulder, pressing his cheek into it and squinting over the sights. He hadn't fired this particular weapon, but the target would only be ten yards out, maybe closer. Even if it weren't properly sighted in, he couldn't miss from this range. He steadied his breathing as the sounds continued getting closer by the second.

Ernesto and the others were still as stones, barely breathing, anticipating the coming action with a mix of fear and excitement. A breeze came downslope, rustling the brush and bending the tall grasses over the trail. At the same instant, a shape formed beyond. A hand went up, pushing the swaying grasses away. At first, Henry thought he saw the khaki color of a Japanese naval officer and hoped the men with him would wait until they were all in the killing zone. Then he saw beyond the first man. He opened both eyes, looking over the barrel. He was about to bring his hand up, keeping the others from firing, but he was too late.

A shot from Ernesto was followed immediately with another from farther back. Henry yelled, "Cease fire! Cease fire! Friendlies!" He risked getting to his knees, waving his arms, "Stop! Stop!" A shot from the men on the trail whizzed past his head. He instinctively dropped but continued yelling, "American! American! Cease fire!"

Silence swept over the area. Gunsmoke wafted along the breeze and Henry dropped his rifle and stood, stepping from cover, expecting to be shot. He waved his arms frantically, seeing men lowering their weapons, and he stepped onto the trail. The Filipinos with him also stood.

A low, keening moan, then an angry, "No!" came from the men up the trail. Henry trotted forward, his hands still up. Miraculously, the lead man was unscathed, but the next man was down, his chest frothing with red-tinged bubbles. His eyes darted side to side and his mouth opened and closed, making high-pitched, ineffective gasping sounds.

Henry pushed past the dazed Filipino still on the ground, shaking badly from his near-death experience, and slid in beside Major Hanscom's quivering body. Lieutenant Commander Staub was on the other side, shaking his head, repeating, "no, no, no."

Henry ripped open Hanscom's shirt, blood spraying his face. The entry wound was small and bubbling profusely. Fresh blood streamed down Hanscom's body, pooling beneath him. Henry placed his hand over the wound, pressing hard. Blood continued to seep, and air escaped through his imperfect seal.

Men parted along the trail as Sergeant Gonzalez pushed his way past, bowling some over into the brush. The sight of Hanscom sprawled out, bleeding, made him pull up for an instant. Then he dropped his rifle and cradled Hanscom's head. "Hey, Zeke, you're okay, you're okay." He couldn't keep the panic from his wavering voice. Hanscom raised his eyes, seeing his old friend's worried face. Hanscom tried to speak but couldn't catch his breath. "M—Medic!" Gonzalez yelled.

Pharmacist Mate Wilkins was already on his way and slid in a second later. "Shit," he stammered, pulling the meager assortment of rags he'd scrounged from his pouch. He pushed Henry's hands away, replacing them with the rags, pressing hard. They immediately turned red but provided a better seal. Hanscom gasped, getting a breath, the awful sound of escaping air still there, but reduced slightly. Wilkins said, "Hold these, Henry. Turn him, I need to see his back."

Henry held the rags as Wilkins reached beneath Hanscom's back, feeling for the exit wound. He cursed again, "Shit, he's losing a lot of blood." He pulled his hand out. It dripped with fresh blood and bits of skin. He used the last of the rags, stuffing them beneath his back.

Hanscom's eyelids fluttered, the pain excruciating. He kept his eyes locked on Gonzalez. Gonzalez held his head, stroking his hair with a shaking hand, muttering, "You're fine, you're fine."

Hanscom reached up, clutching Gonazalez's hand. "Gonzo," he sputtered, sending bloody spittle flying. "Gonzo," he said again, quieter. Gonzalez stopped speaking, focusing all his attention on Hanscom. Hanscom's voice was low and thinning, "You gotta make it outta here, Gonzo. You gotta..."

Gonzalez nodded, "We're all making it out, Zeke. We'll go together."

Wilkins continued pressing into his back, trying to staunch the flow. Hanscom's struggling breaths were getting less robust, his color fading. "Gonzo," Hanscom continued. "You gotta tell her. You gotta tell Ellie..."

"You'll tell her yourself. You'll tell her yourself, dammit."

Hanscom's eyes moved from Gonzalez to the blue sky and he muttered softly, "It's okay, it's..." The gasping breaths stopped, his eyes glassed over, his body suddenly slack. Lifeless. He was gone.

Gonzalez continued rocking him, tears streaming down his cheeks, mixing with his friend's blood. Henry leaned away, leaving the bloody rags on his chest. The Filipinos he'd led here stood in a semi-circle, faces slack, shoulders slumped, barely holding onto their rifles.

15

Tarkington woke to the sound of arguing. He opened his eyes, wincing at the pain still throbbing from the side of his head. He gingerly touched his right temple, feeling the spongy dryness of bandages and the smell of spices. He briefly remembered being hauled back from the jungle upon Carlos's sturdy back. He'd been in and out of consciousness, remembering being laid down and fussed over by many lovely Filipino women. He didn't know what they'd done, but his wound felt much better than it had even a few hours before.

The voices carried into his room, and he jolted fully awake, realizing he was hearing Sergeant Gonzalez, Lieutenant Commander Staub, and the dim drawl of PFC Henry. Henry had done it; he'd found them. Now they could get out of here before the Japanese sent more boats and men.

He pushed himself to a sitting position. His head was still a little woozy, but nothing like before. He actually had to take a piss which told him he'd finally gotten in front of his dehydration. He swung his feet to the floor stuffing them into the boots he remembered the crew of The Eel giving him. It seemed like ages ago, but couldn't have been more than a week, maybe a week and a half.

The tone of the voices outside made him hurry, something didn't sound right. He heard Winkleman, "It was an accident. An unfortunate accident. No one's to blame."

Tarkington got to his feet. A dozing Filipino woman, not one of the pretty ones, stood, jabbering at him and pointing back at the bed. He gave her a lopsided grin, holding up a hand, gesturing for her help. She moved to his side, and he used her as a crutch. She continued berating him, but helped him move toward the doorway.

He pushed the rickety door open and sunlight streamed in, striking him in the face. It alarmed him how low the sun was in the sky. It would be setting in a few hours. He squinted, looking out over the sparkling sea. The Japanese boat they'd captured wasn't visible. A brief flush of confusion, then he remembered that Vick, Stollman, and a few Filipino guides had taken it to a hidden bay south of here.

The Filipino woman, whose name he remembered was Juanita, jabbered Pidgin, making everyone nearby spin around. Winkleman moved to him, looking concerned. "You shouldn't be up yet, Tark."

"Bullshit," Tarkington uttered. He smiled, seeing Gonzalez and waving. Gonzalez waved back, but didn't smile. Tarkington nodded toward Gilson and Staub.

Gilson grinned, stepping forward with his hand outstretched, "You've been busy, Staff Sergeant. We leave you for one day and we come back, you've got your own army and even the start of a navy, from what I hear."

Tarkington took Gilson's hand, stepping away from Juanita to do so. He nodded, "Yeah, something like that." He lifted his eyes to the others. There was something wrong. "What's happened?" he asked.

Winkleman answered, "They lost some people, Tark."

He pointed past the group and Tarkington saw three lined up bodies covered with sheets. Tarkington took a step toward them, "Who?" he asked.

Winkleman's voice was low, "Encentes, Seaman Mankowitz, and..." he paused looking directly into Tarkington's eyes, "and Major Hanscom."

Before Tarkington could say anything, Henry stepped forward, his captured rifle slung over his shoulder. He kept his eyes down as he addressed him, which struck fear into Tarkington; he'd never seen his friend act this way. Henry drawled, "It was my fault. I killed him. I killed Hanscom."

Tarkington was stunned, but before he could ask for details, Gonzalez was quick to say, "Bullshit! You didn't pull the trigger, Henry. It wasn't your fault."

Henry shook his head, "Maybe not, but I was in charge. Might as well have been me."

Tarkington's head hurt worse suddenly, but he asked, "Our own guys killed them?"

Lieutenant Gilson shook his head, explaining, "Just Hanscom. Japs killed the others." He pinched the bridge of his nose, "It was an accident, like the sergeant said." He leaned in closer, "Ernesto and Rodriguez fired the shots."

Tarkington had only known the Filipinos for a matter of hours. He pictured Ernesto but couldn't come up with an image for Rodriguez. "Where are they?"

Gilson pointed to the bodies. Two men sat nearby, their heads in their hands. "Over there. They haven't left their sides."

Tarkington looked at Lieutenant Commander Staub, whose eyes were bloodshot as though he hadn't slept in weeks. Tarkington took a deep breath, steeling himself against the throbbing in his head. He straightened up, thrusting his chest out, addressing Staub. "Sir, we've gotta get outta here. Hell, I thought the Nips'd be here by now."

Staub straightened his back, lifting his chin and nodding his agreement. "What do you have in mind, Staff Sergeant?"

"It'll be dark soon. We need to tidy this place up and get to the boat. We can run all night and get far away from this island."

Staub nodded, "What about the townspeople? What'll happen to them?"

"We can't take any of 'em. Barely enough room for all of us. Probably wouldn't leave anyway. If we clean things up enough, make sure there's no sign of *anything*, maybe they'll leave 'em alone. They can tell 'em the Japs came through here but left north, say they had radio problems. God knows this salty air wreaks havoc on *our* gear."

They spent the hours of daylight remaining burying their dead. They buried the Japanese in a single hole soon after the fight. The Americans and Filipinos had their own plots. They concealed all the gravesites. They took great pains to make the area look as untouched as any other.

The GIs and sailors helped the Filipinos repair bullet holes and scrubbed away blood stains marring the town hall. Special care was given to wiping out any US boot prints, or any left-behind articles of clothing which might tip off the Japanese.

As evening descended, the ragtag group of GIs and sailors marched out of town, the locals whisking their tracks away with long branches. One pretty young woman walked alongside Raker, reminding Winkleman of a lost puppy. When they got to the edge of the jungle, Raker stepped away from the line and stood beside her touching her cheek and smiling. He kissed her soft red lips then stood and marched away, giving her one last wave before disappearing around the corner.

Winkleman growled, "Raker, you dog! You told me nothing happened."

Raker shook his head, "It'd be rude, Wink."

Winkleman shook his head, "I knew it. I knew I shoulda stayed behind with you."

Raker grinned, "Sure hope the Japs don't show up nine months from now. She'll have some explaining to do."

Winkleman erupted, "That's awful, Private. Have some class for crying out loud."

"Meant nothing by it. Make no mistake, I'm coming back here after the war. I'll find her again. I promise you that. Don't you see? I'm in love, Sergeant."

Winkleman shook his head and murmured, "Think the pain from your arm's turned you soft."

After a few minutes, Stollman slowed his pace, allowing Raker to come up beside him. Stollman leaned close, "So, how was it?"

Raker grinned, shaking his head. "I'm not one to kiss and tell, Stolly."

Stollman guffawed, "Yes you are. Come on, spill it."

Raker noticed a few of the others coming closer, hoping for details, "I'll just tell you this: everything's sweeter in the tropics."

Stollman shook his head in disappointment, "That's it? That's all you're gonna give us?"

Raker's eyes sparkled in the fading light, "You'll just have to make your own memories I guess."

"Shiiit," hissed Stollman.

They were standing at the edge of the sea a couple minutes later, looking out over an idyllic bay. The two Filipinos leading them pointed, and Tarkington saw the dim outline of the captured patrol boat tucked against the bank. He nodded, noting that it would be impossible to spot from the air or sea.

He clapped the two Filipinos on the back, thanking them for their help. They nodded solemnly, then stood to the side and watched the sailors and soldiers move along the shore and hop the short span from the ground to the boat deck. There were 20 men, seven GIs, and the rest Navy. There'd been 15 Japanese sailors, so they'd be a little cramped.

Gilson ordered his three machinists into the bowels to check out the engines. He wished his chief engineer was here, but he'd gone down with The Eel. Stollman and Vick went with them, since they'd already run the boat.

After an hour, everyone was in place. The bridge could accommodate five men comfortably. No one knew Japanese, so they had to figure out what the dials and buttons did through trial and error. Starting the engines and steerage were obvious, but other dials and knobs were complete mysteries.

The machinist's mates, along with Petty Officer Yankowski, had little trouble with the engines. They were different, but not so much so that they posed a problem.

Darkness descended, and like the night before, the only light came from the stars. Red-filtered lights shone on Lieutenant Commander Staub and the other men manning the bridge. The engine purred at idle, the stink of fuel and oil making Staub feel more at home than he had in days.

Tarkington was standing near the door. He'd put Henry on the big mounted gun bolted to the roof. Raker was with him, assuring Tarkington that he could help with the ammunition even with his broken arm.

Torpedo tubes adorned the sides, but the crew didn't know how to arm or fire them. Their goal wasn't to engage the enemy, but to slip past them, using the darkness and the many islands dotting the archipelago. If they couldn't avoid contact, they'd do the best they could, but the name of the game was avoidance.

Lieutenant Commander Staub asked, "Are we ready to sail, Gil?"

Gilson, who was bent over the Japanese map, which had far more detail than the ones that went down with The Eel, straightened and nodded, "Yes, sir. I don't see why not. It'll be one for the history books."

"Only if we live to tell about it," Staub replied grimly. He couldn't keep the excitement from his voice though when he ordered, "Take us into open water, Lieutenant."

"Aye, sir." Lieutenant Gilson took the helm, "Let Yankowski know we're moving out, Ensign."

Ensign Walker, the only surviving junior officer from The Eel, picked up the handheld mic stenciled with Japanese characters and passed the order, "Prepare for departure."

Yankowski's reply came quickly, "Aye. We're ready down here, sir."

Gilson goosed the throttles, immediately feeling the powerful engine responding, pushing the boat through the calm, warm waters of the tiny inlet. The excitement on the bridge spread and Tarkington couldn't keep from grinning. His head still throbbed, but not enough to dull the experience of motoring south on a captured enemy boat. Hopefully, they'd get far enough to escape the ever-tightening noose around the Philippines.

Gilson skillfully maneuvered from cover and soon they were on the open sea. He opened the throttles to 20 knots, slowly ramping up the power, getting used to the way the boat responded. He loved being on a submarine and hoped to command one of his own, but the exhilaration he was feeling at the moment made him wonder if perhaps he should look into PT boats.

The wind, which had been negligible in the inlet, was blowing at 15 knots in the open ocean, creating waves and swells which the boat lunged and sliced through easily and with gusto. The men topside moved below or toward the stern, seeking protection from the bridge structure, hanging onto whatever they could to keep themselves from being pitched into the sea.

They passed the little town, seeing the dim outline of buildings, recognizing the bay and seeing the stick-like H shapes of outrigger canoes juxtaposed against the white sand.

Lieutenant Commander Staub had to raise his voice to be heard over the engine and the hull crashing through waves, "Ensign Walker, use the signal light; let 'em know we're out here."

"Aye, sir." Grinning, he aimed the signal light, flashing "thank you" over and over in Morse code. He doubted anyone on shore knew Morse code, but he didn't know what else to do. The signal light the Japanese had taken ashore had been dismantled, the various parts buried in the jungle, but soon lights from house lanterns lit up, waving back and forth like fireflies.

Tarkington grinned and waved, knowing they couldn't see him. As they dashed past, leaving the light show in their wake, he hoped to God they hadn't doomed them to the wrath of the Japanese.

He'd heard Raker's ultimatum that he'd return and find the woman he'd laid with. Tarkington had little doubt that was an empty promise. No matter how much Raker believed it now, the feeling would fade with distance and time. If, by some miracle, he found his way back, would she be alive, or ruined and discarded like so many other civilians in this war?

Tarkington thought his time aboard The Eel would've made him immune to seasickness, but he was wrong. The constant undulations—up, down, and side to side—combined with the darkness and lack of consistent horizon, made him sick. He wasn't the only one. He and Winkleman were both green around the gills.

After leaving the town behind, they'd moved farther out to sea, putting distance between land masses and the Port of Iloilo on the southeastern shore of Panay.

Tarkington started off in the bridge area, but soon realized he was in the way. Lieutenant Gilson, Lieutenant Commander Staub, and the young Ensign Walker had it well in hand.

Before leaving though, he'd perused the chart beneath the eerie red lighting. Walker pointed out where they'd come from and their position and projected track. The boat's fuel stores were nearly full, giving them an estimated range of 300 miles, which would get them to Mindanao.

Staub told him it was unlikely that they'd run into enemy vessels, and if they did, they were—after all—operating a Japanese boat. They wouldn't be able to communicate, either by radio or light signal, so the plan, in case they came across another vessel was to play dumb and get the hell out of there as quickly as possible.

The boat was only about 60 feet long, which meant there wasn't a lot of space for the 20 men. Indeed, the 15 Japanese sailors must've found it cramped too. There were only enough bunks for six sailors. There were two officer's quarters, more like broom closets, with barely enough space for the short, thin bed and a rickety shelf and chair.

Tarkington tried going from the bridge to a bunk but thought it better to be topside, not only for the fresh air but also for the access to vomit over the side, avoiding a mess.

Now he was sitting beside Winkleman, their backs against the hard metal structure of the bridge facing the pitching bow. They were soaked, the sea spray relentlessly pounding them, but it washed the vomit off themselves and the deck. The whipping wind kept the smell from making the entire scene worse.

Tarkington looked up, noting the clear sky shining with stars despite the wind. He shivered, the wind combining with his wetness, finally overcoming the warm evening. He figured he was dehydrated from not being able to keep anything down. He tried drinking water with little success. Being soaked in salt water probably didn't help matters.

The constant hum of the single engine changed pitch and Tarkington felt his back press into the wall. They were increasing speed, which caused the bow to slam even harder into the waves. The booming sound of the hull was like a rifle shot.

He exchanged a look with Winkleman, who'd noticed the speed increase too, "I'm gonna check it out."

Winkleman nodded, struggling to his feet, "I'll join you."

Keeping their hands glued to whatever they could, they moved along the base of the structure until they were at the short set of stairs leading up the side of the bridge. Tarkington was grateful for the handrails. He took each step slowly; his legs felt like they weighed a thousand pounds. He felt as weak as a newborn puppy.

The bridge was full of tension. Staub and Gilson were staring out to sea. Gilson glanced up at Tarkington and Winkleman, and waved them inside. Tarkington immediately felt better getting out of the wind and spray. He evaluated his gut, deciding he could risk it for the moment. Winkleman stepped in too, but wasn't as confident. He stayed near the door, his hand on the latch.

Tarkington leaned close. "Something wrong? We noticed you've increased speed."

Gilson nodded, "We spotted a flash out there. It was big, like a main gun on a ship."

"I didn't hear anything. Are we taking fire?" Tarkington asked.

"No. We didn't hear it either, just a large flash." He kept his eyes glued outside. Tarkington did too and there was another flash. Gilson pointed, "There it is again. Looks to be heading west. Slow us down, Gil. Whatever it is will pass in front of us. Let's not get too close."

Tarkington asked, "Can you tell what it is?"

Staub shook his head, "If it's a weapon firing—and I can't think of what else it would be—it's big. Like something that would be on a Jap Destroyer or Cruiser."

"Does it see us?" Tarkington asked, alarm in his voice.

Gilson decreased the throttle after Ensign Walker notified Petty Officer Yankowski. Staub tightened his grip on Wilkins's shoulder as the speed rapidly dropped off.

Staub nodded, "Depends. We don't know a lot about the Jap navy's technology, but based on my experience aboard the Eel, They've probably got both radar and sonar. They've most likely been aware of us for quite some time. The fact that they're not heading straight for us is a good sign, though." Gilson nodded his agreement. Staub rubbed his chin, "Hopefully us slowing down won't raise any suspicions, but we can't keep our speed or we'd pass too close."

Gilson nodded, "I'll keep it steady at ten knots and maintain course."

Staub considered for a few seconds, "Yes, good idea. If he takes an interest, we're faster—at least I think we are—and can leave him behind."

"What the hell is he firing at?" asked Tarkington.

Staub shrugged, "Maybe just a drill."

The radio crackled, making them all jump and exchange worried glances. Through the static, a metallic, clipped voice said something in Japanese.

Staub shook his head, "Damn, that's probably him. What I wouldn't give for someone that could speak Jap." There was another hail, followed with screeching static.

They all stared at the handset as though it would get up and do a dance. Gilson shook his head, "I don't even know how to turn the thing down, let alone on and off. Afraid I'll accidentally transmit."

Another burst from the radio, this time with more insistence. Tarkington asked, "Can we click it, like we do when we're having radio trouble?"

Gilson shrugged, "Who knows? Fact of the matter is, we don't know how the Japs operate. A click could mean, 'come on over, we'll barbecue.'"

Walker guffawed, not able to stifle his burst of laughter. Staub wasn't amused. "When we don't answer, he's going to investigate. He might not suspect anything, but even the Japs will investigate a non responsive vessel. They might think we're in distress."

16

Radioman Jin, on the bridge of the IJN destroyer Nokaze, pulled the headphones off his ears, "Nothing, Captain. There's no response from the contact." A few seconds later, he tried again, and when there was still no answer, he shook his head.

Captain Kento's mouth turned down at the corners. He and his crew had been zigzagging their way across the Sulu Sea all day and night, searching for an American submarine, which had been attacked a few days before. The attacking aircraft pilot reported a direct hit, but hadn't had enough fuel to loiter, and make sure it actually went down. However, a follow-on aircraft had reported attacking men in the water a few hours later, which suggested a sinking.

The surface contact, which was two kilometers north and moving south, didn't match that of an allied submarine. It was far too small. He assumed it was a friendly Type-14 motor torpedo boat out of Iloilo. But when it didn't reply to radio calls, his interest piqued. Perhaps they were in distress.

Normally, Captain Kento would be in his stateroom sleeping at this hour, but his XO had a fever, so he graciously took his night watch. He could've given the helm to another senior officer, but he'd been meaning to observe the night shift sailors, and his XO's sickness was the perfect excuse.

The forward Type-3 gun crew wanted to fire a few test rounds after refitting a broken part. After two shots, the crew was satisfied with the repair and Kento turned his attention to the contact. "Helm steer to zero six zero."

"Zero six zero, aye, Captain," the young man at the helm spun the wheel and the responsive rudders heeled the destroyer to starboard. The officers and NCOs steadied themselves as the centrifugal force pulled their bodies to port. Captain Kento had been in the Navy most of his adult life and been on countless cruises, both in peacetime and in war, but the feeling of a ship responding to controls still brought a smile to his face.

The Nokaze steadied and cut through the swell, sending water spraying over the deck. The southerly wind had made traveling east to west an uncomfortable rolling experience. He'd barely noticed, but now cutting into the swell at 90 degrees felt more natural. "What's our contact doing?"

The radar operator immediately answered, "They've slowed, Captain. Still bearing 125 at ten knots."

"If they weren't going so fast earlier, I would've written them off as a fishing vessel. Why did they decrease speed, I wonder?" Ensign Morio, standing nearby, knew his captain wasn't actually asking him. He'd learned long ago that Kento had a habit of asking himself questions out loud. He didn't expect, nor want, an answer. "Try hailing them again," he ordered.

"Aye, sir," answered the radio man. A few seconds later, "Still nothing, sir."

"When we're within range, send them a flash signal, Ensign Morio."

Morio straightened his back, "Aye, Captain." Morio asked, "Shall we alert the gunners, sir?"

Captain Kento pursed his lips, then nodded, "Yes. Alert the gunners." He thought it would be overkill, but if nothing else it would be excellent training. He listened to Ensign Morio calling down to the gun crew leads. Soon the Type-3 naval guns would get the target information and would slew and angle. In the darkness, it would be hardly noticeable. If the target turned out to be hostile, it was well within range and would be blown out of the water.

The radar man announced, "Captain, the contact is likely a Type-14 Motor Torpedo Boat."

Captain Kento nodded, but was skeptical of the information. The new radar systems were truly amazing. Some operators boasted that they could distinguish one fuzzy blip from another fuzzy blip, but he thought it unlikely. He agreed with the assessment however, not based on the blip, but the speed the boat had been traveling.

He felt slightly let down, though. The brief, although unlikely, possibility of action had gotten his blood pumping. It had been months since his last combat and he and his crew were itching for more. He desperately wanted to continue moving south to the Solomon Islands, where all the action was, but he still had another week patrolling these confined waters, where it seemed he was never far from points of land. He longed for the open ocean, the raw power of which couldn't be matched. He felt as boxed in and constrained as if he were sailing in a fishbowl.

Ensign Morio announced, "Gun crews are ready, sir."

Kento checked his watch, *under two minutes. Good crew.* "Very well," he uttered. "Standby."

"Standing by, sir."

Aboard the Type-14 MTB, the situation was quickly coming to a head. Staub assumed the Japanese destroyer or whatever he was facing, was likely bearing down on them fast. If he'd been aboard The Eel with an IJN ship bearing down like this, he'd know exactly what to do, but manning a surface vessel was a different matter. Whereas the submarine's best defense was slipping beneath the waves stealthily disappearing, the T-14's advantage was in speed and agility. But could he outrun a modern Japanese destroyer? He didn't know the top speed of this boat, but figured he was about to find out.

He leaned over the map. The red glow from the overhead light made everything look sinister. "He won't be satisfied until he's come alongside and none of us looks like a Jap. It's time to hightail it out of here." He pointed toward an island which the maps told him was four miles off the port side bow. "We'll shoot for that island; he won't be able to follow for fear of hitting a reef. His radar won't be able to see us once we're behind it in the island's shadow."

Gilson nodded, "I think it's our only option, sir. Better safe than sorry." Staub nodded, and Gilson lifted the mic, "We're about to see what this little girl can do, Yankowski. Standby for full throttle."

Petty Officer's Yankowski's voice sounded tinny, "Roger. Everything looks good down here. Hit it, Lieutenant."

Staub barked, "Heading, zero nine zero, full throttle."

Gilson nodded, "Aye, hold on!"

He pushed the throttles steadily until they were pegged. The boat responded, slipping onto a plane, the hull flexing with each wave impact. Gilson turned nearly 90 degrees east, the V hull gripped the water, banking the boat into the turn. The hull slamming into waves stopped, but now the boat rolled side to side, rocking as Gilson made micro-adjustments to each incoming swell. The darkness and wind didn't help, but soon the ride smoothed as they darted due east.

Staub felt exhilarated with the speed. "That Skipper's probably about as confused as he can be. One of his vessels, but we didn't answer hails, and now we're running away."

Tarkington's belly was cooperating somewhat, and he ventured to ask, "Are we in range of his guns?"

Staub nodded, "We probably have been long before we even saw those flashes, Staff Sergeant."

"Think he'll fire on us?"

Staub exchanged a look with Gilson, then shrugged, "I expect we'll find out in the next few minutes. If he wasn't coming for a closer look, then no. But if he was and we're suddenly evading...?" He stroked his chin, "But if I were in his shoes, the last thing I'd want to do was kill a friendly."

Everyone's attention was drawn to a sudden bright flash from starboard. It was while they were cresting a wave, giving them a superb view of the horizon. It was much closer than the initial flashes they'd seen. The arcing, fiery tail of an incoming shell mesmerized them and before anyone could call out, the shell crossed well in front and exploded in frothy whiteness. They dipped into the swell, blocking their view of the explosion, but the sharp boom swept over them like being slapped by an angry mother.

Staub yelled, "Warning shot!" Gilson glanced at him for orders, "Keep it steady, Gil. Give us everything she's got. We just need a few more minutes before we'll be in the island's clutter."

Tarkington grumbled, "We may not have minutes."

Staub raised his voice, "Keep watch south! Call out flashes. Be ready to take evasive maneuvers." He addressed Tarkington, "Tell the men on deck to hold tight, gonna get dicey out there."

Tarkington nodded toward Winkleman, who was still near the door. Winkleman leaned out and yelled at the top of his lungs, relaying the message, but the noise of the wind and engine drowned him out.

Tarkington strained, searching for another flash on the horizon. The boat lifted on another swell, then rolled into the trough. Twice more it happened. "Why aren't they shooting?" he asked.

"Making sure, I guess."

Walker yelled, "I think I saw her!"

"Flash!" called out Winkleman. Gilson immediately turned to starboard, bringing the bow back into the waves at a 30 degree angle. The turn happened just as they crested a wave, and the boat launched off it as though it were a motorcycle off a steeply-sloped ramp. The bow went airborne, the hull out of the water to midship, then sliced back into the sea, covering the bow with a foot of water. The hull shuddered, but the engine kept churning them forward at 30 knots.

There was an arcing flash of fire in the sky, another warning shot sailed harmlessly past them. Gilson maintained course for another 30 seconds, then spun the wheel back to the east, hoping to throw their aim off. Now they were running parallel with the swells, rolling in and out of mini valleys of water.

Tarkington and Winkleman called out simultaneously, "Flash!"

This time Gilson turned the opposite direction, climbing up and over a retreating wave and gliding down the front side as though the boat were a massive surfboard. This time the explosion was on target, or at least it would've been if he hadn't taken evasive action. The explosion was much closer than the last two and the concussive blast vibrated the hull.

Staub yelled, "He's done with the warning shots!"

Gilson nodded at the same time turning the boat back east, but he didn't stop there. He continued the turn, once again making them climb up and over another wave. He cut power as they crested, keeping the hull from launching this time. As soon as they were over, he added full throttle and glided to the bottom of the swell, turning with it, trying to keep in the groove, allowing the wave's inertia to help them along.

The feeling of ripping down the front face of a surf wave was unmistakable for Winkleman, who'd done some long board surfing with his uncle. His nausea persisted, but it had subsided with the shot of adrenaline coursing through his veins. "Flash!" he yelled, gripping the door handle for stability.

Gilson turned straight south, making a sharp 90 degree turn. This time there were four arcing shells, all passing over them, slamming into the backside of the wave they'd just been on. Gilson gritted his teeth, "Damn, they're good." He maintained course for 20 seconds, trying to guess how long between shots, then turned back west, cutting a wide swath, making a full circle before pointing east again. The move kept the guns from firing as they waited for a more constant heading. He kept it steady only for a few seconds before again juking north east.

Another flash. Two arcing shells slammed into the sea off their starboard bow, and another two flashed over them, slamming into the sea just 40 yards off their port side. "They're bracketing us!" yelled Staub.

Gilson continued his random turns, sometimes reacting to flashes with abrupt turns, sometimes with less-violent course changes, and still other times decreasing speed but maintaining course. Shells continued to rain down all around them, but each second that passed brought them closer and closer to the small chain of islands.

Staub and Ensign Walker tried desperately to keep track of all the course changes, but in the end they had to guess how close they were getting to land. Staub yelled to Tarkington, "Tell the men on deck to watch for the island."

Tarkington brushed past Winkleman, who was doing all he could to keep his feet. He opened the door and stepped into the sea spray. In the darkness, he could barely make out the shapes of men clinging to anything bolted down, trying to keep from being launched into the sea. He yelled, "Watch out for land!" He shook his head. There was no way they could hear him—and even if they could, they were too busy trying to survive. He'd stay put and keep watch as best he could.

Captain Kento was getting frustrated. His men were adjusting and shooting well, but the constantly jinking vessel was impossible to pin down. He was no longer concerned that the vessel was friendly. His two warning shots made them take evasive maneuvers, which meant whomever they were, they didn't want contact.

Despite his frustration with the gunnery, he was excited to be engaged in battle again, even though it was a puny and unworthy adversary. He figured it must be an American PT boat; it was certainly acting like one. The radar man identified it as a friendly Type-14 vessel, but he was obviously mistaken. After the kill, he'd be sure to have the sailor punished for his incompetence and excessive hubris.

There was a danger that the PT boat might attack, but so far it only seemed to want to escape as quickly as possible. It was heading mostly east, no doubt hoping to lose the bigger ship in the archipelago of islands dotting the area. Perhaps it would run aground and his gunners could pick it off at their leisure. He'd already wasted too much ammo.

He hoped it *would* attack. It would make the kill that much more satisfying. They had little to fear from the American Mark 14 torpedos. They were known to be faulty and rarely exploded if they managed to actually hit a target. He didn't fear for the safety of his ship.

His mind was wandering. He refocused, "It's time to kill them. I want ripple fire along all potential turning points."

The swell pitching the boat up and down made for tough shooting too, so he'd slowed down, allowing the PT boat to get farther away but also making the firing platform that much more stable. The range wasn't the issue, but the crazy course changes and pitching deck were.

The sailors were chattering, constantly giving updates on changes in course and speed. The enemy vessel was being driven with skill and cunning, but this time all six of his guns would fire, covering any possible course change.

Captain Kento waited for his XO, Commander Shinji, to give him the nod. Shinji looked sick, his face pale and sweaty, but he was a tiger for action and had come from his quarters when he noticed the abrupt and unscheduled course change. He'd been directing the gunners ever since and although he was obviously feverish and not at his best, he was performing admirably.

Shinji gripped his headphones to his ears, then nodded to his captain, who barked, "Fire at will!" The front two guns flashed in quick succession, each angled slightly differently. The Type-3 gun behind the bridge followed suit soon after, sending six shells arcing a mere two kilometers out to sea.

Kento watched their glowing arcs streak across the dark, star-filled sky and disappear into the blackness. There were no flashes, but in these swells he'd be lucky to see any impacts. Instead, he was looking for the glow of a burning ship, the sign of a direct hit.

The radar man yelled out, "Sir, the contact stopped. They're dead in the water, Captain."

Kento leaned over the sailor's shoulder. Sure enough, the contact was no longer dodging and darting its way east. He raised his binoculars, searching for the glow of fire. There was nothing, but in this wind and spray the boat might've already capsized. As though reading his captain's mind, the sailor noted, "Signal's still strong, sir."

The XO, pulled his binoculars from his bloodshot, feverish eyes and scowled at the enlisted man. "The captain didn't ask for your opinion, Radar man. Keep your mouth shut unless spoken to." The fully-cowed Seaman Hu stood and gave a quick bow, keeping his head lowered. He dared not speak again. Shinji ordered, "Man your post." Hu gratefully took his seat, pressing the earphones over his ears and staring at the surface contact.

Even though they called the flash out and Gilson pivoted, two of the shells from the six-shot salvo landed close enough to send bits of shrapnel into the bow. There was no actual damage, but it was obvious the enemy ship wasn't messing around anymore and was using all her big deck guns.

Gilson cut the throttle down to half while they assessed damage. He was about to go full throttle again, but Staub stopped him, "Hold on there, Gil. Cut power, let her drift. We'll make 'em think they got us."

Lieutenant Gilson immediately complied and the engine purred, the hull mushing into the sea, drifting along with its quickly dissipating forward momentum.

Now that the craft wasn't zipping along at 30 knots, the only sound was the wind, but it wasn't nearly as intense. Gilson kept just enough throttle to steer into the waves, not wanting to get rolled by a breaking sneaker wave. Staub ordered, "Get Yankowski and Hurst up here on the double."

Gilson got on the mic, calling the petty officer from the engine room, and telling him to find Gunner's Mate Hurst.

They both entered the cramped bridge and Lieutenant Commander Staub got right to the point. "You know weapons' systems inside and out. I need you to get those Jap torpedos unlimbered, loaded, and ready to fire. Can you do that?"

Hurst smiled. "Yes, Captain. Before we ran into the Jap ship, me and Manny, er—I mean Machinist Mate Unterman gave 'em the once over. I think we can get 'em armed and loaded, sir."

Staub beamed and slapped his shoulder, "Excellent. Get it done. I wanna put one up that Jap's ass." He turned his attention toward Lieutenant Gilson. "We got anything we can light on fire? Something that'll put off a nice glow?"

Petty Officer Yankowski chimed in, "The Japs left a whole pile of oily rags down there plugging a gasket leak, I think. They'll burn."

Gilson added, "The spare torpedos sit on wooden planks, that'll add to it."

Staub nodded, "Good, good. Let's get it done. We don't have much time."

Captain Kento searched the black horizon. He was about to order another salvo on the now-stationary target. The guns were loaded and zeroed and he was seconds from ordering them to fire when he finally saw what he'd been looking for: the soft glow of fire. "There," he said, unable to contain his excitement. "A glow. The swell must have hidden it before. The PT boat is burning." He let the binoculars dangle from his neck. "Take us closer. I want a look at our mystery ship, Commander Shinji."

"Aye, Captain."

The bow turned and their speed increased, closing the two-kilometer separation quickly. Kento kept scanning the horizon. Occasionally he thought he saw the boat's outline, but he couldn't be sure. The ocean swell lifted and dropped the target, frustrating his efforts to pin it down. He'd be happy to record another kill, but they might not get there before the vessel sank. Without proof, he wouldn't be able to add it to his extensive list of verified kills. It would go down as a probable and might even be recorded as a fishing vessel.

"Increase speed to 25 knots and take us straight to target, Commander."

Concern crossed Commander Shinji's face, but he quickly complied. Running headlong toward an unknown enemy vessel was an excellent way to get sailors killed. If the vessel weren't completely destroyed, it could open fire. Granted the small boat's guns wouldn't be able to do much against the Nokaze, but why take the chance? It was an unnecessary risk and very unlike his normally reserved and careful Captain.

He cleared his throat, "Permission to go to full battle stations, Captain."

Kento glowered at him, then nodded, seeing the wisdom of having all guns manned and ready, just in case his prey wasn't as defenseless as it appeared. "Granted, Commander."

The blaring klaxon sounded, sending the rest of the crew to man all stations. Soon every gun was manned and ready to rain terror on whatever was out there.

A few minutes later, with the glow growing more and more obvious, the radar operator said, "Sir, we should be able to see it off the..."

He was interrupted by the sonar man, "Torpedos inbound!"

Kento felt his stomach lurch as he saw two hazy blips approaching fast. He was speeding straight towards them, which was his best option. If he tried to turn away, he'd give the torpedos his broadside. "Maintain course!" he bellowed. "We'll pass between them. Open fire!"

Hu's face was glued to his radar screen, "Target's moving away fast, Captain."

The pitching deck caused the guns to hesitate, waiting for the bow to come back up. Finally, the front two guns fired, lighting up the night, temporarily blinding Captain Kento, who was desperately searching for the incoming torpedos. He wasn't all that concerned about the American Mark14s; they were an inferior weapon. The magnetic proximity charges could be problematic, but they rarely worked. A glancing blow wouldn't set them off.

The sonar man had his hands pressed against his headphones, focusing on how the torpedo's sounded, alarm growing steadily, "Sir, the torpedos sound odd."

Captain Kento tore his eyes from the sea, annoyed. The sonar man was concentrating, trying to pick out the fast screw noises of the incoming torpedos, but the excessive noise of the sea and the recent explosions kept him from elaborating.

Captain Kento looked at the hazy sonar display. The torpedos were coming fast. The sonar man informed, "One will miss to starboard, the other is straight on!"

Kento had to decide which way to turn. He could steer into the starboard torpedo, there was some wiggle room and they might pass to either side, or he could turn to port and make both miss to starboard. He had a second to decide. "Helm, five degrees port, now!" He couldn't afford a bigger turn, or his stern would swing into the starboard torpedo's path.

He felt the slight turn, hoping it was enough. He strained to see through the gloom of the darkness, but with the choppy swell and the darkness, it was impossible. He focused on the grainy sonar scope. The tiny blips were coming fast. He sucked in his breath, unconsciously gripping the back of the sonar man's metal chair.

The bridge went silent, the only sound the wind. Everyone held their breath. The sonar man broke the silence, "Passing now, it's..."

The Type-2 torpedo sliced through the choppy swell at 40 knots. It passed a few meters off Nokaze's bow. The hull was slicing away, but the destroyer's wide belly kept the distance even. At first it seemed the torpedo might slip past, but the rough sea fell away and the torpedo went airborne, bursting through the face of a wave. Whether it was the wind, the current, or a combination of both—upon reentry—the torpedo's angle changed slightly bringing it into contact with the metal hull of Nokaze just enough for detonation.

The sonar man's voice cut off as the sudden rending explosion lifted the destroyer's hull out of the water, sending everyone on the bridge to the floor. Smoke filled the room, and there were screams of wounded and terrified sailors.

Captain Kento pulled himself off the floor. The room quickly cleared of smoke, the shattered windows allowing the stiff wind to circulate. The only sound was the incessant ringing in his ears. He yelled, his voice sounding far away, "Damage report! Damage report!" but there was no response. He realized the others were still on the ground, pulling themselves up. He grasped Commander Shinji's shirt, pulling him to his feet. Shinji bled from a deep cut above his right eye. Blood dripped into the side of his mouth and he spluttered and choked on it as he got to his feet, swaying badly.

Finally, the crew was back on their feet, taking in damage reports, shaking the cobwebs from their heads. Commander Shinji spit a gob of bloody mucus onto the deck. He listened intently as the damage reports flooded in. It seemed an eternity passed before Shinji finally reported, "Sir, we have a single breach, amidships. All flooded compartments are being sealed. Fires are being fought. Engineering reports no damage to the engines but request reducing speed to better evaluate them."

Kento nodded; his ship was damaged but not in mortal danger. "Slow to five knots. No reason to help the flames. Casualties?"

"Still coming in. So far, six confirmed dead, sir."

"Enemy contact?"

The radar operator pulled himself back into his chair, the scope was cracked, the round screen black. "Radar scope's damaged, Captain! It's dead."

The sonar operator had his headphones back on, but the explosion had burst at least one eardrum. He wasn't sure if the sonar array was damaged or if it was his hearing and addled brain, but all he could hear was ringing. He didn't hear Captain Kento, but felt the smack on the back of his head.

He turned, ripping the headphones off his head and glared. Blood dripped from the ear cups. More dripped down his cheeks, wetting his shirt. He could see Kento's enraged eyes and his mouth moving, but there was no sound. The sonar man pointed to his ears, shaking his head. The pain was breaking through the surge of adrenaline and he suddenly felt sick.

Commander Shinji shook his head, "Unknown, sir."

Kento slammed his fist down, cursing. He desperately wanted to smash whatever had just attacked him, but needed to get his crippled ship in order first.

17

After firing the torpedos, Gilson pushed the throttles to their maximum and swung the bow back east. The lithe boat reacted beautifully, the single screw clawing the sea, pushing the hull to top speed in a matter of seconds. He kept his eyes forward, seeing the men pushing the burning rags and slats of wood into the sea. He searched for the land mass which should be coming up fast.

Half a minute passed before there was a flash from behind. Gilson didn't dare look but Staub yelled, "Shelling our last location."

Gilson asked, "Our torpedos?"

There was no answer. He readied himself for more evasive maneuvers. The enemy ship was close enough now that it could bring all her guns to bear, including smaller caliber stuff. Their only chance of survival would be weaving in and out of the ocean swells and hoping they found the island soon.

There was another flash from behind, this one bigger, and the booming clang swept over them. Staub yelled triumphantly, "Hit! A torpedo hit!" Yells of jubilation filled the bridge. Men on deck raised fists, cheering raucously.

Gilson kept the throttles pegged, but chanced a glance back. He could just make out the distant flickering glow. "Outstanding! Good call, sir."

Staub slapped his back, bringing his attention back front. "Hopefully that'll dissuade him." Staub joined Ensign Walker at the map. The smile on Walker's face was ear to ear. "Where are we, Ensign?" Staub asked.

Walker turned away from the soft glow from the red light, refocusing himself. He put his finger down, "Here, sir. Or there abouts."

Staub nodded his agreement, "Yes." He pursed his lips, trying to gauge how far they were from land. Stroking his chin, he said, "Gil bring us to 060 degrees. We don't want to run into the reefs."

The boat swung to port. The glow from the stricken enemy ship was hardly noticeable now. The winds decreased and with it, the swells. The little T-14 glided along smooth and fast. The men on deck still clung to whatever was bolted down, but without the wild maneuvers and near misses, it was a joy. None of them thought they'd still be alive by now.

Stollman, standing near the pitching bow, pointed and yelled, "Land! I see land!"

Gilson saw it at the same instant and immediately cut power and turned farther to port. The hull mushed into the sea, as he took it from 35 knots to 15. The island formed a jagged black silhouette against the starry skyline. It wasn't a big island and probably wasn't inhabited. There were no lights, but that wasn't surprising and didn't mean much. It didn't matter though; they weren't planning on stopping.

Gilson took a wide berth to the backside of the island. The T-14 wasn't a large boat, and the hull didn't cut deep, particularly while on a plane, but if they grounded or tore out the hull on a reef, they'd be in trouble.

Once in the island's radar shadow, they turned back south and increased speed to 20 knots. The swell was nearly non-existent here; the island acting as a buffer from the open ocean. The only wind came from the engine's 20 knots. The men on deck dried out and released their death grips. Men came from below-decks, some green with sickness. Soon, nearly every foot of the small deck was covered with sprawling men, each telling their own renditions of the encounter with the enemy ship.

Petty Officer Yankowski reported to the bridge, "We've done the fuel calculations. We can make it to Mindanao Island, as long as we don't have any more encounters. We burned through a lot, but the Nips left us with full tanks. Wouldn't push it over 20 knots though."

Ensign Walker took the helm, allowing Staub and Gilson to go over the map together. Staub said, "If we go straight through, we'll get to the northern tip just after daybreak." Gilson nodded, agreeing with the assessment. Staub asked, "Any idea what's happening on Mindanao? I know there's an active resistance cell there. Someone named Fertig, I believe. An American."

Gilson nodded, "Yes, we were briefed about him in passing." He put his finger on the northern tip of Mindanao. "There are port facilities all along here. We're in a Jap boat, but that destroyer or cruiser's gonna put the word out. We don't want to be caught out in daylight."

Staub agreed, nodding his head, "None of these islands will be safe for us. We know Mindanao at least has some friendlies."

The rest of the night passed without incident. One sailor thought he heard the low drone of an aircraft, but he never saw it. They'd eaten what they could find on the boat, mostly rice, fish, and beans. Everyone got their share, but the light meal left them yearning for more. The night's events had drained them and some were asleep, rocking side to side with the boat's motion. The steady drone of the engine lulled them to sleep or, at the very least, put them into a relaxed state.

The eastern horizon glowed softly and the predawn air cooled a degree or two. Off the bow, just poking over the distant horizon, a land mass. Ensign Walker saw it first, pointing, "Land ho, sir."

Staub gave him an amused look, "Land-ho?" he teased. "You need to get some sleep, Ensign." Walker grinned as Staub lifted the binoculars, adjusting the focus, "That's gotta be Mindanao."

Lieutenant Gilson nodded his agreement. "Same plan, sir? Heading toward the southeast?"

Staub replied, "Yes. I think Fertig's group's in that area. At least that's what G2 thinks."

Gilson turned the boat to port, increasing their speed to a steady 30 knots. Sailors and GIs alike scanned the skies for enemy aircraft. Enemy vessels were also of concern, but if aircraft spotted them, enemy boats would undoubtedly follow.

Staub and Gilson had discussed the two options open to them: they could either slow down and hope their small size and slow speed made their radar signature seem like a harmless fishing vessel, or they could push the throttles, identifying themselves as a war vessel, but getting to safety quicker. They concluded that, even if they were slow, the enemy would be on the lookout for *any* vessel not identifying itself.

They kept the radio on using it as an early warning system, but so far it had been quiet, save for a few static-filled bursts, probably from distant, unrelated ships.

Petty Officer Yankowski came to the bridge reporting, "Sir, at this speed we've got an hour's worth of fuel."

Staub nodded his understanding, "Thanks, Yan." He addressed Gilson, "Take us closer to shore, Gil. Let's find somewhere to stow this thing." He glanced at the sun, which was blazing through puffy gray and white clouds. "Once we're closer, we'll slow down a bit too. That'll extend our fuel a little." Gilson changed course, angling toward the looming island. Staub ordered, "Tell the men to man their weapons. Put Hurst up on the twenty." Petty Officer Yankowski saluted and left the bridge.

Staub watched Yankowski relaying the message. The GIs were already holding their weapons, and Staub realized he'd never seen them unarmed. *Probably why they're still alive.* He stuck his head out the shattered window, cupped his hand, and yelled, "Staff Sergeant." Tarkington, who was stretching a few yards forward of the bridge, turned toward him. "A word, please."

Tarkington entered the bridge raising an eyebrow, "You wanted to see me?"

"We're moving closer to the island." Staub nodded, putting his finger on the map, "We're here, heading southeast toward this area here." The map was in Japanese, but towns and ports were obvious enough. "We don't want to get too close to this port, so we'll land in here somewhere. We're almost out of fuel, but unless we encounter something, we'll make it okay." He glanced at Gilson, who gave him a confirming nod. "Once we land, I'd like your men to be our point guard. Push in, set up a perimeter. We'll work on hiding the boat."

Tarkington nodded, "We can do that, sir. No problem." He lifted his chin, "Any idea what we're gonna find?"

Staub shrugged, "I expect more of what you found on the other islands: locals and Japs."

"I mean about this Fertig fellow."

"All I know for sure, he worked for a mining company before the war and was in the Army before that. He's an officer, not sure what rank, and like you, he didn't surrender when everyone else did." He held up a finger, remembering, "And he's from Colorado."

"Fair enough. I'll let my squad know what's happening. We'll be ready."

The land mass, which seemed so small and distant, was now huge and looming. Gilson reduced speed to 20 knots, weaving in and out of reefs and avoiding the occasional partially-submerged logs dotting the area. If they hit one of those, they'd risk bending the single screw, either leaving them slow or worse, dead in the water.

The GIs were near the bow, their weapons ready. The smell of the sea changed slightly as the sickly sweetness of the jungle's rot and decay mixed.

Gilson had the bow angled toward a small, glistening white beach. It was horseshoe shaped, the edges choked with overhanging branches and vines. It would provide perfect concealment from both the air and sea. The fuel situation was critical, so it would have to work.

Gunner's Mate Hurst leaned into the gun atop the bridge, scanning for targets along the beach and thick jungle beyond. Ensign Walker stood beside him, ready to assist if needed with the unfamiliar heavy machine gun.

The boat glided into the little bay and Gilson cut the engines, avoiding grounding. He turned to starboard, heading toward the jungle, the beach still 15 yards ahead.

Tarkington glanced back at the bridge. The jungle would be too thick to penetrate, so he signaled they were going over the side. They'd swim to the

beach. Staub extended his hand out the shattered window, giving him a
thumbs up.

Tarkington looked into the beautifully clear, inviting water and leaped
as far out as he could. The others followed and soon they were wading in;
the water coming to mid-chest. Holding their weapons high, watching the
jungle beyond the shimmering beach, they hurried forward. Tarkington
thought, under different circumstances, this little hidden beach would be
paradise, particularly if he had one of those pretty nurses with him. What
was her name again?

He shook his head, cursing himself for his lapse in concentration. His
head wound throbbed; he'd nearly forgotten about it until now. He forced
himself not to touch the bandage, which now seemed heavy and sagging.
He kept his submachine gun out of the corrosive seawater and waded,
every step bringing him closer to the pristine little beach. *Monica? Was that
her name?* He honestly couldn't remember.

At the water's edge, they stopped and crouched, scanning for threats.
Henry, on the far left, pushed forward, staying low. The others followed suit
until they'd crossed the silky-smooth sand, stopping at the jungle's edge.
Being off the boat felt odd and Tarkington felt himself swaying slightly as
though still on the little gunboat. It was disorienting, and he felt suddenly
nauseated. *Sick on the boat, sick off the boat, dammit,* he thought bitterly.

He ambled his way to the edge of the jungle and crouched, sweeping
his submachine gun. Intense shafts of morning sunlight perforated the
jungle like solid pillars. It was beautifully distracting. Tarkington looked to
Henry who was studying the area, all *six* of his senses working. Finally, he
turned to Tarkington, nodding. It was safe. Tarkington turned to the boat
and waved. The sailors relaxed, continuing to tether the boat and camouflage it as best they could.

The GIs stood, keeping watch. Winkleman stepped beside Tarkington
and nodded back toward the boat, "Thought that thing was out of fuel. We
should just sink it. Japs find it, they'll tear this place apart looking for us."

Tarkington furrowed his brow, irritating his stitches. He winced, "Yeah,
you're probably right. I'll mention it to Staub. Maybe he thinks there's a
harbor nearby to refuel it or something."

Winkleman shrugged, "If there is, we can't just pull up," he raised his voice, doing his best Mickey Mouse impression, "'Hey Tojo, how's about a fill—and check the oil while you're at it.'"

The image cut through Tarkington's mountain of tension. He felt laughter building, threatening to burst. He put his hand over his mouth, tears forming and streaming from his eyes as his shoulders shook. He felt like a schoolboy trying to keep his laughter in check while class was in session. Everything seemed funnier when it happened during an inappropriate time and soon he was shaking, his face red as a beet.

Winkleman looked around sheepishly, "Take it easy, Tark. It wasn't *that* funny," but soon he was stifling his own laugh. None of the others heard Winkleman's impression, but the laughter was infectious and soon they were all grinning. It was good to get off the damned boat and back onto firm ground.

With the boat secured and hidden, the sailors and officers leaped or lowered themselves from the vessel, joining the GIs. Everyone was in high spirits, glad to be off the boat. Since leaving Panay, everyone felt exposed and vulnerable. The feeling worsened after their close encounter with the destroyer. They were still in unknown territory, facing unknown dangers, but at least they were off the open sea.

The sailors had brought everything useful they could carry and piled it at the edge of the jungle. Tarkington looked it over. It was mostly whatever food and water they hadn't already consumed, but there were also ropes, radio batteries, and boxes of ammunition for the big mounted machine gun.

Tarkington asked, "You planning on using the boat again, sir?"

Staub wiped sweat from his brow and shook his head, "Out of fuel. We discussed scuttling it, but decided it might come in handy as a bargaining chip with the locals."

Tarkington nodded but said, "If and when the Japs find it, they'll scour this place looking for us. Doubt that Jap ship went down and if it did, there'll be survivors. They'll be gunning for us, sir."

Staub's face flashed anger, but he quickly got control. "I agree. We'll find this Fertig fellow, see if he wants anything off it first. Perhaps he'll have a better place to conceal it."

Tarkington exchanged a glance with Winkleman, then nodded, "Okay. But if we don't find him in the next day or two, I think it's in our best interest to sink her."

Staub nodded, "I agree, Staff Sergeant." He pointed at the pile of gear, "I'll have my men bury this once your men have taken what you want."

Tarkington shook his head, "We've got what we need, sir."

Gilson, who was listening in, directed men to dig a hole and soon the pile of loot was buried in the soft sand near the tree line.

Gilson took a compass heading and pointed south, "The map says the Port of Ozamiz is that way. If I remember the briefing correctly, it's where Fertig's group is."

The GIs led the way, moving cautiously through the jungle. A steep cliff band forced them west a few kilometers before it petered out. So far, there'd been no sign of people. The small trails here and there were too random to be from anything except animals.

The thin jungle was relatively easy to move through. They made good time and when the cliff band ended, they pivoted south. Through the occasional clearing, the sight of a looming mountain rose from their right. The peak, shrouded in a thick layer of fog, made it look as though it had no end. Lieutenant Gilson thought he remembered it being called Mount Malindang.

They'd gone six or seven kilometers when Henry crouched and held up a fist. Everyone froze, the sailors taking longer to react. After a minute of silence, Tarkington moved until he was beside his lead scout. Henry pointed. A few yards in front of him was a well-used path. The sandaled footprints left little doubt who used it. It cut a path back toward the east, back toward the sea, and probably ended at or near the port.

Staub and Gilson moved up, leaving Ensign Walker with the rest of the sailors. Staub leaned close to Tarkington's ear and was about to speak when Henry gave a quick, low hiss. He pointed to his ear, then east along the trail. Someone was coming. They lowered themselves to the jungle floor. Tarkington took in the full aroma of the soil. A three-inch-long centipede was inches from his nose, but he ignored it, focusing on the path. The cold metal of his submachine gun put his mind at ease.

Three Filipino women appeared, dressed in colorful garb and carrying empty baskets. Tarkington didn't see any weapons. When they were close, Tarkington stepped into the path, one hand holding his weapon, the other waving in greeting.

The women stopped chatting and froze. Fear flashed across their faces, their eyes shifting between the machine gun and his face. Tarkington smiled, trying to allay their fears. Henry was up, moving smoothly behind them, intending to block their escape route. They barely noticed him, their attention firmly on the stranger standing in their way.

"Kumusta," Tarkington greeted them. The lead woman's face changed from abject fear to curiosity.

She shook her head, "No Jap?"

Tarkington nodded, "American," pointing at his chest. The others rose from the jungle floor. He pointed at them, "American soldiers."

Her eyes widened in wonder and the women behind her spoke rapidly in their native tongue. The lead woman asked, "Invasion? Kill Japanese?"

Sergeant Gonzalez stepped forward, forcing a smile. He still hadn't recovered from losing the major. He addressed them in Tagalog, slipping back and forth to Pidgin. The women's faces lit up with gracious smiles and they motioned for the men to follow. Tarkington raised a brow, and Gonzalez said, "They want us to follow them back to Ozamiz. It's another few kilometers. She says it's safe."

18

The three Filipino women led them along the trail, smiling and chatting all the way. Tarkington only picked up some of it, Gonzalez a little more. They led them quickly, seemingly without fear of Japanese patrols. It made Tarkington nervous to be moving so fast, but when Gonzalez asked about it, the women waved their hands submissively, as though there were nothing to worry about. Tarkington glanced at Henry, who shrugged, following along but still concentrating on their surroundings.

They smelled the town before they saw it. The savory aromas of cooking permeated the air, making their stomachs grumble. It had been quite a while since they'd eaten and the savory smells made them forget that they were on an occupied island, hundreds of miles behind the lines.

They broke out into broad daylight, the sparkling town beautifully idyllic. The houses were clean and well-maintained. Even the streets sparkled. Very unusual for the Philippines, which suffered from inadequate sewage. Normally, Philippine towns and cities reeked, but this town would put US cities and towns to shame.

Even more surprising, the townsfolk moved around as though the war was a million miles away, or had never happened at all. Their guides waved and greeted everyone they met, happy to gloat over the newcomers.

Henry lifted his chin toward a group of uniformed Filipino men. Tarkington tensed, wondering if perhaps they were Makapili, or Jap sympathizers. Perhaps the entire town was. That would explain a lot. But instead of reacting to the newcomers with alarm, the uniformed Filipinos smiled and waved greetings. One man spoke to another, sending him running the opposite direction.

As they neared, Tarkington realized they were wearing the uniforms of the Philippine Army, the same ones he'd seen countless times before and during the early part of the war. Surely the Japanese would shoot them on sight. But they looked as unafraid as any troops he'd ever encountered.

The three women exchanged happy greetings and explained the events of their meeting. The seven Philippine Army soldiers never once made a move to take their rifles off their shoulders. Instead, they nodded and smiled until the women finished, then the man in charge, an officer with the rank of a first lieutenant, stepped around them and saluted.

Staub, Gilson, and Walker still wore their faded and tattered uniforms and the Filipino must have recognized them as officers, for he directed his salute at them. The naval officers saluted back and the Filipino lieutenant said in near-perfect English, "Welcome to Ozamiz. My name is First Lieutenant Juan Enriguez."

Tarkington felt as though he'd slipped back into a time before December 8th, 1941. It was momentarily disorienting. The other GIs looked just as baffled, exchanging glances with one another, not quite believing what their senses were telling them.

Lieutenant Commander Staub said, "Thank you, Lieutenant. I'm Lieutenant Commander Staub, this is Lieutenant Gilson. Are you in charge here?"

Lieutenant Enriguez shook his head, "No, sir. Captain Guttierez is my company commander and Colonel Fertig is in overall command." Stunned silence.

Finally, Tarkington asked, "Did you say Colonel Fertig?"

Before the beaming lieutenant could answer, a tall Anglo man stepped around the edge of a house, loping their way. He had a sheepish grin and a bright red, well-trimmed, goatee. "At your service," he said. He wasn't in uniform; instead, he wore loose fitting comfortable clothes. Instead of a US Army officer, Tarkington thought he looked more like a businessman on vacation. He looked to be very much still in the role of mining official, despite the war. Adding to this, instead of saluting, he extended a hand to every one of them, welcoming them to his town warmly.

It stunned everyone; it was as though the past eight months never happened. Fertig chuckled and explained, "You must be used to different circumstances." He extended his arms, taking in the scene, "The Japanese don't have a large presence here. Our little slice of Mindanao isn't worth their time. Frankly, I think they're spreading themselves too thin." He shrugged, "But we'll see about that." His smile put everyone at ease, and Tarkington knew he was in the presence of a natural leader. He instantly liked him. Fertig lifted his chin, "We'll get into how you came about stealing a Japanese gunboat...but first, you're just in time for lunch."

Soon they were sitting around a large table in a surprisingly cool building eating an array of local food. Tarkington devoured everything, not realizing just how hungry he was. The savory taste of various meats, roots, and spices over rice surpassed the smells they'd first encountered.

Once they'd filled the voids in their bellies, they asked questions. Lieutenant Commander Staub, seated beside the gangly colonel asked, "How d'you know about the boat?"

Fertig grinned and stroked his goatee a few times, "You were spotted and reported as you came around the corner and into Panguil Bay. We have units up and down the coast keeping tabs on Japanese shipping. As you neared, it was obvious to the spotters you weren't Japanese." He shrugged, "White men on a Jap boat, I just assumed you must've stolen it." Staub scooped a mouthful of rice. Fertig asked, "Well, aren't you going to tell me about it?"

Staub pointed at Tarkington and talked around the rice, "It was his operation."

Fertig turned his way, "Ah, Staff Sergeant Tarkington, is it?"

Staub swallowed the rice and added, "In fact, he and his men are the whole reason we're out here in the first place."

Fertig's interest piqued. Tarkington moved his plate away while clearing his throat. For the next half hour, he told Fertig about the past few months, glossing over large portions which Fertig figured out on his own. When he finished, Fertig leaned back shaking his head, "That's quite a tale, Staff Sergeant. I'm assuming your men call themselves Tark's Ticks?"

Tarkington hadn't mentioned the name, and he exchanged a look with Sergeant Winkleman, who shrugged. He hadn't told him either. Fertig explained, "I'm in contact with allied units as far away as New Guinea. Mostly done through relay stations and whatnot. They asked if I'd had any contact or word about you and your men. They mentioned you sometimes called yourselves Tark's Ticks." He smiled, nodding his head, "Of course I hadn't then, but if I'm not mistaken, that's who I'm having lunch with now."

Staub's face lit up, "You're in radio contact? That's marvelous news. We can call for extraction."

Fertig nodded, "Yes, I'm sure command will be happy to know you're all alive. They were quite worried they hadn't heard from you. They thought you were dead or captured." His grin faded, "I am sorry to hear about your boat and the men you've lost." He looked at Tarkington, "Both of you, I expect."

Staub nodded, pursing his lips. His enthusiasm returned though, and he slapped his hands on his knees, "Hot damn! When can we make the call, Colonel?"

"I'll call as soon as we're done here, but I don't think you'll be leaving for at least a month. We were just resupplied two days ago. The next scheduled resupply is in 30 days. They're bringing us more heavy weapons— mortars and machine guns—if I'm not mistaken."

Tarkington asked, "How is it you can just walk the streets like you do? I mean, on Luzon and even Panay, there's constant enemy traffic. Seems like the war's far away from here."

Everyone went quiet, eager to hear his answer. Fertig nodded, "Yes, you're quite right. We are in an unusual situation here. Most of the Japanese are stationed on the main part of the island, across the peninsula from us, across Panguil Bay. There's a Jap outpost here," he pointed south, "about six kilometers that way. It's a heavily-fortified compound: fencing all the way around, guard towers, manned machine guns—the whole deal. But they don't venture out far. They patrol their immediate area, but we know their schedules and leave them alone. Likewise, they leave us alone."

Tarkington scowled, "So they know you're here? They know about *you*?"

"The local commander does, yes. He's a reasonable man, in fact."

Everyone's mouths dropped open, silence filling the room. The feeling of complacency and comfort shattered in an instant, replaced with fear and distrust.

Tarkington's voice deepened, "You're in contact with the enemy?" He got to his feet, touching the sling to his submachine gun, but keeping it on his shoulder. "You're a *collaborator*?" he asked, the last word dripping off his tongue in disgust. The other GIs were on their feet as well.

Fertig shook his head, holding his hands out for calm. "No! It's nothing like that, Staff Sergeant. I assure you, no one here is a collaborator. The Japanese commander leads two platoons of rather green, inexperienced troops. One evening a few of them got drunk on rice wine and attempted to rape some local women. Juan interrupted them." He pointed to the diminutive Filipino immediately to his right. He hadn't spoken a word, but his eyes held a keen look of intelligence that Tarkington hadn't missed.

Fertig continued, "Through *unimaginable* force of will, Juan and some of our soldiers didn't kill them outright, but delivered them to me instead." He broke his gaze with Juan. "I'd heard that Lieutenant Shigawa— the camp's senior officer—was an honorable man, at least as honorable as a Japanese officer can be during these times." He shrugged, "So, I took a chance. Along with Juan and Captain Gutteirez," he indicated the Filipino officer to the right of Juan, "we tied the offenders up and hauled them to the front gate, demanding a meeting." He laughed, remembering the meeting, "To make a long story short, Shigawa didn't know whether to shit or go blind." There was a smattering of laughs from the audience, "I demanded the men punished. He could've arrested me or killed us where we stood, but he knew it would lead to retaliation. I told him I was an Italian, living in town as the de facto mayor." His smile broadened, "I don't think he believed me, but he didn't want to disturb the peace and possibly have his entire camp overrun, so he did our bidding. The men were punished publicly, and we all went on with our lives. Neither he nor his men have shown their faces here since." He slapped his knee, laughing, "By God, you shoulda seen his face. Anyway, it's allowed us to live free from their control. As a result, we've been able to stockpile quite a few weapons and ammunition, and recruit widely."

The GIs and sailors were mesmerized with the tale. Lieutenant Gilson asked, "Aren't you worried they'll eventually come calling? I mean, perhaps another unit from across the bay? This can't last forever."

Fertig nodded his agreement, "You're absolutely correct, Lieutenant. We're ready. When it happens, we have our defensive plan laid out. Of course, it depends on how and where they come, but like I said, we're ready. And no matter where the threat emerges, we'll know long before they arrive. We have an extensive network of informants scattered all over." His eyes hardened, "They won't be able to sweep us aside easily."

PFC Stollman piped up, "And what if it's your buddy Lieutenant from the camp? What then?"

Staub tensed and was about to reprimand the insolent private but held his tongue when Colonel Fertig smiled, holding up a hand. "It's a valid question." His eyes drilled into Stollman who held his gaze, "The short answer is: he's my enemy and I won't hesitate to kill him and all his men at the first hint of aggression. The long answer? I've been able to get information on the man's history. He got his rank bumped down to lieutenant after he refused to kill civilians they had ordered him to kill. They banished him here." Fertig shook his head, "But that's only half the story, he'd already killed hundreds and only stopped when his conscience finally caught up. I'll have no problem killing the man, son."

Satisfied, Stollman gave him an evil grin, "I'll do it for you if I'm around, sir."

Vick shook his head, murmuring, "For chrissakes, Stolly. Shut the hell up."

Tarkington shook his head, "Italian, huh?" Fertig nodded, his red hair plastered to the side, accented with the nearly-orange goatee and his ruddy, light complexion. Tarkington laughed out loud, "I think you're right about that Jap officer not believing you." Everyone laughed and guffawed—some Filipinos, having no clue why, laughed anyway, cutting any remaining tension.

Fertig stood and bellowed, "Another advantage to this place?" He waved toward another building and women and children carrying skins full of liquid stepped into the circle filling cups. "We make our own alcohol!"

A cheer went up as sailors and GIs clambered over one another to get a taste.

Captain Kento and the crew of the Imperial Japanese Navy vessel Nokaze were limping their way back to Iloilo Port on the southeastern shore of Panay. It was the nearest port capable of patching them up well enough to make the journey to Manila Bay's dry-docking facilities at Cavite.

The final count from the unprecedented torpedo attack, was 10 dead, 19 wounded, two missing and presumed dead.

The torpedo had ripped through the hull above the waterline, which was the only reason they hadn't sunk—the only explanation for the high impact attributed to the heavy seas at the time of the attack. They surmised the torpedo had launched high from the front-face of a wave and impacted the Nokaze's hull while it was low in a trough. Once the seas calmed, the shredded, blackened steel was high and dry, giving it the appearance of a missile strike rather than a torpedo. The high explosive ignited fires, causing more damage and killing and maiming more sailors. Fire swept through two gunnery stations, rendering them inoperable.

The mystery boat got away clean. Captain Kento ran the scenario through his head over and over, trying to piece together how it had happened. He knew he'd acted brashly by running headlong at the target instead of killing it at range, but he'd desperately wanted to know more about the vessel and its crew.

He took full responsibility for his actions and would report his failure to command. He'd had a glorious career up to this point, but he had little doubt that run was ending. He assumed he'd either get demoted to some backwater or imprisoned outright. Either way, the punishment wouldn't come close to his own internal shame.

As they steamed north, toward Panay and Iloilo Port, Captain Kento monitored the airwaves religiously, having all messages playing through the overhead mics on the bridge. He hoped to glean something about the mystery boat, something giving him a clue as to its whereabouts so he could exact his revenge while he was still in command.

It came the day after the attack, when the Nokaze was only 100 nautical miles from the port. Iloilo, which was home to a contingent of T-14 and T-25 motor torpedo boats, was desperately trying to locate one of its own—a T-14 MTB. They hadn't heard from them in days. When they hadn't reported in the first day, they chalked it up to radio trouble, but standard procedure in such an instance was for the boat to return to base for repair. Or, barring that, having a new radio flown out to them. So far, this boat hadn't returned, and air patrols were unable to find it either.

Kento knew the MTB commanders had reputations of being cavalier, often diverting from their filed routes to investigate whatever piqued their interest, but they never strayed from the operational area altogether. The Aichi float planes had thoroughly searched the AO and came up empty, making the minders in Iloilo believe they must have been attacked and sunk. Captain Kento had a different belief.

Until he'd heard this report, he believed he'd been attacked by a rogue American PT boat, who'd scored a lucky and rare hit with a Mark 14 torpedo. But now he realized they'd hijacked an entire Japanese boat and fired the far superior Type-2 torpedo. This would also explain the radar man's conviction that they'd been attacking a friendly. He briefly thought about the sailor. He was currently in the stockade. Kento put it out of his mind. The sailor needed to learn discipline and humility.

Kento wondered if he should relay his suspicions. It might help his comrades find the missing boat, but he decided against it. He was sure this is what happened, but thought they might perceive it as him trying to lessen his punishment. He *wanted* punishment—deserved it. The harsher the better. But he also yearned for revenge, and he'd never get that sitting idly in a stockade or counting ration boxes on some forsaken backwater island.

An hour later, with Panay Island visible on the horizon, the radio message he'd been waiting for came over the airwaves. One of the float planes spotted a T-14 motor torpedo boat all the way down toward Mindanao. There were no patrols that far south; indeed, Iloilo held the only T-14 Squadron in all the Philippines. Mindanao was at the very outer limits of the small boat's fuel range too, with no refueling stations along the way. This had to be the boat that attacked him.

Kento's XO, Commander Shinji, surmised the same conclusion as his captain. He asked, "What are your orders, Captain?"

Kento was due back in Iloilo today; he had superior officers waiting to debrief him about the encounter. Indeed, they wanted him brought earlier by seaplane, but he convinced them he needed to stay with his damaged ship. He slammed his fist onto the map table, making everyone on the bridge flinch and look up. They quickly averted their eyes, concentrating on their non-existent work.

Kento seethed, "I have orders to report to Iloilo. It is my duty to comply." He chewed his lower lip, something he did when concentrating hard, "I will have to convince them to allow me my revenge. They owe me that, at least."

19

Tarkington hadn't been this stress free and comfortable since before the Japanese invasion of the Philippines. Ozamiz felt like living in a quaint little tropical paradise. The food was plentiful. The locals never stopped impressing him with their endless variations of the same ingredients.

Everyone was friendly, even the women, who looked upon the taller Americans with unashamed lust, particularly after a night of drinking, which happened at least three times a week and would've been more but for the scarcity of product. It took time to produce the quantity of alcohol needed to sate the sailors' and GI's appetites. With every passing week, it seemed to take more and more as the men gained weight and built their tolerances back up to pre-war levels.

No one was at all surprised when Raker forgot all about the Filipino gal he'd slept with on Panay at the first hint of more action here. He wasn't alone. Many of the GIs and sailors woke up in unfamiliar houses, nursing headaches and enfolding warm female bodies. Tarkington wasn't immune either. He'd taken to one of the local beauties, and although they could barely converse, they had no problem communicating.

Tarkington didn't allow himself to get too complacent, however. After the first week, he conferred with Lieutenant Commander Staub and Lieutenant Gilson and together they instituted a mandatory daily exercise program. In the morning, but not too early, Sergeant Gonzalez led calisthenics. Gonzalez embraced the idea with gusto, hoping it might assuage the pain of Major Hanscom's death. It didn't, but he kept the men in decent shape.

Tarkington also insisted on the occasional patrol. Not only did it allow them to keep their edge in the jungle, it also provided them a familiarity with their surroundings. Essential and invaluable if and when the Japanese decided they wanted to kick the hornet's nest.

They ventured near the Japanese compound occasionally, promising Fertig that they'd be careful. Lieutenant Shigawa would have little choice to act if he knew there were American fugitives living in Ozamiz. They were careful; the added danger of seeing the enemy up close, kept them sharp and their heads in the game. Living this lifestyle could get them killed if they allowed themselves to relax too much.

Fertig was in contact with allied command at least once a week. It relieved them to know the fates of The Eel crew and were ecstatic to hear that all Tark's Ticks were off Luzon and with Fertig. They'd be taking them off Mindanao—along with the sailors—during the next delivery. Tarkington and the others would have been happy to spend the rest of the war in place, but orders were orders—and frankly, Tarkington wanted to know why they thought they were so damned important. He was wondering what was in store for them.

The days and weeks felt like a vacation, one which might never end. By the third week, the Americans were fully rested, well fed, and happy. Tarkington felt the old nagging in the back of his head. He needed to be doing more. He needed to be actively helping to bring the war to an end. He needed to be killing Japanese.

His brother was on his mind more and more. The Army promised they'd notify his parents when they found out he was alive, but how would his brother Robert take that? Was he already in the service? He'd been in college when this whole shindig kicked off, but did he stay in or join up, thinking his brother dead or captured?

He had to get word to him, tell him to stay in school. Robert was a tough son-of-a-bitch when he wanted to be, and Tarkington knew he'd make an excellent officer, but he had an aloofness to him. A softness which he'd have to shed fast if he hoped to survive in combat. For the thousandth time, he prayed that Robert was safely stateside.

With the expected resupply and evacuation only a week away, disturbing news arrived from a contact from the more northerly island of Cebu. There weren't specifics, but the mention of the town of Ozamiz automatically brought it to Fertig's attention.

Fertig hadn't lived as long as he had behind enemy lines without being careful, so he sent runners across the bay, asking his second, Colonel Rodrigo, if he'd heard any rumblings. To Fertig's dismay, the answer was quick in coming. Something was brewing.

Rodrigo explained he'd been finalizing a report when Fertig's men showed up. Fertig doubted that was true; Rodrigo was a self-serving son-of-a-bitch and would first see if there were an advantage to withholding the information. But, with his hand forced, he'd traveled back with the runners, delivering what he knew in person.

Rodrigo took great interest in the American presence. He'd heard about their journey, but hadn't actually met them until now. Tarkington was immediately on edge, sensing the young man's self-centered personality. Rodrigo reminded him a lot of another Filipino back on Luzon who'd betrayed him and his fellow Filipinos for the sake of power. Things hadn't ended well for him or his followers. Rodrigo's demeanor was eerily similar.

Once Rodrigo met with Fertig and his closest confidants, he left, surrounded by Filipinos that could best be described as body guards. Tarkington and Henry watched him strut down main street as though he were a visiting dignitary. Henry shook his head and spat a long stream, "Damned peacock with a corncob shoved up his ass."

Tarkington nodded, "I don't trust him and I hardly know him." Once Rodrigo and his entourage were out of sight, Tarkington turned toward the central building where the meeting took place. "Let's go see what's up."

They'd only gone a few yards when Fertig, Juan, and Guttierez emerged. Instead of Fertig's normally happy-go-lucky face, he looked deeply concerned. He saw Tarkington and Henry approaching and before they could ask him anything, Fertig said, "Find Staub, Gilson, and Walker. I'll fill everyone in at the same time."

Henry trotted off, leaving Tarkington with the three resistance leaders. Tarkington pointed the way Rodrigo'd gone, "I'm a pretty good judge of character and that Rodrigo rubs me the wrong way."

Fertig stopped stroking his chin, nodding his agreement, "Your instincts are good, Staff Sergeant. He's a necessary evil though. He was a rival, but now he's with us." He grinned, "Where I can keep an eye on him. Believe me, when the time comes, *Colonel* Rodrigo will turn against us, but only when it serves him. I won't worry about him until the Allies are close. When the Nips are beat, or nearly so, that's when Rodrigo will make his move and not before."

"You're an optimist. The Nips are kicking our butts, far as I can tell."

"They're overextended. Their supply lines stretch thousands of miles. No army or navy, for that matter, can keep that up. They were hoping for a knockout punch, hoping we'd sue for peace." He shook his head, a sly grin showing through his goatee, "But that hasn't happened. Yeah, we're on the ropes, but it was a lucky punch. The tides'll turn against them, and soon."

From around the corner came the naval officers, led by Henry. Behind them, Winkleman and Gonzalez followed. Fertig waved them over, then led them back inside the central building and into a sizeable room they used for meetings. Spread out on a large teak table was a map of Mindanao Island. Overhead, a tired-looking fan spun lazily, shifting the stale air around.

Fertig got right to the point, "The rumors are true. The Nips are planning an operation. I don't know what's changed for them, but something's put them off and troops are being mobilized across the bay, here." He placed a long finger on a spot on the map across the bay and slightly north. "They're staging from this area near Iligan City. Observers have reported ships offloading troops via landing crafts. As you can see, it's a quick boat ride across the channel and they'll be on us. There's no reason for them to be bolstering their troops on the main island. There've been no incidents, and the Allies are still far to the south. The only thorn in their side is us." He let that sink in.

Staub took advantage of the pause, "It may be something altogether different, perhaps they needed a place to practice and train for some upcoming landing."

Fertig shook his head, the small tassels on his wicker hat slapping one another, sounding like tiny sea shells clinking. "Our people are telling us the Nips aren't acting like it's a training exercise. Many of them are marines, hardened veterans. Regardless, we'll be activating our defensive maneuvers in anticipation. If nothing comes of it, we can put it down as a good exercise."

Gilson lifted his chin, "If you're dealing with marines, you should consider leaving the area. No offense, but they'll mop the floor with you. They'll come with plenty of support, mortars, heavy machine guns, maybe even tanks."

Fertig stroked his goatee, nodding, "It would be the wise thing to do, fade away and fight another day, but my men are proud and we've been preparing for this day. We have some surprises of our own."

Tarkington shook his head, "If you stand and fight, the town'll be destroyed along with everyone in it. Women, children, and old men. The Japs'll kill 'em all."

Fertig nodded, "The town will be empty; it's part of the plan. Those not fighting will fade away; we've built bunkers and shelters in the mountains. Everyone knows the plan and is in agreement. We can rebuild the town."

Staub asked, "And what about our evacuation? We should contact command and tell them to push up the schedule..." the room went silent and Staub added slightly embarrassed, "You'll need the supplies to help with the fight."

Fertig nodded slowly, "This isn't your fight. We've been planning this for months; there's no reason for any of you to risk your lives here. You've already gone beyond the call of duty just getting here." He placed both hands on the sturdy table, looking each man in the eye, "We'll be fine." Tarkington shook his head and was about to interject, but Fertig looked away, "Now, if you'll excuse me, we have a lot to do."

Fertig went off with his men, leaving the sergeants and naval officers still looking over the map. Tarkington shook his head, "We can't just leave them, sir."

Staub closed his eyes, taking a long breath and blowing it out slow. He finally answered, "My mission is to get you men back to our lines. I'll be damned, when I'm this close," he held two fingers so they were almost touching, "to achieving that mission, that I'll throw it all away." The others stared at him until he continued, "Fertig's been ready for this long before we arrived. He knows what he's doing. He said so himself; he doesn't need us."

Tarkington and the rest of the GIs felt torn with Staub's decision not to help Fertig in his hour of need. As promised, Fertig contacted command asking them to hurry the resupply and evacuation if at all possible. The two-submarine convoy was already en route, but command said they'd relay the new situation when they checked in next. They also advised Fertig to do what he had to do to remain a viable source of intelligence. They didn't want to lose him or the steady stream of information he provided. They didn't go so far as to order him to retreat, but they implied it.

Tarkington had already seen the defenses Fertig had set up in case of an incursion, but most of the concealed positions assumed the attack would come from across the spit of land connecting this section of Mindanao and not from an amphibious landing from across the bay. So, in order to give the Japanese marines as hard a time as possible, Fertig and everyone able to wield a shovel was busy digging new hidey-holes and trenches. Dug-in mortars were relocated back and recalibrated for direct fire onto the beach in front of Ozamiz City. It was the most likely landing point, providing an inviting, gradually-sloped beach with few obstacles...at least no visible ones.

The Japanese T-14 MTB didn't run as well on the lower grade fuel stockpiled at Ozamiz Port, but despite the excessive smoke and rough-sounding engine, it worked well enough. At night, the Filipinos used the port facility cranes to load large boulders onto the stern of the compact boat. They dropped them into shallow water, creating obstructions.

Hopefully, a few of the Japanese landing craft would hang up on them, allowing mortars to rain shells upon them. Machine gun pits were constructed along key choke points, designed to funnel the Japanese into gullies which were laced with all sorts of nasty surprises.

After a full day of back-breaking work, the sailors and GIs sat along the beachfront, sitting on porches drinking water by the gallon and eating a huge boar one of the local men had killed.

Tarkington wiped his greasy chin with the back of his grimy hand and said, "You've got a good thing going here, Colonel. Those marines are in for a surprise."

Fertig swallowed the succulent piece of meat he was chewing and said, "Thank you, Staff Sergeant. Course, it's never been our intention to hold the town. Ideally, we want to hit 'em hard and fade into the jungle before they're able to hit back."

Tarkington nodded his approval, "True hit-and-run guerrilla tactics are near impossible to defend against. The key is to break off before you get too engaged."

Fertig nodded, "That's the plan." He took another long swig of water, "By the way..." he looked to where Staub was sitting. He'd been working just as hard as everyone else. Tarkington thought he was probably trying to make up for insisting they leave before things got hot. "...heard from command. They passed along the update, but it's unlikely they'll be able to get here much earlier. It seems the Japanese Navy has tightened things up out there beyond the Sulu Sea. You may be here for the fireworks after all."

Staub shook his head, then nodded and wiped his brow. "Well, if that's how things go, we'll do whatever we can to help." He leveled his gaze at Fertig, "But getting these men out of here is my priority. My mission hasn't changed."

Fertig nodded, "Indeed it hasn't. Command reiterated it, in fact." He grinned at Tarkington and the other GIs, "You men are certainly being given the service."

Tarkington lowered his gaze, feeling embarrassed with all the attention. "Any idea why?" he asked.

Fertig shook his head, "They don't tell me these things, but someone high up's involved."

Tarkington mumbled, "Doesn't make any sense." He shifted, stretching his back. "Any word on the Jap Marines?"

Fertig answered, "Only that they're still there and they're on alert status, which I guess means they could go at anytime."

Staub asked, "What about the Jap garrison? What're they doing? It must involve them."

Fertig stroked his goatee, "I have men watching their camp and yes, you're right. There's definitely been more activity there. In fact, Lieutenant Shigawa sent a patrol farther out than he ever has before. My men tailed them. They observed the port facilities for an hour, then left." There was silence as they thought about that new development. "I've sent more men to watch them, enough to ambush them if they make a move."

Lieutenant Gilson, who'd been quiet up to this point, stated, "I'd guess they'd try to coordinate with the Marines, trap us in a pincer move."

Fertig agreed, "Yes, if they move, I think we can expect the Marines are on their way. My contacts in Iligan City will alert us long before that, however."

Staub added, "Too bad the subs won't be here before the attack, could've used their supplies."

Fertig answered, "We'll need them even more after all this is over. We'll likely shoot through most of our ammo."

The sun set, turning the day to night as though by a light switch. The tired men sat around, allowing their food to settle before getting back to work. Nighttime was the perfect time for digging trenches, setting booby traps, and sinking obstacles without being observed. During the day, there'd been a few passing fishing vessels that weren't familiar, whose occupants seemed to take an inordinate amount of interest in the insignificant port town. The added scrutiny only added to Fertig's and everyone else's belief that Ozamiz beach was the target landing area.

20

Two more days passed without incident, bringing the expected resupply and evacuation date to within two days. The hard prep work—done mostly at night—was complete. Now all they needed were enemy soldiers.

Tarkington's squad, along with the sailors, had taken the time to familiarize themselves again with the entry point to the trail which would lead them to the pickup point. They'd walked the ten-kilometer trail before and seen the little cove to the southwest where the resupply happened every month.

It would have been more convenient for the townsfolk if the subs came directly into Ozamiz Port, but that would involve another day to sail around the cape and enter Panguil Bay, which was shallow and often patrolled by air. Even a submerged submarine would be easy to spot in the clear water and could not maneuver well enough to get away from an aerial attack. In short, it would be suicide. The well-used, but well-hidden trail would be their escape route when the time came.

Just after dinner, word came from a breathless runner; the Japanese were mobilizing. Fertig looked at his watch, "Well, I suppose this is it," he said, somewhat breathless himself. "I suspect they'll be landing right at dawn."

Everyone sat up straighter. The long wait was finally coming to an end.

The familiar flush of nausea passed quickly through Tarkington, as he exchanged a worried glance with Henry.

Part of him wished they'd miss the attack. The last few days, as the subs got closer and closer and the Japanese Marines lingered, he'd entertained the idea that perhaps they'd get off this rock and head home before the invasion force arrived.

Despite the idyllic setting and the incredible hospitality of the last few weeks, Tarkington yearned to be somewhere completely away from the war, if even for a day. He knew no where was truly safe, but some places were safer than others. The journey on the sub would be fraught with danger too. Perhaps it would be better to die here and not put himself through the agony of another submarine cruise. Could he put himself back into a submarine? Perhaps he wouldn't even get the chance.

Japanese Marines, like their counterparts—the US Marines—were fierce, from everything he'd heard. Perhaps they'd sweep through Fertig's men like sweeping away dust. Then what? Fight to the death, or flee to the pickup point? He closed his eyes and blew out a long breath. Only time would tell. The one thing he was sure of: nothing ever went as planned once the lead started flying.

The rest of the night passed slowly. Tarkington surprised himself by falling asleep. He awoke with a start after a solid few hours. His back was propped against the back wall of a foxhole. Beside him, barely visible, sat Winkleman and Raker. Raker's arm was healing well, or as well as could be hoped for. It still hurt and he couldn't extend it all the way, making shooting his weapon difficult. Normally, he'd be on the fringes near Henry, identifying and sniping likely officers and NCOs, but with his arm only halfway functional, he was along the main line. He had his rifle, a captured Type-38 Arisaka, propped on the edge of the foxhole.

Tarkington cleared his throat, "Anything happening?" he asked.

Winkleman startled, "Nothing yet, Tark."

"How long was I out?"

"Couple hours. Go back to sleep if you want. I'm too wound up."

Raker added, "Me too. We'll wake you when it's time."

Tarkington adjusted his position. The incessant sounds of insects and distant screeches and yowls of night animals mixed with the soft lapping of water against the sand. The night air was warm and muggy. Tarkington gazed up at the stars, bright and thick. "Wonder what's happening back home?"

Winkleman chuckled, "What time would it be? Daytime?"

Raker nodded, "Yeah, it's three AM here, so around noon on the west coast—but yesterday."

Winkleman shook his head, "Weird to think about. Seems like another life time." He adjusted his position, "Noon in northern California, assuming there're no Japs..." he chuckled, "June, right?"

"July eighth, dumbass," Raker said, shaking his head.

"We missed the fourth? Damn, how'd that happen?"

Raker teased, "You missed the fireworks? Too bad, quite a show." He slapped Winkleman's shoulder, "Don't worry, you'll get a show in a couple hours that'll make up for it."

Winkleman chuckled, "It can get pretty foggy on the coast in summer. The best time's spring." He looked up at the stars, "I suppose everyone's probably inland a mile or two. We used to have picnics in the redwoods, get out of the dreary fog and swim in the rivers. They're clear and warm by now. So many crawdads," he shook his head, "Takes no time to fill a pot. My Uncle Wyatt has this recipe—well, I can't even describe how good they taste, fresh like that."

Raker asked, "What the hell's a crawdad?"

Tarkington answered, "Like a mini-lobster. You eat the tail section."

Raker grinned, "I do like eating tail on occasion," he leered.

"For crying out loud, Private, thought you never kiss and tell," complained Winkleman. "What about you? What would you be doing if you were back home, Rake?"

"Fishing most likely. Trout fishing on the lakes this time of year's good. Big browns and rainbows. Creeks are good too, fly-fishing mostly. You talk about good—fresh trout cooked in butter...?" He shook his head, "nothing better." There was a long pause as they all thought of home. Raker finally added, "Except tail." They all laughed quietly in their hole.

Someone appeared alongside the edge of their hole, giving them all a start. Lieutenant Gilson whispered, "Japs are on the move. We've got reports from Iligan City, the Marines have launched. There's also been movement from the Jap compound. We can expect a two-pronged attack right at dawn."

Tarkington stood, stretching the kinks from his back and neck. "I'm gonna check on the others." He slung his submachine gun, and Gilson gave him a hand up. "How're your men doing?" Tarkington asked.

Gilson shrugged, "Good as can be expected. This isn't their kind of fight; they'd rather be ten fathoms down shooting torpedos, not dug into foxholes waiting for the hammer to come down."

"Need anything from me, Gil?" They'd become friends over the last month, each having respect for the other's natural ability to lead men. Tarkington still called Staub, "Lieutenant Commander Staub," however.

Gilson shook his head, "Nah, think we're as good as we're gonna be at this point. I'm heading to the boat now."

Tarkington nodded, "I'll walk with you."

As they turned toward the docks, Winkleman and Raker wished him luck. Gilson turned back, "Thanks. You too. Keep your heads down."

They strode along the edge of the beach toward the pier and the captured Japanese T-14. They watched sailors hustling around making final preparations to launch.

Lieutenant Commander Staub stood on the dock watching his men work. Seeing his XO, he said, "There you are. Better hurry, Gil, don't want the Japs to hear you. That damned engine makes a lot of racket."

"Aye, Skipper," he responded, saluting.

Staub returned it, bracing smartly, then extended his hand. They shook and Staub said, "Be careful out there, Lieutenant. You've got a skeleton crew, hit 'em hard and get outta there, and remember if anything seems off, abort and get yourself back to shore. No heroics."

Gilson released his hand, "Yes, sir. Don't worry, we'll be okay."

"Wish I were going with you."

Gilson waved it off, "You're needed here, sir." He nodded to Tarkington, then stepped onto the boat. The sailor at the bow pushed off and as the boat drifted away, Gilson said in a half-whisper, "See you at the rally point."

The harsh sound of the engine starting made his whispering seem comical. Smoke billowed across the pier, nearly choking the onlookers. The throttles engaged and the boat turned and disappeared into the gloom, leaving a trail of acrid smoke.

Staub shook his head, "I hope this works." Tarkington said nothing. It either would or it wouldn't.

The glow from the east, normally the hopeful beginning to a new day, brought dread and the unmistakable droning of engines pushing landing crafts their way. Tarkington hunched low, just his eyes above the lip of the hole he shared with Winkleman and Raker. He had his submachine gun in hand. Spare magazines arranged neatly side by side upon a shelf he'd cut out with his K-bar knife.

In the gloom of the early morning, he still couldn't see the oncoming boats, but he knew from first-hand reports, there'd be ten of them, filled with 15 men each. 150 veteran Marines were bearing down upon them fast. Even if he'd had the entire support of the 32nd Division, he wouldn't have been confident of their chances.

Winkleman and Raker were also at the lip, searching the waters. Raker had his rifle propped between a notch in a log he'd hacked out, swinging side to side, testing his range of motion and visualizing himself firing, working the bolt and firing again. With only one arm, he was slower but still fast. He'd practiced the move thousands of times, knowing it might save his or a fellow soldier's life. His arm ached after those sessions, but he figured once the lead started flying, he'd probably work right through the pain as though his arm were uninjured.

Minutes later, Raker tensed and uttered, "There they are."

Sure enough, Tarkington saw the dim outlines of squared-off boat prows pushing through water, making white wakes. The engine noises were muffled, but as they approached they grew, soon overriding everything else.

The sky lightened, promising another gorgeous sunrise, but no one noticed the subtle changes in the light except that they could see the landing crafts better with each passing second.

Tarkington lifted his head, trying to see farther east, "Any second now," he grumbled. As if on cue, another engine, this one much louder, joined the others. Tarkington took in a sharp breath, "Here we go. Get ready."

From the east, the sound grew and soon a new white wake was cutting through the morning light, streaking directly at the most-easterly-positioned landing craft. Tarkington pointed, "There."

The others looked, seeing the outline of the little T-14 gunboat streaking toward the landing crafts. A blindingly bright muzzle flash erupted from the top of the boat's bridge. The muzzle flash, even from this distance, was huge. Red tracer fire, every fifth round, lanced into the first landing craft. The sound of rending metal and splitting wood joined with the heavy thumping of the heavy machine gun.

It took only a moment for the gunners manning the mounted machine guns on the landing craft to respond. More red tracer fire, this time outgoing, searched for the T-14, which had turned away, darting into the dawn gloom.

The sudden blinding explosion of a boat vanishing in flame and smoke caused the men in the hole to duck below the lip. A wave of heat swept over the beach, slamming into the trees, making them lean over as momentary monsoon-force winds swept over them.

Tarkington hunkered beneath the lip, smiling. He yelled, "Torpedo! Direct hit!" He'd wanted the T-14 sunk when they'd first arrived. He thought perhaps the Japanese had located it, and it was the reason they were invading. He'd kept that assessment to himself, but he was glad they'd kept it now, for it had evened the odds slightly.

The incredible explosion seemed to have shunned the night for good. When Tarkington dared look out, it was light and the rest of the landing craft were only 50 yards from the beach. Despite one riddled with machine gun fire and another obliterated, the other landing crafts continued churning forward, their high prows cutting through the calm waters of Panguil Bay. The T-14 was nowhere in sight, but the craft that had taken the brunt of the machine gun fire was sending quick bursts to dissuade further attacks.

The hollow sound of mortar tubes firing from behind made Tarkington look up. He saw the arcing shells gracefully flying to their apex then descending, gaining speed, before slicing into the sea and exploding. Huge geysers of water spouted 30 feet into the sky. The first two landed on either side of the middle boat. In response, the Japanese gunners opened fire—stitching the sand, the dock and pier, and every building in sight—with lead.

Winkleman chanced a glance over the lip but immediately ducked again, "They're about 30 yards out."

The crack of a rifle off to their left made Tarkington grin, "Henry's found a target."

Raker cursed, "Dammit. I should be with him." Another rifle crack from Henry.

Raker lifted his head, sighting his own rifle, but Tarkington pulled him down, "Not yet. Wait till they drop the ramps. Remember one clip, then we're outta here."

A new roar from farther out in the bay made them all exchange glances. Tarkington chanced a look, seeking out the T-14. The growing sounds of many weapons firing at once was too far around the corner for him to see, but it was in the general vicinity of where he assumed Gilson and his sailors were. He ducked back down, shrugging and shaking his head, "I dunno what that's all about, but it can't be good."

More whistling mortars followed by explosions. There was a loud grinding metal sound, and Tarkington risked another look, seeing the mortars had landed in the water spraying the entire area with water. The grinding sound he'd heard was a landing craft hitting one of the submerged rocks. The bow had run up on it and now it precariously tilted to the left, momentarily stuck. Tarkington ducked down and chuffed, "One of 'em's stuck."

The mortar crews must've gotten the word too. It was a pre-sighted location. Soon, two more shells arced overhead, and this time there was a rending explosion. It sounded different from the water strikes. Everyone in the hole looked. Japanese Marines were crawling over the sides of the pinned, burning landing craft, falling into the water. It was neck deep, and they struggled under packs and weapons toward shore. Tarkington saw a soldier standing on the side, waving his hand, directing men out of the boat. A rifle crack from Henry's vicinity and the Marine's chest bloomed red, and he fell back into the boat.

Two more shells arced over, one slamming into the stern with a great clanging explosion, the other landing alongside, killing many of the men already struggling in the water.

They all went into cover again and Tarkington said, "Two down, that's better than we could've hoped for." He clutched his submachine gun, checking the safety was off and the bolt was engaged. "Wait for the heavies, that's our signal."

The sound of boats churning into sand and the sudden slamming of front ramps lowering was the signal for the heavy machine guns to open fire. Two .30 caliber M1919 Brownings were dug in, Vick and Stollman manning one, the other by a crew of eager Filipinos. Tarkington imagined Stolly would be chomping at the bit to open fire and now he'd get his chance.

He didn't have long to wait. The Brownings opened up simultaneously. "Now!" yelled Tarkington. Winkleman and Raker were already up.

Tarkington saw the effects of the .30 calibers. Bullet strikes shredded the Marines as they tried to sprint forward directly into the withering fire. With their attention on the heavy machine guns, Tarkington aimed his submachine gun at a Marine coming off one of the landing crafts not in the Browning's line of fire. He squeezed off two rounds, spinning the Marine. He stumbled backward and sat down hard in the water. Tarkington squeezed a longer burst into the men coming behind the first man before ducking down.

Winkleman and Raker were firing, dropping, working the bolt actions, and coming up and firing again. Japanese were down everywhere, but they continued to press, crawling forward, using dead comrades for cover. Soon the return fire intensified, and Tarkington knew it was time to disengage.

He yelled, "Pour it on, then get the hell out!" He rose and emptied the rest of his magazine into the onrushing Marines, then dropped under the lip. Winkleman and Raker each fired one more shot, then sank down too. Tarkington quickly swapped out his magazine and yelled, "Go! I'll cover you!"

Raker and Winkleman sprang out the back of the hole at the same instant Tarkington loosed a sustained 30 round burst. Grabbing the last of his magazines, he sprinted out the back, buzzing bullets chasing him all the way. He weaved in and out of trees and soon there was only the occasional whiz of bullets.

The Browning machine guns were battling it out with the gunners on the landing craft. Tarkington's gut told him they were taking too long. They should've stopped firing and abandoned their positions by now after booby trapping the gun emplacements. *Dammit, Stolly! Retreat!*

The occasional mortar shell continued raining terror upon the Marines; they'd be the last defenders to pull out, being positioned the farthest back. As Tarkington exited the short strand of jungle and entered the streets of Ozamiz, a familiar sound made his bowels turn to liquid; the shrieking of incoming artillery. He dove for the closest cover, yelling, "Incoming! Incoming!"

Captain Kento's destroyer, the Nokaze, nudged its way into Panguil Bay in the darkness soon after the Japanese Marine's launched from Iligan City. Captain Kento wanted to personally watch the invasion force storm the town of Ozamiz, where the renegade T-14 MTB had been spotted a few weeks prior.

As soon as Kento heard about the spotting, he'd implored Admiral Ukada to allow him to avenge his killed and wounded sailors. The Province of Misamis, which included the town of Ozamiz, had been a thorn in the sides of the Army units deployed on the larger Mindanao Island for some time now, but since there were more pressing matters, and the region didn't cause overt problems, the town's open defiance of Japanese authority was ignored. But when the news of the stolen Japanese vessel came to light, there was no other choice but to set things right. Otherwise, where would it end?

Captain Kento spent a week at Iloilo Port getting the gaping hole in the hull patched. It would take longer to replace the two forward deck guns—time he didn't have if he hoped to partake in the mini-invasion.

Admiral Ukada assented to Captain Kento's request to provide the landing force with back-up since the replacement guns were still weeks away from being ready for fitting, and because Ukada saw a little of himself in the fiery captain. By overseeing a successful operation, Kento would prove himself to the general staff, and perhaps the smudge on his perfect record would be ignored.

Now Kento was on the bridge in the dead of night, creeping into the relatively-shallow and ever-narrowing bay. The radar man kept him apprised of the landing craft's progress as best he could. With the nearness of the land masses, and the landing craft's small size, it was difficult to break out contacts from the clutter. No matter, they'd have a front-row seat as soon as the sun peaked over the eastern horizon.

Kento checked his watch. Only minutes until the landing crafts turned toward the beach. The radar man suddenly stiffened, staring at the new scope that had been installed in Iloilo. Kento noticed. He stared at the sailor, waiting.

A few seconds passed, then the radar man turned in his steel chair, "Sir, Surface contact approaching the landing craft from the northwest." He hesitated, "It—it's small and fast, Captain." He hesitated, "Much like the T-14."

This time, instead of doubting the young sailor, he searched for the boat in the dim light. "Alert the gun batteries," he ordered. The radar man was quick to call out location, speed, and course. The XO relayed the information to fire control, and every operable gun on the ship slewed toward the contact.

The night lit up with sudden flashes in the distance. Red lines of tracer fire lanced out from a point of darkness. From this distance of nearly a half mile, it looked like a modest fireworks display. The sound came a few seconds later, the steady hammering of a heavy machine gun. Answering red tracer erupted from the darkness farther away. It was obvious the clashing vessels were close, too close for Kento to risk firing, though he wanted to give the order with every fiber in his being.

The sonarman yelled, "Two torpedos in the water!" Kento felt his bowels churn, the oddly reminiscent scenario of the prior month, still fresh in his mind. "They're targeting the landing craft!" the sonarman concluded.

The heavy exchange of tracer fire continued, but the enemy contact was turning, speeding away fast. Kento could see the white wake in the growing light of morning. His adrenaline surged when he recognized the boat for what it was: the renegade T-14. It was quickly separating itself from the landing craft, giving him a golden opportunity to destroy it once and for all. The guns tracked the now obvious gunboat. Deck gun officers and NCOs directed the gunners with long pointing rods, and soon every weapon with an angle was ready to blow it out of the water.

The sudden explosion turned any remaining darkness to stark light. The flash was immense, momentarily transfixing everyone on deck. Captain Kento's jaw rippled as he realized the 350 kg warhead on the Type 2 anti-ship torpedo had vaporized one of the landing craft and every Marine aboard.

Kento's attention returned to the fleeing T-14. It was still coming at them, clearly unaware of their presence. He dropped his hand, "Fire at will!" he ordered.

Instantly the deck of the Nokaze lit up with massive muzzle flashes. Every weapon—from smaller caliber machine guns to the big rear 120mm guns—opened fire at once. The first few shots were behind the streaking boat, sending up huge geysers and sending skipping ricochets into the beach beyond, but they adjusted quickly and soon the T-14 disappeared behind a curtain of exploding water, fire, and smoke.

Kento had his binoculars to his eyes. A grim smile creased his lips. All he could see of the little gunboat was the bow, pointed straight up, sinking fast. His guns had cut it in half. It would be a miracle if there were any survivors. "Cease fire," he ordered. The guns immediately went silent, their smoking and glowing red muzzles still tracking the destroyed target. Kento nodded, "Excellent shooting."

The radioman raised his voice, "Sir, the Marine Commander says they're being hit with mortars. He's asking for a fire mission."

Kento nodded somberly, "Very well. We'll flatten this damned town if we have to."

21

Tarkington staggered to his feet. Dust, smoke, and debris filled the air, making him hack and cough. Winkleman and Raker were pulling themselves off the ground.

Raker gasped, "What the hell was that?"

Winkleman shook his head, chunks of dirt and plaster from the shredded buildings falling onto his shoulders. "The locals didn't say anything about artillery."

Tarkington coughed hard one last time, clearing his lungs. Through a raspy throat, he said, "Has to be something to do with all that shooting we heard from the bay. Some kind of supporting ship, maybe." Rifle fire from the beach whizzed and ricocheted off the ground, creating bizarre zings and twangs. Tarkington pushed them forward, "Go! Japs on our tails."

Winkleman and Raker took off, running between two buildings, both holed by the exploded 120 mm shells. The holes smoked, and there were licks of flames inside. Tarkington raised the submachine gun to his shoulder and fired toward darting shapes, just coming off the beach, sending them ducking for cover. He took off, running as fast as his wobbly legs would take him.

The fire from the town had virtually stopped. Now, most of it was coming from the invading Marines. A concerted yell rose from them as they ran and fired at retreating shapes.

Tarkington weaved in and out of the streets. Another shrieking overhead sent him sprawling for cover. No one needed reminding. Everyone dove to the ground. The big shells slammed into the streets, sending hot shrapnel in every direction, lighting nearby buildings on fire.

Back on their feet, Tarkington saw Henry and Gonzalez standing at the corners of buildings half a block in front. Henry waved for them to hurry. Henry suddenly crouched, bringing his rifle to his shoulder, as though aiming at Tarkington. He fired, worked the bolt, and fired again. The outgoing bullets passed close to Tarkington's left shoulder, but he kept running, knowing Henry wouldn't have risked it unless it was urgently necessary.

Tarkington dove in behind Henry. Across the road, Gonzalez leaned out and fired, then ducked back when the wall beside his face splintered and covered his dark face with white dust.

Winkleman and Raker slid in behind Tarkington, who rolled to his knees and leaned out with his submachine gun. Two Japanese Marines were darting along the wall of a storefront. Tarkington fired a short five-round burst. Blood splashed the white wall behind the lead Marine and he fell, skidding to a halt, unmoving. The second Marine dropped to his knees and scurried toward the fallen man. Tarkington readjusted his aim, but Henry pulled him back before he could fire. The wall behind him was suddenly stitched with bullet holes.

Henry yelled, "These guys are good. We gotta break contact. Now!"

Tarkington yelled at Gonzalez across the street, "Meet at the rally point." Gonzalez gave him a quick nod then took off through the alley, disappearing around the corner.

Another shrieking wail of incoming shells made them all hit the deck. The shells exploded between themselves and the advancing Marines, the shock wave and concussive blast lifted, then dropped them to the ground like toys. Tarkington had the wind knocked out of him. He gasped, trying to fill his lungs. His head suddenly hurt again and his ears were ringing, but he still had the sense to know that the shells must have had the same effect on the Marines.

He stumbled to his feet, swaying. He croaked, "Now. Move out! Our chance!" The others were in similarly bad shape. Winkleman swayed so badly, he reached for the crumbling wall beside him and fell through it as though it were made of dust.

Raker, despite his broken arm, helped him to his feet. Winkleman was covered, head-to-toe with white dust and bits of charred bamboo. Tarkington looked across the street where Gonzalez had been moments before. The entire block on that side was leveled, as though dropped by demolition.

Tarkington pushed Henry, and they ran through the choking dust, feeling their way with their hands out front as though blind. The day, bright a moment before, now seemed dark and foggy. They put their shirts over their mouths and noses, trying in vain to keep from inhaling the thick air.

They kept moving, pushing through until the air cleared. Through ringing ears they heard gunfire, mostly coming from behind them. They moved past the last block of buildings. The sparse jungle beyond looked like salvation. Once there, they'd feel relatively safe, but there was a long 50 yard stretch of open ground between them. The shots from the Marines were getting ever closer. Thankfully, there'd been no more artillery, but the damage was done, stalling their retreat, keeping them in contact much longer than was healthy.

They got to the edge of town. The rendezvous point was up the hill and west about a mile. It had seemed far enough from town to keep them from being spotted before, but now he wondered. The Japanese were close and would most likely be able to follow them—assuming they could get across the open ground in the first place.

Henry moved back down toward the corner they'd just come from. Tarkington shook his head, "We've gotta cross now. All together." Tarkington knew Henry was planning on stalling the enemy, but there'd be no way to give cover when it came time for him to cross.

Firing from the right, about two blocks over, made them duck lower. Henry peaked around and drawled excitedly, "It's Gonzo. Crazy spic's alive."

Tarkington's eyes lit up, and he leaned around the corner too. Sure enough, Sergeant Gonzalez, still covered in white dust, was leaning out firing down the street. Tarkington cupped his hand around his mouth, yelling, "Gonzo!" Gonzalez looked up after chambering another round. He smiled and gave him a tired wave, as though greeting him while passing through the aisles of a grocery store. "You okay?" Tarkington yelled. Gonzalez brought his hand up and tilted it side to side; not great, but okay.

Tarkington growled, "He doesn't look okay. We gotta cross the street and go to him." He clutched Henry's arm, "Go to the corner you were heading for. When you've got a target, kill the son-of-a-bitch then come right back. Nobody else is dying out here." He looked at Raker and Winkleman, "As soon as he fires, you two head for Gonzalez. We'll cover you as you cross with him, then you do the same for us. Check weapons and ammo." Winkleman and Raker nodded their understanding.

Henry stayed low as he trotted to the corner. Tarkington covered his move with his submachine gun. He had half a clip loaded and a full one in his pocket.

Henry sat with his legs crossed, his elbows resting on his knees, supporting the rifle. It wasn't his trusty '03 Springfield, but he was getting accustomed to the heavier trigger pull. Whoever had owned it before him had kept it clean and in excellent working condition.

A few tense minutes passed and Tarkington wondered if he'd have been better off crossing from the get-go. He shook his head. It would only take one man with a rifle to take all of them out, and he knew the Marines were probably already spread between the buildings, waiting for them to be flushed out.

Henry tensed. Tarkington watched his finger move off the trigger guard to the trigger. He put his hand on Winkleman's shoulder, readying him. The instant the rifle cracked, Winkleman and Raker were running along the backside of the building toward Gonzalez. Henry fired again, then rolled back behind cover smoothly. There was return fire, but not directed their way. Good, they didn't know where the shots came from.

Tarkington kept him covered as Henry hustled back to him. Henry grinned and whispered, "One more dead Jap Marine."

"Head along this wall to the next corner. Cover them as they cross the street to Gonzo. I'll stay here in case they try an end-around."

Henry nodded, adding, "Watch the windows on the second floors; that's where the one I got was."

Tarkington nodded, glancing up at the four top-floor windows he could see. He desperately wished he had a canteen of water. His mouth was sticky with dryness. He refocused, *stay in the game, Tark.*

Out of the corner of his eye, he caught movement where Henry and the others were. He kept himself from looking, keeping his concentration on the corner and the windows. There was no shooting from the others, which he took as a good sign.

Something plopped around the corner where Henry's sniping position had been. For an instant, Tarkington tried to discern what it was, but instinct kicked in and he rolled around the corner, pulling his legs in right as the grenade exploded. Shrapnel pinged past. Tarkington went to a knee, listening at the corner. The scuffling of boots and Japanese voices told him all he needed to know. He positioned himself and his muzzle so he'd come around the corner as one.

He took a deep breath, his finger on the trigger, and leaned out quickly. Two Japanese were only yards away. Their eyes went wide, seeing their doom. Tarkington depressed the trigger, holding the submachine gun's stock in his armpit, not needing to aim properly. He emptied 15 rounds into them and they bucked and jolted, falling into a bloody mess of twisted, broken limbs.

He clawed for another magazine, taking his eyes from the scene and finding the last mag. When he looked up, a silhouette in a second-floor window got his attention. Tarkington didn't have time to react. Like the men he'd just killed, he knew he was too late. He saw the flash and felt the searing heat of the bullet lancing through his woefully-delicate body.

Suddenly he was staring at the sky above, wispy white clouds against an impossibly-blue background. A seagull drifted by, completely unfazed by the war or his dying in it.

Winkleman turned when he heard the grenade explosion. He saw Tarkington roll out of harm's way. Winkleman hesitated, exchanging a quick glance with Henry, wondering if they should follow his last order or go help.

They watched Tarkington dart from the corner and empty the rest of his magazine. That was all Winkleman needed to see. He pushed Henry, who was already moving back that way, "Give him a hand."

Winkleman focused his attention back toward Gonzalez across the street. Gonzalez was pressed against the wall, his rifle barrel pointed down, and even from here Winkleman could tell he wasn't doing well. He kept wiping his eyes and shaking his head, as though trying to keep himself awake or focused.

He was about to yell for Gonzalez to give them covering fire when he heard Tarkington suddenly grunt. He'd heard the sound so many times, he knew immediately that he'd been hit. Forgetting about Gonzalez for the moment, he spun, along with Raker, in time to see Henry dragging Tarkington out of the line of fire.

A flash of fear swept through him, and he swallowed the bile rising in his throat. Raker looked at him with wide eyes and was about to run to Tarkington's aid, but Winkleman gripped his shoulder, "Get Gonzalez. I'll help Henry and Tark." Raker licked his lips, then nodded and turned back toward Gonzalez.

Winkleman ran toward Henry. He was frantically assessing Tarkington's wound. Winkleman cursed. There was blood everywhere, darkening Tarkington's faded blue sailor's shirt. His eyes glazed over, but there was life there. Tarkington fixated on the sky, muttering something unintelligible.

Winkleman dropped his rifle and tore open the front of Tarkington's shirt, sending bloody buttons flying. The wound was low and seeping blood. Winkleman exchanged a worried look with Henry. Winkleman said, "Take care of the Nips. I'll patch him up." He used the discarded shirt to wipe the blood away and found the puckered hole in Tarkington's gut. Blood immediately covered the area again. He pushed the shirt hard into the wound and wrapped the sleeves around Tarkington's back, tying them off in front. It wasn't perfect, but it might stem the blood flow somewhat.

Henry peaked around the corner, but pulled back as a shot rang out and the ground a few inches from his foot exploded in a dirt geyser. "Shit, he's got us pegged."

Winkleman sat Tarkington up and he winced in pain. "Sorry, old buddy, this is gonna hurt." He put his shoulder into Tarkington's gut and with Henry's help hefted him over his shoulder. Tarkington didn't call out, but his eyes widened then shut and Winkleman felt him suddenly go slack. "That's it, Tark. Just relax." He raised his voice, "We gotta go now, Henry."

Henry nodded, then went rigid. He cursed, "Shit." The urgency made Winkleman turn. Henry took a step, planted his foot as though he were kicking a soccer ball. That's when Winkleman saw the grenade. Henry's foot kicked it back around the corner. The blast came a second later—the sound and concussion rocking them despite the building's protection.

Henry cursed, "Son-of-a-bitch." He stepped around the corner, his rifle leading, and fired. He quickly pulled back, his white teeth shining through his gun-powder blackened face. "He's down," he uttered matter-of-factly, "But there'll be more."

Behind them, from the jungle, came a new sound. At first they both cringed, then smiled. A heavy machine gun was firing, sending slicing yellow tracer rounds down the street. Raker had made it across the street and was standing beside Gonzalez, pressed into the wall. The heavy machine gun fire looked like a physical barrier between them.

Winkleman yelled, "It's now or never!"

Henry pushed him, "Go!"

Winkleman didn't wait. He trudged away from the protection of the building, and immediately felt exposed. Tarkington's dead weight was cumbersome, and soon his lungs were on fire. His legs threatened to fail him, but he pushed on, counting each step methodically. The bark of the machine gun barely cut through the roar of the blood pounding in his ears. He heard shots behind him where he'd left Henry, but dared not turn, knowing if he tripped he wouldn't be able to get back up.

Through his hazy, sweat-stung eyes, shapes appeared like apparitions and soon Tarkington's weight was off his shoulders. He wiped his eyes, seeing Filipinos and sailors urging him on. Tarkington's inert form was draped over a makeshift stretcher and he thought he recognized Petty Officer Yankowski's massive shoulders holding the front end.

They were yards from the jungle. The machine gun continued firing.

Winkleman remembered Henry. He turned in time to see him sprinting straight at him, chewing up the ground like a trained Olympic sprinter. Winkleman dropped to a knee, pulling his rifle off his shoulder and aiming, searching for targets in the windows. His efforts were for naught. The windows were already shredded with bullet holes from the machine gun. Henry sprinted past him. He got to his feet and followed.

He pulled himself behind a tree and put his hands on his knees, catching his breath. The machine gun fire stopped and there was yelling. It was time to go. Winkleman looked around frantically, "Where's Gonzo and Raker?"

He heard Colonel Fertig's voice, "They're fine. Both of 'em are retreating along with the others. Come on! We gotta go!"

As though to increase the urgency, they heard the shrieking roar of another incoming salvo. The shells landed in the open field, sending up great geysers of black dirt.

The next few minutes were a blur of dodging trees, bushes and boulders. Winkleman kept Henry in sight. He hadn't seen Tarkington since offloading him to the stretcher. He hadn't looked good at all. They stayed ahead of the advancing artillery and eventually turned west, avoiding it all together.

Their pace slowed as they found the trail leading to the coast. They continued to trot, and it relieved Winkleman to see Vick and Stollman ahead. He caught up with them, and still trotting, slapped Vick's back, speaking between breaths, "You guys on that machine gun saved our bacon back there."

Vick's eyes lit up, "Wink!" He turned, seeing Henry too, "Good to see you two!"

Stollman turned, slowing. "You made it!" he exclaimed. His face went from joy to serious in an instant, "How's Tark? He okay? Didn't look good."

Winkleman's face dropped, shaking his head, "I don't know, Stolly. He was gut-shot. Lost a lot of blood."

Vick added, "There's a doctor with him. Fertig said he's the best surgeon in the Philippines. Once they're on the beach, he'll operate. Got a whole surgical ward all set up for this sort of thing."

"That's great news!" exclaimed Winkleman.

Henry nodded, "Tark's too damned stubborn to die. He'll pull through, I just know it."

Winkleman asked, "That your sixth sense working?"

Henry nodded, "Damned right."

22

Six hours had passed since arriving at the beach. The GIs and sailors sat around outside the long thatch hut, which had been converted into a makeshift operating room. There was a constant flow of Filipino women in and out and every time they asked them for news, the answer was always the same, "not yet."

Staff Sergeant Tarkington wasn't the only one wounded, although he was the most serious case. Blood was needed, so Winkleman, Stollman and Henry volunteered for transfusions.

Gonzalez was inside too, his injury a serious concussion. He told them the last thing he remembered was an explosion which sent him airborne. He must've hit something for when he'd awakened, disoriented and in pain, he was being dragged by two hefty Japanese soldiers. He'd tried to break free, and they punched him mercilessly for his efforts.

Two locals saved him. They'd jumped from cover, hacking the Japanese to death with machetes, saving him from certain death. The blood-soaked Filipinos delivered him to the corner of the building then went back into the town and no one had heard from them since.

Lieutenant Commander Staub came from the radio hut and joined the men on the ground surrounding the hospital. He looked as though he'd aged ten years over the past few hours. No one had the energy to stand or salute, even if he'd insisted, which he didn't. He blew out a lengthy breath and ran his filthy, shaking hands through his hair. "Just got off the horn with the resupply sub. They'll be here tomorrow night."

Despite the good news, no one looked happy. Petty Officer Yankowski asked, "Any word on Lieutenant Gilson and the others, sir?"

Staub sighed heavily, "Fertig says his sources describe a Jap destroyer in the mouth of the bay. No doubt that was the damned artillery that..." his voice faded. "There's no sign of the torpedo boat." He lifted his chin, looking Yankowski in the eye, "There's been bodies pulled out." He shook his head. "Parts of bodies," he corrected quietly. He rubbed the back of his neck, "They're all gone, Ski."

Silence and a heavy grief hung over the men. Minutes passed without a word. It seemed even the birds stopped chirping.

Staub finally broke the silence, "Any word on Tarkington?"

Winkleman gulped against a dry throat, shaking his head, "'Not yet' is all they'll tell us."

Staub got to his feet, "Look, it'll be dark soon. Fertig's got the entrances to this place locked down tight. Let's get cleaned up and get some food." The sailors nodded, getting themselves to their feet.

None of the GIs moved and when Staub gazed at him, Winkleman squinted up at him, "We're gonna stay here in case they need more blood, sir."

Staub nodded, "I'll have some food delivered your way."

Winkleman muttered, "Thanks." He got to his feet, staggering as he dusted his butt off. He looked Staub in the eye, "Gilson was a good man, sir. All of them were. If they hadn't taken out those landing crafts, we would have been overrun."

Staub dropped his gaze, "I have no idea what I'm gonna tell his wife."

"Tell her the truth: he saved all of us."

Two more hours passed before the surgeon, a short man named Dr. Hulong emerged, rubbing his blood-soaked hands on a wet towel. He wore an apron like you'd find a chef wearing, but instead of food and grease stains, it was streaked with blood. The GIs sprang to their feet, watching him in anticipation. His expression was impossible to discern until he finally saw them in the fading evening light.

His face lit up with a slow grin, "The surgery went well. Your sergeant lost a lot of blood but the transfusions worked and I stopped the bleeding. I was concerned with his bowels but didn't see any major tears. Time will tell. If he suffers an infection, I may have to open him up again."

Winkleman asked, "So he's gonna make it? He's all right?"

Dr. Hulong shrugged, "The next week will tell, but I am optimistic."

Vick asked, "Will he be able to travel by tomorrow night?"

Dr. Hulong shrugged again, "He'll have to be. The medical personnel aboard your subs are top-notch. They're not surgeons, but..." he let the phrase hang.

Winkleman asked, "Can we see him?"

Hulong nodded, "Of course, but I'll warn you he looks worse than he is."

Stollman grinned, "Say, since he's got my blood pumping through his veins, does that make him my brother?"

Dr. Hulong shook his head and gave him a tight grin, "I'm going to the beach for a swim," and with that he left them to storm the building.

The men who'd donated blood had already been inside, laid down next to him, in fact, but there'd been a curtain separating them. Hulong was correct: seeing their rough-and-tumble leader reduced to little more than a waif was disconcerting. He was pale and his cheeks were sucked in, which accented his cheekbones as if he were starving. But his chest rose and fell steadily, and they could see his strong heartbeat pulsing in his thinned neck.

They surrounded his bed, none of them saying a word, but each placing a hand on him, reassuring him of their presence. A Filipino woman walked over, intending to limit the number of visitors, but stopped seeing the display of affection. She turned back to her other patients, men and women with cuts and gouges from shrapnel, mostly.

None of the GIs moved or spoke, and after an hour passed, the Filipino was going to break it up. As she approached, she heard a croaking sound, like someone who desperately needed a drink of water. She started and clutched her chest when she realized it was the patient's voice. She peered between the bloodied, war-torn men, seeing Staff Sergeant Tarkington's eyes flickering open.

The GIs looked up too, equally astonished. "Tark? You're awake," stated Winkleman.

Tarkington couldn't lift his head, but he shifted his eyes to each one of them, then croaked, "Tark's Ticks. Ugly sons-of-bitches."

Winkleman and the others grinned, the stress of combat and loss overcoming them all at once. Instead of crying, laughter rolled over them and nurses and patients alike looked on as though the Americans had lost their minds.

VALOR BOUND
Tark's Ticks #4

**Tark's Ticks have escaped the Philippines,
only to be thrust into the hell of New Guinea.**

The US Army needs a better way to gather intelligence on Japanese movements and concentrations. They envision an elite force of commandos that can match the enemy's intensity and brutality.

Tark's Ticks are perfect candidates. Rigorous weeks of training shapes the already deadly squad into Alamo Scouts.

In late 1942, the Allies are desperate to contain the indomitable Japanese. Going on the offensive, the Allies attack the northeastern coast of New Guinea. Their goal: retake the heavily fortified region of Buna.

The newly trained Tark's Ticks enter the action. Far behind enemy lines, they must rely on their training—and each other—to make it out of the brutal quagmire and unforgiving jungles of Papua New Guinea.

The faced-paced 4th book in this gritty WWII series will keep you turning the pages.

ABOUT THE AUTHOR

Chris Glatte graduated from the University of Oregon with a BA in English Literature and worked as a river guide/kayak instructor for a decade before training as an Echocardiographer. He worked in the medical field for over 20 years, and now writes full time. Chris is the author of multiple historical fiction thriller series, including A Time to Serve and Tark's Ticks, a set of popular WWII novels. He lives in Southern Oregon with his wife, two boys, and ever-present Labrador, Hoover. When he's not writing or reading, Chris can be found playing in the outdoors—usually on a river or mountain.

From Chris:

I respond to all email correspondence.
Drop me a line, I'd love to hear from you!
chrisglatte@severnriverbooks.com

**Sign up for Chris Glatte's reader list at
severnriverbooks.com/authors/chris-glatte**

Printed in the United States
by Baker & Taylor Publisher Services